ONE OF THE GUYS

LISA ALDIN

Spencer Hill Contemporary / Spencer Hill Press

First Edition: February 2015
Lisa Aldin
One of the Guys: a novel / by Lisa Aldin – 1st ed.
p. cm.
Summary: A tomboy rents out dates with her male friends to students at an all-girl prep school and ends up falling for her best friend.

The author acknowledges the copyrighted or trademarked status and trademark owners of the following wordmarks mentioned in this fiction: ChapStick, Christmas Vacation, Cloverfield, Darth Vader, Diet Coke, Discovery Channel, Dr. Pepper, Dunkin' Donuts,Family Guy, Fight Club, Ford Focus, Ghost, Go Fish, GoPro, Hello Kitty, Home Alone, Honda Civic, Ice Spiders, Indianapolis Colts, James Bond, Junior Mints, King Kong, Mario Brothers, Mario Kart, Maxima, McRib, Moby Dick, Monday Night Football, Mountain Dew, My Bloody Valentine, New England Patriots, No Country For Old Men, Pale Blue Dot, Peach, Post-It, Road House, Skittles, Snickers, Texas Chainsaw Massacre, The Proposal, Titanic, Tupperware, Tweety Bird, VW Bug, White Castle, Yoshi

Cover design by Jenny Zemanek
Interior layout by Jenny Perinovic
Author Photo by Christopher Aldin

ISBN 978-1-939392-63-3 (paperback)
ISBN 978-1-939392-64-0 (e-book)

Printed in the United States of America

For Chris and Charlotte

. . . .

one

· · · · · · · · · · · · · · · · ·

I LOVE THE BEGINNING OF A HUNT. No one is tired or hungry or complaining yet. Plus the start is so full of *maybes*. Like maybe we'll capture our town's legendary lake monster on film tonight. Maybe we'll put to rest any doubts of his existence. Maybe we'll become the legend.

As Lake Champlain wrinkles with miniature waves, I imagine Champ swimming underneath, looking up at us and smiling. My knees bounce with the excitement of a kid waiting to see Santa. I can't sit still. But the guys are so relaxed and quiet, staring off into the night, waiting. The gentle *slosh, slosh, slosh* of water petting the side of Ollie's pontoon boat rises and falls. The scent of algae lingers.

Come on, Champ. Show yourself. I dare you.

I look up at the sky dotted with clouds and hope for rain. After a hunt, I like to walk into my house smelly and soaked. The night somehow feels wasted unless I'm dragging mud into the living room.

I wish I knew what would entice the old monster to appear. Bread crumbs? Serenading the water with an enchanting song? Performing some weird dance? We've tried it all, but we haven't spotted Champ since the summer before fifth grade. The summer that forged our friendship. The summer all four of us noticed the giant, black tail grazing the surface of the lake.

A massive belch escapes me. Loch shifts in the driver's seat and shoots me a stern look over his shoulder, his plain white T-shirt flapping in the breeze. I smile sheepishly. Not the best time to showcase my talent.

Strike one. After three noise violations, we will end the hunt. Champ likes quiet. Why else would he hide at the bottom of a lake for centuries?

"Sorry," I whisper, holding back another burp. Maybe I should lay off the Mountain Dew.

After a moment, Loch smiles and mouths the words, "Good one."

I stifle a laugh. Yeah. The best ones sometimes come out of nowhere, as my dad would say.

Ollie slaps his arm. "Stupid bugs," he grumbles.

I sigh. Let the complaining begin. I could sit here all night without saying a word, bugs swarming, heat crawling up my neck, but Ollie can barely go thirty minutes without whining about something. I dig through my duffel bag of monster-hunting goodies until I find the bug spray and toss the bottle across the boat to Ollie.

"Thanks, McRib," he whispers. He sprays his arm until it shines with wetness.

Cowboy coughs and whispers, "Take it easy with that poison." He scoots a few inches away from Ollie, covering his mouth and nose.

"Bugs carry diseases." Ollie leans over to spray his thick hairy legs. He should really consider shaving those things. They look like fuzzy caterpillars. "I'm not taking any chances."

"This coming from the kid who flies down mountains on a board for fun." Cowboy rests his elbows on his knees. A huge bug crawls between strands of his blond hair. He casually shakes his head, and the bug vanishes into the dark.

"You can't get a disease from snowboarding," Ollie adds, his whisper growing louder. I cringe, wishing he'd keep it down. It's too early to scare off the monster.

Cowboy rests his head back and closes his eyes. *Is he bored?* How could anyone find this *boring?* We're monster hunting! An uneasy feeling bubbles in my stomach, like I'm watching my favorite movie but it's nearing the end. And I can't rewind.

"Careful," I say, keeping my voice low. A mosquito lands on my elbow and proceeds to chow down. "You'll scare Champ away with your paranoia, Ollie."

"I prefer winter." Ollie wipes his hands on his cargo shorts. "Bugs hate winter."

"*Champ* hates the *talking,*" Loch whispers, fidgeting with the GoPro dangling around his neck.

"Agreed," Cowboy says softly, eyes still closed.

Everyone shuts up. I scratch at my bug bite and breathe a little easier, pleased with the silence, however fleeting it may be. But Cowboy is irritating me. I mean, this is ridiculous. His eyes are *closed.* On a monster hunt. How does he expect to *see* anything?

I take a deep breath. Try to relax. I don't want to scare Champ away with any bad vibes. As the breeze ripples the water, my gaze wanders to the mountains surrounding the lake. I bet those mountains have seen Champ a million times over hundreds of years. Witnessed every sighting. Every story. The mountains know our story, too. If only they could talk. Because no one believes what we saw.

Eventually my gaze lowers to Loch. His fingers rest on the wheel, guiding the boat with ease. I never get tired of seeing him in his natural habitat, on the hunt for a legendary beast, working to prove skeptics wrong. After a few minutes, he cuts the engine, stands, and slides his hands into the back pockets of his jeans.

On second thought, this is my favorite part of a hunt. Watching Loch hold his breath. Studying his lips as they move in a prayer-like fashion. I know he isn't really praying, though. He's talking to Champ, making deals and promises with the monster in exchange for a glimpse.

"Hey, McRib. Can you toss me a bag of sour cream and onion chips?" Ollie asks.

The request startles me. Ollie doesn't even bother whispering anymore. I pull my stare away from Loch and fumble through the bag. No chips. Oh, right. I ate them on the way here. I throw over a can of delicious Mountain Dew instead. Now the silence can continue. I hope.

"Hey," Cowboy says, his voice soft and quiet, but not quite a whisper. "Throw me one?"

Or maybe not. I should probably just hand Cowboy his drink, but I'm too lazy to get up. I'm comfy. So I toss it. But the can slips from Cowboy's clumsy hands and hits the floor of the boat with a *thud* before rolling toward me. Quickly, I step on it. Loch's shoulders tense. His dark eyes focus on the dark water.

Strike two.

Suddenly, there's a splash behind me. Ollie and Cowboy jump up and peer over the edge of the boat so quickly I think someone might go overboard. Cursing, I search the bag while Loch aims his flashlight and GoPro at the water. After I find my flashlight, the two pale strips of light roll over the water together.

My heart pounds.

I hold my breath.

The only sound is the *slosh, slosh, slosh* of the waves.

Wedged between Ollie and Cowboy, I smell the stench of bug spray on Ollie's arms mixed with Cowboy's eye-stinging cologne. I suspect Cowboy wears the cologne on hunts because he secretly hopes we'll run into Katie Morris, his long-time crush. Like she'd happen to be out monster hunting one night.

A few minutes pass as we search the water for the source of the splash. Maybe Champ will show us his face this time? Or a shoulder? A claw? That'd be sweet.

Ollie steps back from the railing, sighing. My heart drops. *No. Don't give up yet. He's under there. Just wait.* Seconds later, Cowboy plops down and opens his dented Mountain Dew can. The *pop* of the tab echoes. I cringe again. *Strike three?* I look to Loch. Not yet. His tall body's a statue.

Loch and I remain fixated on the lake. I don't understand why Ollie and Cowboy have given up already. It's freaking early. We've survived so many false alarms over the years. Big deal. False alarms don't mean we just *give up.*

A thick branch floats by the pontoon on a wave. Loch turns off the flashlight and scratches the stubble on his chin. I sigh and turn off my flashlight, too. If Loch's given up, the hope is dwindling. His shoulders slumped, he returns to the driver's seat. I feel like saying something encouraging, anything, but I'm afraid the hunt will officially end if I do.

Before I sit down, I give the water one more good look. Nothing.

Ollie chuckles. "Hey, Loch. You could add that to your hours of floating twigs footage."

I sink further into my seat, annoyed. And there it is. *Strike three.*

Loch starts up the engine. "That shouldn't count," I say, sighing.

"Champ could be swimming circles around us and we'd miss it," Loch says, steering the boat back to the dock. "What's the point of being out here if we're scaring the guy away every two seconds?"

I look down, press my lips together, and fidget with my black basketball shorts. I hate the end of a hunt. Everyone's so crabby and pessimistic.

Cowboy yawns. "Maybe we just saw an eel or something that day, you know? Maybe we're wasting our time with this."

Ollie nods. "Yeah. Like maybe my eleven-year-old imagination saw a giant tail, but in reality, it was probably just a stick."

No. No. No. These are not the *maybes* I love. I snort and try to lighten the mood with a stupid joke. "Good point, Ollie. You do like to pretend certain snake-like things are larger than they actually are."

Cowboy laughs, squirting Mountain Dew out of his nose. Ollie breaks into a grin and shakes his head, swatting at a bug. I look to Loch for his reaction. He curls his fingers around the wheel over and over again, lost in thought, quiet. I'm kinda hurt. Loch usually laughs at my lame jokes.

No one speaks for a while. Of course. *Now* everyone is quiet. The hum of the boat's engine sounds. For a second, I think the hunt might be salvaged, but Loch doesn't turn around. The dock grows closer.

"We've spent almost the whole summer doing this," Ollie says. "Searching for monsters. Bigfoot. Champ. Batboy. Giant cats. And for what? This is our senior year, guys. We can't keep chasing after something we thought we saw when we were eleven. We can't chase things that aren't real anymore."

"We'll get the evidence on film," Loch says. "We just need to pay attention at the right time."

"We were all there." Cowboy runs his slim fingers over the collar of his short-sleeved flannel. "We all remember. What's the big deal about proving it to everyone else?"

Loch pauses. His voice lowers. Shadows play across the profile of his face. "Because some of us are forgetting."

When we arrive at the dock, Ollie and Cowboy jump off first and tie up the boat. I really want to say something to Loch about hope and all, but he won't look at anyone as he climbs off the boat. So I let it drop.

I'm last off the pontoon. The boys are still bickering about Champ so I hang back a little, annoyed. By my feet, I notice our four names—real ones, before any of the nicknames caught on—carved into the wooden dock, laid out like a welcoming mat, each letter jagged and sloppy.

Toni. Micah. Luke. Justin.

When I look up, the guys are halfway down the pier leading to the parking lot, still arguing about whether or not Champ even exists. Last year we had all undeniably believed in the monster beneath the water. What's changed?

"Hey! It's still early," I call out, rocking from foot to foot.

"I'm done looking for monsters," Ollie yells over his shoulder. "So unless you've got a better idea, I'm headed home."

Cowboy stops, turns, looks at me. He smiles and stuffs his hands into the pockets of his jean shorts. "I've got to finish *Moby Dick* anyway."

He starts walking again. Each boy gets smaller, farther away, and suddenly it feels like this is it. The last hunt. Our ending. Not the one I had hoped for.

"I have a plan!" I announce. "It's epic! Huge! Exciting! Different!"

The boys stop, turn. All eyes are on me now. Sweat forms under my armpits as I search for a lie to feed them. Anything to keep them from leaving. I take a deep breath and march forward.

"Get in the car." I grin. "This is gonna be a night you won't freaking forget."

two

. . . .

THE PASSENGER'S SEAT OF LOCH'S old Honda Civic knows me well. As Loch drives, I sink into the frayed fabric and fidget with the loose thread beside my knee, careful not to pluck it out. I don't actually have a plan. I'm bluffing big time, and I wonder how long I can keep this up before the guys realize I'm stringing them along just because I don't want to say goodnight yet.

But this is the summer before our senior year. A time to hold on to everything—not to let go. Next fall, too much will change. We should savor what we have now. For as long as we can.

"Which way?" Loch asks, his fingers tapping the steering wheel as we roll up to a stop sign.

"Left." I raise my chin and try to speak with confidence, but my voice wavers. The rattling dashboard drowns out the faint sound of the radio. I punch the volume button a few times, but it's eternally stuck at low.

My seat jostles as Ollie leans forward from the backseat and asks, "So where we going, McRib?"

"I don't want to ruin the surprise." I watch the dark tree-lined street outside. Hot air causes sweat to form along the back of my neck. On occasion, the Honda's air conditioner will grace us with its presence, but tonight isn't one of those nights.

Cowboy sits next to Ollie in the back, his forehead pressed against the window, his nose stuck in a book. Tonight he's reading my torn copy of *Moby Dick*, a summer assignment for our English class in the fall.

"Let me ask you something, Cowboy," Ollie says, leaning back. "Are you a masochist?"

I glance at the rearview mirror. Cowboy doesn't look up from his reading as he replies, "I know what we can do tonight. We can play the quiet game."

"That book is torture," Ollie continues. "Pure torture. Like anyone needs to read hundreds of pages about sperm whales."

"*Moby Dick* has one of the best monsters in all of literature," Loch says, shaking his head. "Don't knock it."

Ahead, the movie theater appears, the marquee aglow with this week's cinematic choices. Instantly, I think of all of the times my dad took me to weeknight shows. I ignore the knot in my stomach, but it's not an entirely *bad* knot. Good memories are tangled with it, but I miss my dad. It's been three years since his death, yet his presence remains strong, especially in familiar places such as this.

"Um, turn here," I order.

Loch steers the car into the parking lot, the pavement still shiny from that afternoon's rain. He parks the car in an empty spot near the entrance. I rest my elbow on the door and play with a strand of hair that's fallen free from my ponytail. I think about all the times Dad and I would scoop up old movie posters on Thursday nights before they were thrown away, many of which decorate my bedroom now. I hate *time*. It can really screw things up.

"So I got a serious question to ask you guys," Ollie says.

I turn around, wondering if he's feeling the same thing that I am, that this year doesn't have to be an ending. It could be a promise. A promise to always be there for each other. A promise to stay the same when so much else seems to change.

Ollie pauses, takes a deep breath, and asks, "Who farted?"

He rolls down the window and attempts to wave the stale air into the outside world. I chuckle and glance at Loch, who just smiles and drums his fingers along the steering wheel.

"That's classic car smell," he says. "Either that or the milkshake I spilled in here last week."

"Is this the big plan?" Cowboy glances up from his book. "A movie? We could watch one in Loch's basement. My turn to pick. I choose *The Proposal*."

Ollie high-fives him. "Agreed! Such a good movie."

Loch groans. "Oh, man. Shoot me now."

"Better than those horror movies you and McRib are obsessed with," Cowboy says.

"Please, Toni. Save me from the dreaded romantic comedy," Loch says, glancing at me. "Tell me you've got something else up your sleeve."

I sigh, ready to admit defeat, I've got nothing here, until someone I recognize exits the movie theater. Principal Rogers stands at the curb, illuminated by the glow from the building behind him. He wipes his glasses on his blue polo shirt and examines the clear night sky. He slides his glasses onto the bridge of his nose and then runs a hand through his thick, gray hair.

"Principal Rogers." Ollie sounds intrigued, spotting him. "Wow. He exists outside the halls of Burlington High." He playfully kicks at my seat. "So what's the plan here, McRib?"

"There is no plan," Cowboy states. "You do all realize that, I hope."

"Not true," I interject. I study Principal Rogers, an idea forming. A dumb idea. Juvenile, really. But an idea nonetheless. "I have a plan. An epic plan."

"Let's hear it then, McRib," Cowboy says. He closes his book and smiles. "Now or never. What are we doing?"

I scratch at the mosquito bite on my wrist and blurt out, "Gentlemen, we're going to moon Principal Rogers."

Silence. Stunned silence. My heart pounds. I've never *mooned* anyone before. But it'd be harmless at least. Could I even do something like this? Expose a piece of myself? Yes. Yes, I could. If I had the guys beside me, I could do just about anything.

"This will be unforgettable," I continue. "Come on, guys. We're *seniors*. This could be, like, a senior prank thing." Or this could be our new bonding moment. After tonight, maybe we won't need Champ to hold us together anymore.

Ollie excitedly pounds the back of my seat. "Genius! I love it! Let's do it!"

Cowboy sighs. "I like my butt to remain private."

"You still saving it for Katie Morris?" Ollie asks, ruffling Cowboy's hair. "One of these days, she will know you exist, man. Even though you never talk to her. Or text her. Or acknowledge her presence in any way."

Cowboy's cheeks go red. He sinks into his seat and buries his nose inside Melville's pages. At the mention of Katie Morris, he'll be lost to us for at least five minutes, probably dreaming of her.

Loch leans toward me. I catch a whiff of vanilla. As he looks pointedly at the principal, he raises his eyebrows. "So this was the plan, huh? How'd you know he'd be here?"

I shrug and avoid eye contact. Loch knows I'm making this up as I go along. He can always tell when I lie. But he lets it slide. "Well, he's not alone," Loch says, pointing.

A slender woman with brown hair and pale skin walks up beside Principal Rogers, hooking her arm into his. She wears a beautiful red sundress and leans her head on his shoulder. She looks all dreamy, happy. Principal Rogers smiles wide, a rare and odd sight, and gently caresses her cheek.

"Oh my God. He's on a *date*," I whisper.

"Weird." Loch shakes his head. "Like I'm watching a bizarre mating ritual on the Discovery Channel. I don't want to see it yet I can't seem to look away..."

"He'll recognize me." Ollie tries to flatten out his wild curls with the palm of his hand. "We need something to cover our faces."

"I've got some extra sweatshirts in the trunk." Loch sinks lower into his seat. Hard to do, considering his height. "Thought we would need them for the hunt tonight."

I pat his shoulder to let him know that if it were up to me we'd still be out on that lake. He gives a soft smile, but I can sense his disappointment. This plan better work.

"Move the car," Ollie says. "He'll see us from here."

Loch drives around to the other side of the parking lot, a safe distance from the principal and his date.

"If we're going to do this, we need to move fast," I say, my pulse quickening. "Right now, Principal Rogers and his special lady friend appear to be stargazing. No big hurry to go home. But they could leave at any minute."

Ollie grabs the sweatshirts from the trunk and hurries back into the car, out of breath. He throws me a gray hoodie with the words GONE SQUATCHIN on the front below a silhouette of Bigfoot and tosses a plain blue sweatshirt to Cowboy. But Cowboy just stares at it like it's covered in slime or something.

"Cowboy?" I pull on the sweatshirt, which practically swallows me up. It smells like mud and cake. Like Loch. "You in?"

"I don't think I can do it." Cowboy scratches his thin nose. "Just the thought makes me want to puke. You sure no one's up for watching *The Proposal?* I can be flexible. Anything with a happy ending."

Ollie yanks on his sweatshirt and says, "Another time, my friend. Another time."

I tuck a hair behind my ear, pull up the hood, and run my fingers over the soft fabric. Man, this sweatshirt is comfy. "Loch?" I ask.

Loch rubs his dark stubble. "There should be a getaway driver," he says. "Just in case. But I'm here for moral support."

"Guess Ollie and I will be the classic pranksters tonight." I force a smile as my stomach flips. It's a holy-crap-is-this-really-going-to-happen kind of flip. There's a reason we don't do things like this. A reason we stick to tradition. Monster hunts or movie nights at someone's house. It feels so unnatural to stray from the normal, but if Ollie wants a different sort of adventure, here we go. Bottoms up. Ha.

Ollie shoves his hair beneath the hood of his black sweatshirt, which is about two sizes too big for him. "On three, McRib," he says. His sharp green eyes glow like jewels in the darkness, and shadows fall across the light freckles on his nose.

I reach for the door handle and say, "One."

"Two," Ollie adds.

The *pop* of the back door opening. I hear Loch's gentle breathing and Cowboy turn a page in his book. *We should have thought this out more. Too late. Can't back out now.*

"Three!" I shout.

I open my door and leap onto the cement. I run toward Principal Rogers, my cheeks warm with exhilaration, my armpits slick with sweat. Ollie runs beside me, his breathing loud and ragged. The principal pays us no attention—not until I jump in front of him and his date, my back turned, and yank down my basketball shorts, presenting a full moon for the adorable couple.

To my right, Ollie leans over, his shorts down, his face hidden beneath the hood. I can't believe I'm here, pants pulled down, my butt exposed to my high school principal and some woman I don't even know.

I'm frozen like a deer in headlights. Actually, a deer would be much more dignified right about now. I'm a joke. A terrible, lame joke. I think I hear a gasp behind me. The date, I assume.

Ollie whispers, "Sooooooo...how long do we do this for?"

Someone grabs the back of his sweatshirt and pulls. Ollie scrambles to pull up his shorts before he stumbles backward, arms flailing.

"Good evening, Luke Brown," Principal Rogers says, anger in his voice.

Yeah. This was a bad idea.

I hike up my shorts, but it's too late to run.

Principal Rogers grabs my elbow, his huge nostrils flaring. Ollie and I exchange a look, mine pure terror, his mild amusement. Rogers folds his arms across his chest, sniffs, and says, "And Toni Valentine. Well, I hope you both enjoy the rest of your evening." He sighs and takes his date's hand. "Because I will be informing your parents about this."

I feel like I might puke. I dry-heave a few times. The date in the red dress looks at me with disgust.

"Please don't do that—" I begin, but Principal Rogers isn't listening. He's walking away with his date.

"Toni. Relax," Ollie whispers to me, rather pleased with himself. At least someone had fun tonight. "What's the worst that could happen?"

Yeah. Famous last words.

three

. . . .

ONE MONTH LATER, I'M SITTING IN a brightly lit classroom at the Winston Academy for Girls. My dad used to joke that the day I wore a skirt would be the day the zombie apocalypse rolled into town. Two hours in and I have yet to see a zombie, but I do feel like the living dead. Someone bathed in raspberry perfume this morning, causing a war to rage inside my nostrils. I might fall to the floor and convulse, the smell's that thick. Maybe it's not the perfume. Maybe I'm allergic to all this estrogen.

"You okay?" the girl next to me whispers.

I respond by covering my mouth and sneezing so hard that a giant wad of snot lands in the palm of my hand. Carefully, I move my hand under the desk and smile.

"Fine," I reply. "Just tired."

The girl chews on a strand of her honey-colored hair as she attempts to write down every word of the lecture. A leather day planner rests at the edge of her desk, a name embroidered in pink curly letters at the bottom: *Emma Elizabeth Swanson.*

I'm definitely not in public school anymore.

Our Business Mathematics teacher pity-smiles at me from behind her glasses and dives into a discussion about supply and demand. I continue to wonder what I should do with the snot on my palm. If I were sitting beside one of the guys at Burlington High, like I should be this year, the snot wouldn't be an issue. I would wipe it on Cowboy, the least likely of the group to retaliate, and laugh.

But what would a "lady" do?

Here at Winston, boys feel as mythical and mysterious as unicorns. There's no sign of them anywhere. No obnoxious belches. No stupid high-fives. No talk of monster hunting. It's unsettling, like I'm walking among a race of polite aliens wearing plaid jumpers and lip gloss.

How am I supposed to survive a year on another planet?

The girl sitting in front of me suddenly turns to the aisle, flips her head over, and spritzes her brown curls with a bottle of raspberry-scented hairspray. Ah-ha. Found the source of the overwhelming stench. She flips upright again and smiles at the teacher, who gives her a stern look before continuing on with the lecture.

A more frightening question: What if I become one of them?

I keep my palm turned up, shifting uneasily as I decide what to do. They didn't cover snot-related problems during orientation this morning. I'm about to ask Emma Elizabeth Swanson for a tissue when the bell rings. Quickly, I wipe my palm on my plaid skirt and pray that no one notices.

"I saw that!"

I spin around, but the redheaded girl rushing through the aisle isn't talking to me. She's chatting with her group of friends about a film on African cats she watched over the weekend. She walks by me as if I were a mere shadow. I should probably make an effort at friend-making, but Emma Elizabeth Swanson, my best option so far since she's the only one who's actually spoken to me, has already left the classroom.

I pick up my books and move with the crowd into the hallway, where the raspberry smell finally lifts. The mass of plaid-wearing bodies thins as everyone zooms to their lockers and hurries off to their next class. A sense of loneliness settles into my stomach as I pop open my locker and switch out my Business Mathematics textbook for Carl Sagan's *Pale Blue Dot*. I have to read it for my English elective about space and time or something.

That's another thing. The classes here all sound like college courses.

I sigh and retie my ponytail. I shouldn't be a Winston girl. Yeah, Principal Rogers talked to my mother about the mooning incident, let her know the kind of shenanigans I was up to with the guys, but it didn't have to lead to *this*.

As much as my mother would love to see me wear a skirt or paint my nails or talk about my feelings, she would never sever me from my childhood friends and send me to a new school for my senior year because of one little incident like that. Mom isn't evil. Brian, her new husband, is. Brian brought home brochures full of smiling uniformed girls and told Mom that an all-girls school would keep me out of trouble, get me away from the bad influences, and turn me into a lady.

What Brian doesn't know was that mooning the principal was my idea. I *am* the bad influence. I don't get it—butt-revealing is innocent compared to most activities that take place inside the secret nooks of high school. Yet somehow, I am punished.

For the rest of the day, I concentrate on keeping the basketball shorts underneath my knee-length skirt from riding up my thighs, which proves to be quite the distracting challenge. And they keep peeking out so I roll them up a little, which doesn't help the comfort factor. But I would feel too naked without them. When the last bell rings, my head throbs, and I long to make Brian's life as miserable as possible. I receive more homework in the first day than I would in a month at Burlington High.

Before I'm released back into the wild to tackle the pile of assignments, I stop by the guidance counselor's office for a check-in.

"Did you meet any cute boys today?" Mrs. Kemper laughs and waves her hand in front of her face like she's swatting at a fly. "An old joke, forgive me."

"Funny," I mumble, shifting my weight to adjust my shorts again.

"Tell me about your first day. You fitting in?"

A quiet snort escapes me, but Mrs. Kemper doesn't acknowledge it. Her hair cascades in thick curls around her pixie-like face. Several loose brown strands stick to her navy blazer. She picks one off, letting it fall to the floor like a delicate feather as she waits to hear what she wants to hear: that, yes, I am fitting in oh-so-wonderfully with the most privileged and sophisticated female students in the state of Vermont.

Me. The girl with permanently skinned knees and dirt under her nails.

"I'm fine." I force a polite smile. I wish Winston offered a *Perfecting the Fake Smile* class. After all the practice I'd had today, I would ace it. "Everything's great."

Mrs. Kemper nods, obviously not believing my lie. "The first day is the hardest. Hang in there, Tonya."

"Toni."

"Who's Toni?"

"I just prefer to be called Toni."

Mrs. Kemper turns her chin up. "But Tonya is such a pretty name."

I shrug, knowing this is a lost battle. Here, I am Tonya. Everywhere else, I am Toni. This place doesn't even accept boy *names*.

"I suppose we're done here," she says, clearing her throat. "Oh, don't forget about your first group session on Friday."

I blink a few times. "Group session?"

Again, she chuckles. "Hard to remember it all, isn't it? Once a week, you meet in the library with a small group of your peers to discuss whatever may be bothering you. It's a way to learn how to express yourself eloquently."

My jaw hangs open. "You mean we talk about our *feelings*?"

Mrs. Kemper stands and grins. "Yes. That's not a bad thing. Have a good afternoon, Tonya."

Oh my God. She's not kidding. I stand, my knees shaking. According to my mother, this year is about *growth* and *the future*. In other words, *no fun*. This was supposed to be the year to hang out with the same guys I've known since the second grade, avoiding as much responsibility as possible.

So much for that.

. . . .

On the drive home (an hour commute, another perk of attending Winston), I crank up the radio in hopes that a dose of good country music will erase my headache. I sing along to a sad ballad, belting out the tune so loud my neck veins pop. It doesn't help.

The scent of raspberry hairspray still tickles my nose as the green hills surrounding the Winston campus shrink in the rearview mirror. I sink further into the seat of my Maxima, the one comfort from my old life that I took with me. It used to belong to my dad. Fast food wrappers sprinkle the floor and the backseat is full of various clothes and books and Mountain Dew cans. No one can force me to act like a lady in here.

I glance at the stack of intimidating textbooks on the passenger's seat and roll down the window to keep the panic attack settling into my chest at bay. At Burlington, I had accumulated enough credits to take afternoons off or graduate early, but there's no such thing as an afternoon off at Winston.

Instead, I'm taking classes like "The Community Ecology of the Forested Landscape," where you basically walk around the campus woods studying Vermont plant-life for a semester. Which wouldn't be bad, actually, if I had Loch by my side. He would find potential Bigfoot tracks or something cool like that. He'd make it fun.

I resent my GPA, and Brian, for landing me on this strange planet.

Alone.

When I get home, I park in the driveway and jog over to Loch's house next door. I shed my plaid skirt halfway across the lawn, stomping on it twice, finally able to breathe. I'm excited for the evening ahead. We're going to the lake for the first time in more than a month.

Over the last few weeks, I have felt a disconnect with the guys. We've been to a few movies, played some video games, but something doesn't feel quite the same. Something changed after I announced my transfer to Winston.

When we do manage to hang out, Loch shows up late but avoids telling us where he's been. I just hope he isn't seeing his ex-girlfriend again. And Ollie spends way too much time talking about the excitement of senior year, one I won't be a part of anymore, not completely, no matter how hard I try. Even Cowboy seems quieter than usual. Sullen.

I'm worried the guys are distancing themselves from me because I'm no longer one of them. I'm a Winston Girl. I don't know. I hope it's just all in my head.

I wind around to the back of the Garrys' household, excited to see my boys. After much texting last week, we agreed on the monster hunt tonight. I don't want to miss out on the pre-hunting activities, including an epic battle of *Mario Kart*. If they started playing without me, Yoshi is likely taken, which means I'll be stuck with Peach again.

As I slide through the basement window, I breathe in the familiar scent of dry wall and stale chips. I land on the shaggy carpet with a giant thud and let out a belly-shattering belch that could put any beer-guzzler to shame.

"Aw, that's better! I've been holding that in all day!" I exclaim, rubbing my stomach.

I turn and find that I'm staring at the horrified face of Amy Garry, Loch's little sister. She's painting her nails on the coffee table, a group of freshmen girls scattered around her, all doing the same thing. The four girls stare in shock, their glittering nails reflecting the dim basement light. I once nicknamed Amy Garry "My Adorable Shadow" because she used to follow us around everywhere. But now she's got this look on her face that suggests she'd very much like a sinkhole to swallow me up.

"Oh," is all I can say at first. "Where's Loch?"

Amy's cheeks burn red. "You mean Micah? He's at work."

I shake my head, certain I've heard incorrectly. Loch doesn't have a job. A job would only get in the way of his research. Plus, we have plans.

Amy's hand pauses mid-air as polish drips onto the table, her heart-shaped face now beet-red. Oh, man. I've mortified the poor child. Quietly, I crawl out of the window without asking questions, although I have plenty. Before I slide the window shut behind me, I overhear one of Amy's friends say, "I bet she's never had a boyfriend!"

Ouch. I ignore the pit in my stomach—they're *freshmen* girls for crying out loud—and grab my skirt from the lawn. I climb back into my car and settle in behind the wheel. Amy was mistaken. Confused. Loch wouldn't bail out on a Champ search like this. Definitely not without telling me. Maybe he thought we were supposed to meet at the lake. Maybe he's there now. I check my phone. No texts. No calls. No big deal. Loch isn't attached to his phone.

I hate feeling like this—so out of control. I pull out of the driveway and head toward the lake, the windows rolled down, trying to keep calm. I imagine the guys waiting for me on the dock, laughing, ready to start a new hunt. Bags full of junk food beside them. I bet they're wondering where the heck I am.

But when I arrive, Ollie's pontoon boat is empty, gently bobbing in the water. I scratch the back of my neck as I walk along the dock and study the bordering mountains. After I sit down and pull out my phone, I send a group text: *Where are you guys? Champ awaits...*

I set the phone beside me, my knees bouncing, unable to shake away this horrible feeling of abandonment. It grows in my chest like a balloon. Seconds later, my phone vibrates. One. Two. Three times.

The first, a text from Cowboy: *KATIE MORRIS TALKED TO ME TODAY.*

The second, a text from Ollie: *A hunt? Today? I can't make it.*

The third, a text from Loch: *I'm so sorry. I forgot to tell you that I'm working tonight. Will explain later. Rain check? How was your first day, Winston Girl?*

They aren't coming.

They forgot.

ALL THREE FORGOT.

I scroll through my saved text messages. Yep. There it is. I'm not crazy. *We planned this.*

How could they just forget?

· · · · · · · · · · · · · · · · · ·

I collapse face-down on my bed. An annoyed meow comes from my pillow. I look up to encounter Tom Brady the cat. I've clearly disturbed his slumber. He glares at me and then begins to lick his black fur.

"So sorry to interrupt," I say.

Like a bad sofa, Tom Brady came along with the stepfather a year ago. Brian's a huge New England Patriots fan, hence the cat's horrid name. Turns out, Tom Brady the cat also doubles as an alarm clock. Every morning at 7 AM, he bites the crap out of my hand until I get out of bed and feed him.

I shower and zone out in front of my laptop for about an hour. I try to forget about the stressful first day at Winston. I try to forget how my friends abandoned me and the feeling that they're slipping away. That's the thing though. Unlike them, I don't forget.

I shut off the lights, crawl under my covers, and unload panicked sobs into my cat hair-covered pillow.

Four

· · · · · · · · · · · · · · · · · ·

OVER THE NEXT FEW DAYS, I SEND about one hundred text messages trying to organize another hunt. On the days Loch can go, Ollie has to help his older brother, Jason, rearrange the basement. On the days Cowboy doesn't have a test to study for, Loch is working. It seems impossible to get the four of us together in one place anymore. Are they avoiding me on purpose?

At least today is Friday. Oh, wait. Friday means it's time to share my *feelings* with total strangers. Super.

"I think we should hear from Tonya Valentine next." Mrs. Kemper folds her hands over her knees, turning her attention to me, but my mind is back at Burlington High.

The guys see each other every day—in the halls, in class, at lunch. They don't have to send a million texts or whatever to communicate. They *are* together. I want to be with them. Technically, Winston is not a punishment. That's what Mom said when she and Brian sat me down to inform me of my new educational pathway. I should be grateful and happy to be here. I feel like a total jerk because I'm not.

"Tonya?" Mrs. Kemper raises her voice, snapping me back to reality.

I shift my weight, regretting the basketball shorts again, but I'm having a hard time parting with them. "My name is Toni, actually. Hey."

The girls study me like I'm something they might be tested on later. The library smells like cinnamon, and comfortable arm chairs form what I've dubbed the Circle of Feelings. Beautiful hunter-green walls surround us as we pour our hearts out. Mazes of books that look older than Earth listen to each confession. The snapping fireplace fills awkward silences, which, until now, have been few.

As everyone stares, I get a wicked itch on my left butt cheek.

"Tell us a little bit about your background," Mrs. Kemper says, pushing for more.

"I'm from Shelburne." I shift my weight again, hoping that might extinguish the itch. "I used to go to Burlington High. My stepfather wanted to send me here. So. Yeah. Here I am."

I don't know what else to say, other than to express the need to scratch my butt, and that's probably unacceptable here.

"Does anyone have a question for Tonya?" Mrs. Kemper scans the group.

The red-haired girl from my Business Mathematics class, whose name I learned this morning is Shauna Hamilton, raises her hand and asks, "Is your last name really Valentine?"

"Um, yeah." What an odd question. Why would I make something like that up?

"That's so romantic." She sighs and crosses her ankles.

Shauna started off the group session today by proclaiming her love for a boy named Ryan, who goes to boarding school in Connecticut. Ryan has blue eyes. Ryan likes poetry. Ryan smells like fresh linens. That's already more than I care to know about Ryan.

I recognize a few other girls from my classes. The girl with the black bob is in my French class. Her name is Lemon, which is easy to remember because, well, I don't hear that name every day. Emma Elizabeth Swanson, the only girl before now who has spoken to me all week, is sitting directly across from me, staring at her shoes, a sour expression on her face. She's stayed silent the whole time.

I wonder what I must look like to these pretty, delicate, poised girls. I itch my knee and lean forward, back aching. I feel beaten down after another long day, and the throbbing behind my eyes won't go away. There's just so much freaking work. I'm worried I won't be able to keep up with it all.

"A lady should always cross her ankles or legs," Mrs. Kemper says with a kind smile.

I cross my ankles, surprised that no one laughs at me. Everyone must be accustomed to posture-corrections, not that any of them need it.

When the group session ends, I run to the bathroom and scratch my butt in peace. I splash water on my face for a pick-me-up and then slip my cell phone from my sock. My fingers hesitate on the keys as I debate whether or not to text Loch.

I need more than a text. I need to hear his voice. I need to feel his stable presence beside me as I complain about the demanding expectations of Winston Academy. I need to look him in the eye when I tell him that I miss our hunts, our former lives, which are evaporating so quickly, and that I still believe, will always believe, that Champ lives in Lake Champlain, waiting to be discovered by us.

. . . .

I forgot that Loch isn't home. He's working. So my after-school routine consists of homework and sulking. After an hour of calculus, my brain feels like it might explode so I watch some *Family Guy* reruns on my laptop and chow down on Snickers ice cream. But I'm so stressed out that I don't laugh once.

"What're you doing?" Mom asks, leaning in the doorway. "Why aren't you out with the guys?"

"Should I be climbing trees or rock-skipping or something?" I set the empty ice cream bowl on my night stand, next to a forgotten pizza plate that's starting to smell.

"It'll get easier." Mom plops down beside me on my bed. There's a ketchup stain on the collar of her gray T-shirt that's been there forever. "Change can be good."

I scoff. "Change sucks."

"Why don't we go grab a coffee?" she asks, brightening. "My treat."

"You're my mother. You're legally obligated to pay for me until March 1."

"Comb your hair, smart ass." She slaps my shoulder. "You're leaving this room."

. . . .

A few minutes later, we're driving down Shelburne Road on our way to Dunkin' Donuts. My mom car-dances to an overplayed rap song. I try to ignore this by staring out the window, but I'm offered only crisp, green lawns and places that remind me of my friends. The bowling alley. The drug store. The movie theater.

When I can't take it anymore, I switch the radio to the country station. The beautiful sound of Tim McGraw fills the space.

"I was wondering how long that would take," Mom says, grinning.

I wonder if this entire trip is some kind of test. "What's the point of this outing?"

"I refuse to let you drop into a hole," Mom replies cheerfully. "You've sulked all week. I allowed that. Today, you move on. And smile."

"Ladies don't smile," I grumble. "Ladies cross their ankles."

Mom frowns as we pull into the Dunkin' Donuts parking lot. She cuts the engine, unclasps her seatbelt, and turns to me. "Give me the word then," she says. "One word. And I'll put you back in Burlington."

For a moment, a flutter of excitement, but this has to be a trick. I ask, "Are you serious?"

She nods, pieces of her curly auburn hair breaking free from her ponytail. The older I get, the more I realize how much our looks differ. Her skin is flushed with colorful freckles while mine is pale and smooth. Her hair kinks into curls while mine is a sleek black. Her eyes? Dark brown, chocolatey. Mine? Light gray, the color of a darkening sky. Everyone says I look like my dad.

"I want to go back to Burlington," I say. I hold my breath. *Please. Say yes. Set everything right again.*

"Ugh! I can't let you do that, Toni." She shakes her head, smiling. Ha. I knew it was a trick, but I'm still disappointed. A simple yes would've solved everything. "Winston is an amazing opportunity for you. Burlington was stunting your growth."

Annoying. I don't need to grow. I think I'm good as I am, thanks.

Inside, we each order an iced latte—I inherited my mother's taste in all things beverage—and choose a table by the window. I press my head against the glass and sigh dramatically.

"How did group go today?" she asks.

Oh, that group and sharing feelings thing. My nightmare. "I've been transformed into a woman who eloquently expresses her feelings," I say. "I'm cured."

"We're not trying to *cure* you..." Mom stops and takes a break from trying to raise my mood as she sips her latte in silence.

When a red VW Bug arrives in the parking lot, I sit up a little straighter. My spirits raise. The Bug belongs to Ollie. I wonder if the guys have come looking for me.

"Wouldn't you know it. Your gentlemen have arrived." Mom sounds less than thrilled. "Which reminds me. Have you met any nice girls at school? It couldn't hurt to have at least one female friend."

I'm not really listening. I'm watching Ollie and Cowboy climb out of the Bug, joking around, happy as can be. Ollie puts Cowboy in a headlock. Cowboy wiggles to get free with no success, so he stomps on Ollie's foot. Ollie howls, laughing as he grabs his neon orange sneaker. Cowboy punches Ollie in the shoulder.

I chuckle. Those guys. Okay. So now they should march right in here to apologize for flaking out lately. All will be back to normal again. But they don't even look my way. As they walk toward the pizza place a few doors down, I tap on the glass, confused and a little panicky. I feel pathetic, but I don't care. I need them to notice me. Finally, they spin around and spot me.

Ollie walks right up to the window, lifts his shirt, and presses his stomach against the glass, shouting, "McRib!"

And then he starts sliding down, his belly fat screeching against the glass. Mom almost chokes on her latte. I don't laugh. I refuse to laugh. I'm mad at them for forgetting me.

Ollie beats the glass with his fists.

"Hey! Stop that!" The strung-out man behind the counter shouts. "I'll call the cops, you punks!"

Ollie skips to the door, and Cowboy trails behind. I sip my latte, masking my hurt. What are they doing here? Without me?

"McRib! What's up?" Ollie announces as the door swings shut behind him.

"Luke," Mom says to Ollie and then nods at Cowboy. "Justin."

Ollie nods back. "Mrs. McRib."

Mom leans back. "Please don't call me that. Aren't you all a little old for nicknames?"

"You don't mess with tradition," Cowboy says.

"Why does my sweet, lovely daughter have to be named after a sandwich?" Mom asks. "Why can't you call her Princess? Or Daisy? I don't know. Something cute."

"Mom," I protest. "Do. Not. Give. Them. Any. Ideas."

Ollie places his palms flat on the table and says in a low voice, "Your daughter ate ten McRibs in one sitting, Mrs. McRib. She is a bad-ass."

"Not my finest moment, Ollie." I press my lips together, annoyed. My stomach aches just thinking about those sandwiches.

"Oh, good. You're acknowledging my presence again." Ollie sweeps a hand through his dark curls, his signature just-rolled-out-of-the-sack look. In reality, he spends an hour in front of the mirror every morning to achieve such an artful hairstyle. His hair looks longer than normal, wisps of curls flirting with his narrow forehead, a sign we haven't been seeing each other as often.

Cowboy shoves his hands into the pockets of his jeans and pretends to be studying the menu. He chomps on a toothpick, squints, and then fidgets with the cuffs of his flannel button-down.

Why does seeing them feel so weird?

After the mooning incident, everything changed so quickly. One minute, I was a Burlington High senior. The next, I was accepted into Winston and swept into a different world. I hung out with Loch on his nights off, texted with everyone, but this run-in with Ollie and Cowboy feels so awkward, like I'm seeing them after a year apart or something. Maybe because Loch is missing from the equation.

Or maybe for a different reason altogether. Maybe we're growing apart.

Cowboy's cheeks appear fuller, more flushed, his blue eyes fresh and bright. I wonder if I look different to them, too. Or maybe this is all just my imagination.

Yet I feel that little empty space in the middle of my chest. A space growing wider every second, every day.

I must look uncomfortable because Mom gives me a strange look, clears her throat, and stands. "You know," she says. "I have to make a few calls. Be right back."

She goes outside and pretends to dial a number on her cell phone, stealing glances at me. Yes, she would like for me to collect at least one friend of the female variety, but she knows how much the guys mean to me. Despite her distaste for the old nicknames, Mom approves of the boys. They were beyond amazing to me, and her, when Dad died. I was fifteen when he had his accident. I needed my friends then, and they didn't fail me.

Ollie plops down across from me and asks, "What's your problem, McRib?"

My latte is empty, but I continue to sip through the straw.

"You're pissed," Cowboy says. He pulls up a chair beside me, the metal legs squeaking against the tile, and leans his elbows on the table.

"You guys forgot about the hunt," I say. "Like it was no big deal."

Ollie frowns and rubs the back of his neck. "My parents were mad about what happened with Principal Rogers, Toni. I can't go running off doing whatever I want. I'm in parental suck-up mode."

"I'm sorry." My throat tightens. A rush of guilt hits me.

We should've just gone home that night. Oh, the irony. I'd been trying so hard to hold us together for a few more hours, and now it feels like we're headed in different directions.

"You didn't make me do it," Ollie says, sighing. "But I have to come up with tuition for this snowboarding camp I want to try out next summer. The parents insist I pay for half now. Something about responsibility, blah, blah, blah..."

"Snowboarding camp?" This is the first time I'm hearing about this.

Ollie nods. "Not sure it'll even happen anyway. It's pretty expensive."

"And I'm sorry about missing the hunt, McRib. I got distracted," Cowboy says. "Katie Morris. She *spoke* to me."

Ollie pulls the sleeves of his long blue T-shirt over his hands. "He could barely function after that," he says, laughing.

I grin, tasting a hint of the old times again. Maybe he's forgiven me for the prank. "What'd she say?"

"*Excuse me.*" Cowboy sighs.

I wait for more, but that appears to be it. I shrug. "Well. That's a start."

"She bumped into me." Cowboy blushes. "It was awesome."

Ollie jumps out of his seat. "Anyway. Hope that clears stuff up. I'm starving! Later, McRib."

"Wait. Where you going?" Just when things feel comfortable again, they're leaving. I stand up so fast my chair tips back, hitting the floor with a loud *clank*. As I scramble to turn the chair upright, the man behind the counter gives me a dirty look.

"Just getting some pizza," Ollie replies.

Cowboy stands, shifting his weight from foot to foot, acting like he wants to say something else to me. I wait for an invitation to join them. Instead, Cowboy nods goodbye, and I watch them leave. They joke around outside and wave goodbye to

Mom, laughing and hollering all the way to the pizza place two doors down.

I feel like Loch's little sister. The old Amy, anyway. I feel like a shadow.

five

. . . .

THAT NIGHT, I'M DETERMINED
to wash away the memory of the horrible week
by saturating my mind with horror flicks. Images
of stupid teenagers being chased down by
indestructible killers mixed with awful special
effects and bad decisions will surely lift my spirits. I
stack five movies next to my laptop that I know will
melt my brain, slide in the first DVD, and settle in
for a night of wallowing in misery.

It's not even dark out yet, so I close the curtains
to create atmosphere.

I'm about halfway through *The Texas Chainsaw
Massacre* (the original) when there's a knock on my
door. I'm twisted up in my comforter, lying in the
fetal position at the foot of my bed, watching the
small screen on the floor with vague interest.

"Can't you tell I'm sulking in here?" I shout. The
door opens and a slit of light creeps into the room. I
hiss like a vampire. "Augh! No light!"

The shoes that step in are a pair I recognize but
hadn't expected to see. Two dirt-smudged sneakers
decorated with an ink-drawing of a cartoonish-
looking Champ. The right sneaker has Champ's

body and tail, the left his smiling head and cute eyes. When I sit up, my tangled hair falls over my face.

Loch closes the door, bathing the room again in a dull glow that matches my current outlook on life. "How *dare* you have a horror-fest without me," he says.

I cover my mouth with the blanket to hide my smile.

He's alive.

He's here.

He hasn't forgotten me.

"I thought you'd be too busy enjoying your senior year," I say, clearing my throat. "One of us should."

Loch sits down beside me, smelling like vanilla as always. I lean over and sniff him, breathing in the reminder of a past life.

"Sorry," he says, smelling his armpit. "I came from work."

I sit back, aware that I'm smelling my friend. "Yeah, about that. What the hell?"

Loch stares at the laptop. The sound of the chainsaw echoes from the speakers. He rubs his head in one quick movement, like he's wiping it clean, a habit he picked up last year after he shaved it. Specks of black hair cast a shadow across his skin as it grows back in, matching the whiskers along his cheeks.

Everything about Loch suggests a work-in-progress. His smudged shoes. His ripped jeans. His worn T-shirt with "The Lake Monster Lives" scrawled across the front in black magic marker. His appearance doesn't give off the impression that he's a neat freak. But he is.

"You're looking at the newest cashier of the Vermont Teddy Bear Factory Gift Shop," he says, leaning his head against my bed.

My eyes widen. "Do you get free teddy bears?"

"I get a discount. You want one?"

"That depends. Do they have a Texas Chainsaw Massacre Teddy Bear?"

He laughs. "If they don't, that's a crime."

Despite my determination to sulk all evening, I end up grinning again. We sit like that for a few minutes, side-by-side, watching the movie, until Loch clears his throat.

"Can you keep a secret from the guys?" he asks.

I look at him, surprised. "It would be my pleasure."

"This is kind of embarrassing," he adds as he reties his shoes. I pinch his knee, letting him know that I'm here. His cheeks redden, his brown eyes cast downward as he speaks. "My parents had to dip into my college fund to pay the mortgage. If I want to go to UVM next year, I have to contribute. A lot."

"Seriously?" I'm almost at a loss for words. Loch nods. His mom was laid off from her job two years ago, but I never realized how serious that was. Whenever I saw her, she looked happy. Loch said she decided to take some time off so I figured they were good. Amazing what people can hide.

"And your parents are just now telling you this?" I ask.

"They thought they would have the money back by now," he says. "It wasn't part of the plan. They're both upset about it. They feel shitty, and I don't want to make them feel worse. It is what it is."

Loch and I always planned to attend UVM together. He would major in Zoology while I took general ed classes for a year, trying to decide who I wanted to be, what I wanted to do. He had promised to help me find my way. I applied to other colleges, including Purdue University in Indiana, where my dad went. But I haven't told Loch that I'm considering going there. It pains me to think about being completely on my own.

I shift my weight. "What about scholarships?"

He shrugs. "Do they give scholarships for desperately average C-students?"

"If they don't, that's a crime," I mimic.

Loch slugs my shoulder. "So that's my life now, Toni. When I'm not in school, you can find me selling stuffed animals to tourists and kids. My path to a better future."

"And you can find me crossing my ankles, wearing plaid skirts, and talking about my feelings. Not exactly what we planned for our senior year, huh?"

Loch rubs his head again. As the chainsaw grows louder on screen, I want to give him a hard time for missing the hunt this week. I want to complain about Winston. I want to whine. But he's got real problems. I'm lucky. Mom wants me to concentrate on my grades, not work. I attend the best private school in the state, and I might have my choice of colleges in the spring without having to worry about tuition.

I don't have to claw my way into a good future. It's waiting for me on a silver platter.

I feel like shit.

On the screen, a scared girl runs through a Texas field, a chainsaw spitting into the air. I listen to the sound of Loch's breathing. I wish he could always be here. My constant presence. Up until now, he's always been around, reminding me of who I am, who I was, who I will be: a girl who doesn't cross her ankles. As we spend less time together, will I forget who I am? Will I lose myself?

I hold my stomach and burp, releasing the frustration from the week. Loch laughs. "Nice one." He tries to compete, but his burp comes out weak.

As the sun bleeding through the curtains fades, the glow from the computer screen illuminates the dirty laundry in the corner, the neglected dishes, the empty Mountain Dew cans lined up along my desk like an aluminum army of sugar. The chainsaw massacre ends, and Loch chooses the next flick. *Cloverfield.* I'm not surprised.

He reaches for my hand—at least I think he does—but then looks away and returns his attention to the movie. As my skin warms, I wonder if the stress of Winston is taking a toll on my immune system. I pull the blanket over my shoulders.

Loch's voice turns low, sweet. "Maybe we can make it through this year together, Toni."

I lay down, hiding my smile. "That would be nice, Loch."

After a few minutes, I float off to a comfortable sleep.

. . . .

I wake up with my head on his soft shoulder. A puddle of drool decorates the collar of his shirt. Loch is slumped against the bed, his mouth slightly parted. I jump up and wipe leftover drool from the corner of my mouth.

Loch doesn't stir. He sleeps like the dead. I look down at my basketball shorts and white tank top. My cleavage spills out. Embarrassed, I find an old sweatshirt on the floor, yank it on, and run my fingers through the knots in my hair.

Stepping over Loch, I head down the hall to the bathroom. I brush my teeth, wash my face, and comb my hair into a low ponytail. I take a deep breath and tell myself to calm down. There's nothing to get worked up over here. Loch has spent the night at my house before. He's seen me at my worst, smelled my morning breath, poked fun at the crust in the corners of my eyes.

This is nothing new.

So why does it feel different?

As I creep back into my room, Loch stirs and groans. I linger in the doorway and watch as his eyes open. For a moment, he looks confused, like he's forgotten where he is. Then his eyes find mine and a smile spreads across his face.

"Morning," he says. I don't know how he finds the strength to always be so pleasant in the morning.

"Caffeine," I grumble. "Must. Have. Caffeine."

A few minutes later, we descend the stairs together. Loch yawns and stretches, his long fingers scraping the ceiling on the way down. In the kitchen, Mom hovers over a bowl of cereal at the kitchen table. Brian grabs his keys from the hook by the garage. He freezes when he sees us, staring from beneath his New England Patriots baseball cap.

"Good morning, Mr. and Mrs. Richards," Loch announces, grinning sleepily. Most people forget this, but Mom took Brian's last name when they married a year ago. I kept Dad's name. I will always keep Dad's name.

43

"Micah." Mom wipes milk from her chin. "Did you sleep well?"

He smiles again. "Don't I always?"

Brian cracks his knuckles and says to no one in particular, "We'll discuss this later." He slams the door behind him. The sound of the garage door opening and closing blankets the confused silence.

"He's still not used to having a teenage daughter," Mom explains. "It makes him nervous."

"I don't belong to him," I snap.

Mom claps her hands. "Change of subject— Micah! How did your first week of senior year go? Everything you hoped it could be?"

"Sucked big time." Loch keeps on smiling. "Thanks for letting me stay over, but I better get going." He slaps me on the back. "Later, Toni."

"Later." Seconds after he leaves, I pop open a Mountain Dew and lean my elbows against the kitchen counter. As I twist the tab on the can, back and forth, back and forth, I can feel her eyes on me. Finally, I look up.

"Go ahead," I say. "Lecture."

"I probably shouldn't allow boys in your room anymore," Mom says. "Overnight. With the door closed."

"Mom." I pop off the tab and clasp it between my fingers. This new concern of hers is clearly Brian's influence. "He's not a boy."

Mom's eyebrows raise. "And how, may I ask, do you know that?"

I sip from the can. "I haven't seen his man bits to know for certain, but he's slept over here a thousand times before."

"But you've both grown up—"

"It never bothered Dad," I interrupt.

Mom looks up, her eyes full of surprise. She picks at her chipped red nail polish. "It *did* bother him." She takes a bite of her cereal. More milk dribbles down her chin. "But it would bother him more now. Micah grew into that manly chin of his. He transformed over the summer. He's kind of movie-star pretty now. Don't you think?"

"Mom. It's *Loch*."

As she tosses the bowl into the sink, leftover milk splatters onto the countertop, but she leaves it. "Things can't stay the same forever, Toni. Everything changes, whether you pretend to see it or not." She kisses my forehead before she disappears into the living room.

After I gulp down the last of the Mountain Dew, I toss the can into the recycling bin. I know things change. She doesn't have to tell me that. Once upon a time, I had a father. Now I don't.

If that's not living with *change*, I don't know what is.

six

· · · · · · · · · · · · · · · · ·

OVER THE NEXT FEW WEEKS, THE weather shifts and cold air swoops in to replace the last remnants of summer. Crunchy, crisp leaves spread across town like a seasonal plague. The lake water trembles, and the sky's mood darkens. Weather I would normally welcome on a Saturday morning, sinking beneath my covers, warm and cozy. Today, however, a special homework assignment calls.

"I must be seeing things," Brian says when I walk into the kitchen, the early morning light shuffling through the blinds. "It's Saturday, and Toni is awake before noon? Wow." He sips his coffee.

I set my book bag on the counter, groaning, and head for the fridge. I gulp down a Mountain Dew and grab another for the road.

"You headed out?" Brian asks.

"Yeah." I try to leave, but he just keeps talking.

"Searching for Champ with your boyfriend?"

I stop, embarrassed. "Loch isn't my boyfriend."

"Oh. Hard to keep up. Sorry." Brian cracks his knuckles. "Do you *want* him to be your boyfriend?"

Brian makes it sound like Loch could be a first boyfriend (oh, how cute!) to write about in a diary or something. How do I explain my relationship with Loch to Brian? Loch's my best friend. I can share things with him that I could never share with a *boyfriend*.

I take a deep breath, telling myself to be nice here. "I'm going to campus to finish a lab I didn't complete in my Community Ecology of the Forested Landscape class. I ran out of time."

Brian leans forward, faking interest. "You liking Winston?"

"Nope." It is my hell.

"It'll get better," he says.

"Sure," I lie, humoring him. "You're right. I bet it will."

I leave, dragging my feet. The fall air tastes cold and fresh, the only perk of rising so early. As I open the door to my Maxima, I see Loch making his way across the lawn, book bag on, wearing a blue sweatshirt and mud-stained jeans.

"Now there's a sight that needs to be documented," Loch says, holding up a flip camera, filming me as he walks. I picture the bags under my eyes, my messy hair, my tired look.

I block my face with my hand and say, "It's too early for the paparazzi."

He laughs and slides the camera into the front pocket of his jeans. "Seriously," he says. "I'm concerned here. The sun's barely up. And yet, here you are."

I tell him about my class, about the lab, about my inability to finish things on time at Winston. Loch leans against the hood of my car. "You know, I was just headed to the lake for a quick scan, but a stroll in the woods sounds intriguing," he says. "Can I come with you?"

"I'll just be wandering the woods, taking photos of trees," I say.

His eyes light up. "I could search for Bigfoot tracks."

I smile. Only Loch. I'm relieved by the idea of familiar company. "You driving?"

He takes his keys from his front pocket. "Naturally."

Loch just gets it—how important it is to continue traditions, however insignificant they may seem. I hide my excitement as we walk to his driveway.

As I climb into the Honda, I yawn again, my eyes still heavy with sleep. I tuck my book bag near my feet and pop open a second Mountain Dew, taking a few sips before setting it in the cup holder.

The empty backseat acts as a stark reminder that Ollie and Cowboy are slipping into new lives, away from me, away from this. It's not quite the same without Ollie kicking my seat, without Cowboy's quiet presence, without all of my friends surrounding me, our own miniature community. Pieces of the puzzle are missing.

"It should be illegal to be awake this early on a Saturday," I say.

Loch's chin looks extra stubbly this morning. "I'll wake you when we get there," he says.

I give him a thumbs-up and rest my head against the window, closing my eyes. Despite the ache in my heart, it isn't long before I drift back into a beautiful Saturday morning slumber.

. . . .

When I wake up, Winston's campus appears in the car window. Golden-leaved trees surround the brick building. Rolling green hills act as the backdrop. The moody sky has brightened, and rays of sunlight warm the side of my face. Fresh drool trickles out the corner of my mouth. I sit up, wiping it away, and glance over at Loch.

He's looking at me, an amused expression on his face.

"What?" I ask.

"Nothing." He turns away, grinning. "We're here."

We park in the front lot, and I lead the way into the woods behind the main building, following the worn path walked by many girls before me. Smarter girls. Girls who can finish an assignment on time. Girls who fit in here.

I forgot gloves, so I pull the sleeves of my sweatshirt over my cold hands as we trudge forward, the morning silence like a fog around us, ever-present.

"What are you supposed to be looking for?" Loch asks.

"I need to identify three different species of tree. I found two, but I still need a photo of the yellow birch." I kick at a pile of dead leaves and shift my book bag to the other shoulder. "I sure picked a fun elective. *Trees.*"

"This campus is pretty cool." Loch glances around. "Better than Burlington anyway."

I snort. "The hallways smell of stress, pretension, and nail polish."

Loch shrugs. "Better than the smell of White Castle burgers in the morning."

"Gross." I laugh. "Ollie still eats that stuff for breakfast?"

"The man loves those little burgers," Loch says, laughing.

I picture the excited look on Ollie's face as he walks the hallways each morning, the grease-stained bag in hand, the stench of onion strong. I miss that look. I miss that disgusting onion-y smell.

I stop to pull my camera from my bag, snapping photos of a few sugar maples, ignoring my wave of sadness. Such a silly thing to miss, Ollie's terrible taste in breakfast food. This is why I have to stay busy and concentrate on what's laid out in front of me. If I allow it, I will become a mourner, lost in a pit of grief over my former existence.

Loch takes out his flip camera and films the scenery.

"Bigfoot could be watching us right now," he says, scanning the area.

"Isn't he more of a Pacific Northwest monster?" I ask.

"He's seen around these parts." Loch lowers the camera. "A few years ago, two kids saw a big hairy monster on a camping trip."

"Too bad they forgot their camera," I say.

"These creatures can appear out of nowhere." Loch brightens. "It's the unexpected. The unknown. Not everyone is filming things all the time. No one can live like that." He sighs. "I wish I'd filmed what we saw. It was Champ. I know it. We could be millionaires or something."

"Doubt it," I reply. "Some people don't believe something even when it's right in front of their face. Just look at Ollie. He saw Champ. Yet—*denial*."

Loch stops walking. "You're cynical today."

I shrug. He's right. Lately, I just haven't been in the mood to believe in legends. I hate to admit it, but Ollie and Cowboy painted some doubt in my mind. What if we didn't see Champ that summer? What if our friendship is based on a floating twig or something? Not exactly a strong foundation. Maybe it's best not to know. Maybe we shouldn't be hunting for legends. What if we discover none of it's real?

I sigh. "Maybe these creatures shouldn't be found, Loch. Maybe Champ should remain a mystery. I don't know. Sometimes mystery is good. Take these group sessions I have to go to every week. They want us to share our feelings, expose ourselves, but maybe it's best to just keep things inside and locked away."

Loch starts filming again. "Best for who?"

"For everyone," I say. "Knowing every little thing could upset the balance of things." I look away, shivering. This time next year, what will we all be doing? Who will our friends be? Am I even capable of making a new friend? I've had the same ones since forever.

"Toni, look." Loch points to something in the dirt. I move in next to him, leaning forward, trying to see what he sees. My arm brushes his arm.

"What?" I'm staring at a pile of leaves.

"Don't you see that?" Loch points his camera at the ground like it's the most interesting piece of earth on, well, Earth. All I see are the leaves and dirt. "There." Loch points again.

Beneath the leaves, what looks to be a footprint is stamped into the mud. I nod. "Looks like someone's footprint."

Loch straightens and grins. His teeth are super-white. I don't think he's gone a day without flossing. "Not just anyone's footprint. *Bigfoot's!*"

I laugh and punch him in the arm. He punches me back, grinning again. I start walking, and Loch follows, shortening his long strides to keep pace with mine.

"I just want to know everything I can about this world," Loch says after several moments of silence. His eyes are cast downward. "I want to discover the stuff thought to be unreal."

"You want to recapture something from fifth grade," I say.

"Maybe." Loch fidgets with his camera. He doesn't look at me. "Don't you?"

A twig snaps behind us. We both turn, on high alert. I search the trees for the culprit but find nothing. When my pulse quickens, I feel stupid. Not like an axe murderer would attempt to kill us in broad daylight, but the sense of isolation out here, tucked away amongst the sugar maples, is sort of creepy. Maybe it's best I lay off the horror movies.

"BOO!" Someone drops from the tree above us. I scream and wrap my arms around Loch's waist, burying my face in his chest. He curls his arms around me, squeezing tight.

"I got you guys so good!" a voice says, laughing.

I look up to see Emma Elizabeth Swanson grinning back at me, her sequined pink sweater reflecting the sunlight, her honey-blonde hair pulled back into a neat ponytail. Her jeans are light blue and shredded at the knees.

"What are you doing?" I try to catch my breath, embarrassed I screamed so loud.

"Same thing you are." Emma's eyes twinkle. "These woods are a great make-out spot."

I look up at Loch. He looks back, his cheeks red. We're still holding each other. Quickly, we take a huge step back, peeling ourselves apart.

"Sorry if I interrupted. I'm Emma, by the way." She extends her hand to me, then Loch. We each shake it. Her nails are painted a pale purple and specked with glitter. She points to me and says, "You're in my business class, right?"

I nod. "Toni Valentine."

"Right. The new girl with the romantic name." Her eyes shift to Loch. "Now I *know* you don't go to Winston."

"This is Loch," I say. "My buddy. My pal. My platonic friend—"

"In other words, not her make-out partner," Loch interrupts. "My name's Micah."

"Oh. My mistake. Nice to meet you both." Emma looks around. "You haven't seen anyone else roaming the woods, have you? Perhaps a short guy with messy hair and adorable eyes?"

"Nope. Sorry," I say, exchanging a look with Loch. He just shrugs.

"Sometimes I think Kevin avoids me on purpose." Emma chews on her lower lip. "Am I being paranoid?"

All I can muster up is, "Huh?"

"He's probably around here somewhere," Loch says. "You never know what you'll find deep in the woods." He winks at me. "Keep looking."

Emma smiles. "Thanks!" she says. She prances off into the woods like an elegant deer, her pink sweater vanishing behind the trees. We watch her go in awe, like we'd just witnessed a legendary creature.

"She seems nice," Loch says.

I don't know what to say. Emma Elizabeth Swanson *does* seem nice, but that doesn't mean I can relate to her. At all.

Leaves break beneath my sneakers as I continue to walk. Loch follows, quietly filming the woods as I try to concentrate on finding the elusive yellow birch. I sense Loch's presence behind me and briefly feel close to my past life again. A past life that doesn't seem so out of reach.

"I think I found what you're looking for," Loch says.

I turn, following his gaze. He points to a tree with yellow leaves several feet to the right. The bark along the trunk is smooth, shiny, and separates into layers, giving it a shaggy look.

I snap a photo but, for some reason, I'm not excited about the find. "Thanks. That's just what I was looking for," I say, hoping Loch doesn't notice the reluctance in my voice. If he does, he doesn't say anything.

seven

· · · · · · · · · · · · · · · · ·

THE FRIDAY BEFORE HALLOWEEN, rain slams against the windows of Winston Academy while my brain swims with calculus equations. The last bell rings and bodies swarm and voices rise. I've acquired a talent for ignoring the loneliness that wraps around me during these busy moments.

Today, instead of fighting the crowd, I linger in the classroom and send a text to the guys about getting together for a Champ hunt this week. I don't care if my fingers bleed from texting them so much; we've got to get together soon. Eventually, they'll run out of excuses.

Seconds later, Ollie replies: *I'm sorry. I can't. Plans.*

Frustrated, I tuck my phone away. I'm starting to wonder if he's really mad at me because of that stupid prank.

The weekend just seconds away, I'm heading for the door when my bag bursts open, sending my books skidding across the floor. I round them up like lost cattle, but my French book is missing from the pack and I've got an essay about the history of Paris due on Monday.

I clutch my bag to my chest and power-walk down the empty hallway, surveying the dark wooden floors, the metal lockers, and the burgundy wallpaper. Thunder rattles the building. Spooky. Sometimes I wonder if this place is haunted with the souls of girls who cracked under the pressure.

I find my French textbook in my locker and wind my way back down the stone staircase. I stop before I reach the bottom. A girl sits on the last step, hunched over, her knees pressed against her chest, her shoulders heaving. I wait for her to sense me there, but she's so lost in her own grief that a bull horn could sound and she wouldn't hear it.

I turn to go back upstairs, but something holds me in place. The girl's honey hair falls over her shoulders in thin waves. She shakes her head, as if arguing with herself in her head. There is something familiar about her small frame, her milky skin, her pressed skirt.

"Emma?"

She turns and looks up at me with bloodshot eyes. Her sobs echo against the empty space and her lower lip trembles as she tries to speak, but all that comes out is a high-pitched *something.*

I can't describe the sound. It should be studied.

Emma buries her face in her arms and lets it all out. I mean *all* of it. I remain at the top of the staircase, extremely uncomfortable.

"Are you okay?" I shake my head. "Dumb question. Clearly, you aren't okay."

Emma says nothing and continues to sob. I approach as if she's a bomb and sit beside her, keeping a safe distance. I hold my bag in my lap and yank on the bottom of my shorts peeking out from beneath my skirt.

They didn't cover this in orientation. They should have.

"Do you want to talk about it?" I ask, trying to channel Mrs. Kemper in group session. She should handle this. She's a professional. I look around, praying someone else appears to step in, but the school is abandoned at this hour. Everyone is off to their after-school activities.

"He told me he loved me," Emma chokes out, wiping her nose with her sleeve.

"Oh. Cool." I pick at my thumbnail. How do I make her stop crying? I could do a funny dance. Sing a silly song. Make a dumb face. *She's not a baby.* She's just a teenage girl. Like me. Sort of.

Emma shakes her head, her cheeks red with sadness. "But it's over. He said he loved me. Then... he ended it."

"Oh," I mutter. *Please. Stop. Crying.* "Not cool then."

"He's a jerk." She waves her arms. "A beautiful jerk that I'm completely in love with!"

I have nothing to offer here, but I can't leave her alone, bawling in the stairwell over some guy. I wish there was a magic button I could press to make this all better. *Words. I should say more words.*

"I don't have a lot of personal experience with ex-boyfriends," I admit, considering a list of my romantic entanglements with the opposite sex could fit into a matchbook. "But I know how guys operate."

Emma sniffles. "You do?"

"I was the only girl on my neighborhood street growing up." Good ol' Newbury Lane. "I understand the male brain."

"What should I do?" Emma's eyes widen. She looks like a lost puppy. A puppy with dripping mascara. *Advice?* Should I really be giving it?

"Guys are clueless." I shrug. "Girls are clueless. I'm not trying to be insulting. It's a fact. A lot of things get lost in translation, I think, because no one's paying close enough attention. What's this jerk's name?"

Emma's tears have slowed. "Kevin."

"Oh, right. The guy in the woods. I'd bet money Kevin is blissfully unaware of how much he's hurt you. Hold on one second." I stand up, slip out of my skirt, straighten out my basketball shorts, toss my skirt into my bag, and plop back down. "Sorry. The skirt was bugging me. Where was I?"

"You said that everyone is clueless." She blinks a few times. "Even girls like me."

I shake my head again. *I am so, so bad at this.* "Let me try a different approach here. Okay. Remember Loch?"

"Your platonic friend?" I nod, pleased. Emma Elizabeth gets it. Loch. *My platonic friend.* Why can't Brian understand that?

"Right!" I say, sounding way more excited than I should. "Anyway. He dated this girl, She-Who-Shall-Not-Be-Named, for two years. He was madly in love with her. It was sickening." My stomach turns just thinking about it. "She cheated on him. A lot. He hated her for it so he ended it."

Emma frowns. "I didn't cheat on Kevin..."

I hold up a finger. "I'm getting to my point, I swear. A few weeks later, She-Who-Shall-Not-Be-Named began dating this guy who wore too much leather and talked with a lisp. Now how do you think Loch felt about that?"

Emma pulls a pink tissue from her bag. "Pissed."

Loch should've been pissed. God, I get so mad just thinking about that girl and what she did to my loyal Loch. Well, not *my* Loch. He doesn't belong to me or anything. Still. I want to punch She-Who-Shall-Not-Be-Named in the face.

"Worse," I say. "He was sad. It's like he completely forgot what a bitch she was. Like his memory was wiped clean. He forgot how much she hurt him, how she cheated. Seeing her with someone else—anyone else—stirred old feelings up again, and logic was thrown out the window. He wanted her back. We had to talk some serious sense into him."

Emma wipes her nose with the tissue. "So I need to make Kevin forget that he doesn't want to be with me? How do I do that? I don't want to date someone else."

I chew on my bottom lip. Maybe I should end the conversation before I do any permanent damage. But I want to help. She shouldn't be jerked around by some guy.

"You don't have to," I say after a moment. "You just need to make Kevin *think* that you are."

Truth is, I'm not one for mind games, but I don't know what else to say. It could work.

Emma shoves the dirty tissue into the front pocket of her pink-plaid book bag. "That's impossible."

"Pretending is easy. I do it here every day." I don't intend to be so revealing, but I can't shove the words back into my mouth. Emma looks at me, kindness behind her blue eyes. I feel bad that I haven't made more of an effort to get to know her until now. Maybe I'll change that.

"You're doing better than I did my first year," she says. "I was a wreck."

I look at her perfect manicure and perfect hair and perfect skin. Despite the fact she's just had a major cryfest, I still wouldn't describe her as a "wreck."

"Do you feel better about Kevin now?" I ask, changing the subject. "Your problem is fixable."

Just when I think I've done something good here, Emma starts crying again.

Advice. I suck at it.

"I'm sorry!" I stand. "I shouldn't have said anything. I don't know what I'm talking about. I've never had a boyfriend."

Why do my confessions keep spilling out around this girl?

"It's not that. It's just that I don't have anyone to pretend with." She wipes a gloop of mascara from the corner of her eye.

"Use a guy friend," I suggest, breathing a little easier. "Bribe him with, I don't know, food or something."

Emma crosses her ankles. "I never meet any boys. Kevin's an exception."

I pick at my thumbnail and lean against the banister, thinking. I should run before she starts bawling again. I look at her wide, bright eyes brimming with tears.

"I guess you'll just have to borrow one of my friends then," I say. It's a promise that I'm not sure that I can keep.

Emma sniffles, and I think she's going to start wailing again. Instead, she squeals so loud that the windows might shatter. She hugs me and skips down the stone steps in gleeful little spurts.

"THANK YOU, TONYA VALENTINE!" she shrieks. "YOU ARE MY NEW BEST FRIEND!"

I smile, blushing, and sling my book bag over my shoulder. For the first time at Winston, I feel like I might make a friend. "My mother would be so happy to hear you say that. And, hey, call me Toni."

eight
·················

EMMA ELIZABETH SWANSON IS cleaning my room while dressed like a black cat. Well, sort of dressed like one. The only indication that she intended to be a feline for Halloween lies in the set of black furry ears on top of her head. The remaining parts of her cat costume consist of a strapless black dress, fishnet stockings, and black knee-high boots.

Tom Brady lies in the middle of my bed, watching her with disdain. I think he's insulted. He would never wear knee-high boots.

After Emma dumps the army of Mountain Dew cans lining my desk into a trash bag, she kicks my dirty clothes with her heels until my various sweatshirts rest in a neat pile in the corner. The embarrassingly girlie pale pink carpet shows underneath. Emma arrived five minutes ago, but she's made more progress than I would in a week.

"I'm sorry," she says, out of breath. Her cat ears are crooked. "I hope you don't mind. I love organizing things."

"No problem," I reply. "We've all got our thing."

Emma's influence on my room is another reason for my mother to love her. Mom nearly fainted from happiness when I asked if Emma (a real live GIRL!) could come over before we headed off to Ollie's Halloween party.

"Time to put on my costume," I announce, heading to the bathroom.

When Ollie sent the text inviting me to the party at his house, I thought it was a joke. Ollie's never thrown a party before. None of us had, unless I count the brief hangouts before monster-hunting expeditions. Which I don't.

At least the four of us will be in the same place at the same time again. *That's* what matters right now.

The party's also the perfect setting for Emma to win her boyfriend back. I chose Loch as her fake date because he's the most reliable. We haven't seen much of each other over the last few weeks—he's been so busy with work—so I'm looking forward to seeing him tonight.

I inspect my costume in the bathroom mirror, pleased with my choice this year. There's no way the guys can beat this. It's simple. It's classic. It's comfortable. It's stereotypical Vermont. I skip down the hall and burst into my bedroom with a giant, "MOOOOOO!"

Emma stares at me, a tube of lip gloss in her right hand, a compact mirror in the other. She snaps the mirror shut, tucks it away, and crosses the room. The heels of her boots leave marks in the carpet like footprints in snow.

"Is that really your costume?" she asks.

As I spin around, presenting my outfit, the rusty bell around my neck produces a hollow clank. "Isn't it awesome?"

"You're a cow."

"Oh, good. I was worried you wouldn't be able to tell." I adjust the pink plastic udders on my stomach. The black-and-white-spotted jumpsuit hangs loose, but I don't mind. The hat, complete with pink fuzzy ears and a pair of horns, fits perfectly, but the best part is I can wear sneakers. I'll be comfortable all night.

"I can't see your *body*," Emma says, tilting her head. "You might as well be wearing a garbage bag."

"And?" *A garbage bag.* Could be a good costume for next year.

"There will be boys at this party." She fiddles with her silver stud earrings. "Cute boys. Right?"

"If people show up. Ollie isn't exactly Mr. Popular." Ollie flies under the radar at Burlington High. We all did. So I have a hard time picturing him as a Party God. Plus he's not a crowd person. He once told me he likes the alone time he gets on his snowboard, how he can't hear anyone telling him what to do. The fact that he's throwing this party still feels weird.

"Don't you want to show off your assets?" Emma asks.

I study my body. "I didn't know I had any."

"Blasphemy! You've got a banging body, Toni! I'm sorry, but I can't in good conscience let you hide those legs!" She advances toward me.

I take a step back. "Um...this isn't where we cue to the Movie Makeover montage, is it?"

Emma grins.

. . . .

An hour later, my cow costume's mutilated. Poor cow. It happened so quickly. Scissors and fabric flew through the air. Makeup brushes dusted my cheeks. Lip gloss sparkled under the bedroom light. I stare at the remnants of the black-and-white jumpsuit lying dead on the carpet, feeling naked.

"You're still a cow," Emma says, slipping on a pair of purple high heels. She doesn't go anywhere without at least two outfits. "You're just a cute cow now. Ha. That rhymed."

The knee-high boots I borrowed from Emma pinch my toes, dig into my heels, and make me dizzy. I'm not a tall girl, and I don't want to be. It's not natural for me to see the world from way up here. The fishnet stockings itch my thighs, and the lip gloss tastes like fruity chemicals. My boobs spill out of the black tank top (an old piece of my wardrobe from junior high that Emma found in my closet), and Emma's black mini-skirt is at least two sizes too small.

I'm exposed. At least she let me keep the cow bell around my neck.

"Your crush will faint when he sees you tonight," Emma says, studying me like I'm her masterpiece. She finishes cutting up the hat and ties the ears in my hair like a headband.

I adjust the underwear riding up my butt. "My what?"

"You don't have to tell me who he is." Emma powders my nose. "We don't know each other well enough to be trading secrets yet."

"I don't have a crush." I pull up the tank top. Immediately, Emma yanks it back down. I have some serious cleavage. Did my boobs grow two sizes in an hour? Emma must be some kind of boob magician.

"Seriously?" She tilts her head. "Not even a little one?"

"It's possible to go through life without being love-crazy," I say. I'm proof of that. I've survived this far.

Emma's eyes widen. "Yeah, but what a sad way to go through it."

I'm not lying. I don't have a crush at the moment, but I've had my share of them before. Those boys blend together in my mind, a merry-go-round of passing faces, and I barely remember some of their names. I pretend not to remember the boys who quickened my pulse, drove heat to my cheeks, and invaded my dreams because not one of them returned my feelings. I'd prefer not to recall the sting of rejection from the boys who preferred the girls in high heels, the girls who used hair products, the girls who sat on the sidelines during impromptu basketball games before gym class.

Boyfriends could wait until college.

"You don't know how lucky you are to know so many guys," Emma says. "I met Kevin by accident. He came to my house, passing out fliers for his lawn-mowing business. It was fate."

I picture an unsuspecting boy ringing a doorbell and the next thing he knows Emma Elizabeth Swanson is wrapping her legs around his waist, planting kisses all over his face, desperate to cling to a male.

Emma rips another piece of fabric from the dead cow costume and ties it around my thigh. "Um... what is that?" I ask.

"It's sexy. It's like a garter," she says. "The boys will stare at it all night."

"What's a garter?"

Emma laughs. She thinks I'm joking. She smooths the top of my hair, which is pinned into a high sophisticated bun. "You have amazing shoulders," she says. "Thin. Pretty. Classic. You should wear your hair up like this more often."

My cheeks redden. I wear it back often, but in a low messy ponytail. Just something to keep it out of my face. Nothing like what Emma's done. "Let's go over the plan again," I say.

Emma plops down on the bed and crosses her legs, ready to listen.

"You sure Kevin's coming?" I ask.

She nods. "I invited him. He accepted. He goes to a Catholic school in Shelburne so I think he's eager to mingle with the public school crowd. Truth be told, so am I."

"Perfect." I try to pace as I speak, but I stumble in the unfamiliar heels. I steady myself. "So Kevin shows up. When he does, you dance with Loch. Flirt. Talk. Whatever. Make sure Kevin sees you do this. I'll chat casually with Kevin about what a great couple you and Loch make. Blah. Blah. Blah. I can make up some juicy, but classy, stuff. After which Kevin will become steaming jealous and beg for your forgiveness."

Emma beams. "And we all live happily ever after."

"Yep." I wobble over to the mirror and check myself out. Embarrassed at what I see, I glance back at Emma. She's leaning back on her elbows on the bed and swinging her legs back and forth, staring at the ceiling. She looks so hopeful like that, lost in her own thoughts, her own dreams, her own romances. I think we might be, like, friends.

A nervous itch sprouts up on my right butt cheek.

I hope I don't screw this night up for her.

nine

· · · · · · · · · · · · · · · · ·

GREEN PASTURES AND VARIOUS rose bushes border Ollie's beautiful ranch-style home. A gravel road leads to a small horse barn behind the house, where his mother keeps her prize possession, a Morgan mare named Goldie. Across the fields, navy-soaked mountains line the sky, a thought-halting sight, even for a seasoned veteran. I would take longer to admire the moonlight spilling onto the grass, but my legs are freezing.

"I'm going to get frostbite in this outfit," I say to Emma as we make our way up the cobblestone steps, heavy bass music beckoning from behind the green door.

"Quit being such a baby." Emma applies another layer of lip gloss before slipping it back into her tiny black purse. "You'll be inside most of the night. It's not like you're out trick-or-treating."

As I reach for the door knob, Emma stops me. I feel my lips going blue as she places her hands on my shoulders and pushes them back.

"The entrance is everything," she says. "Walk into that house like you own it. Don't hunch over."

My teeth chatter. "Can you see my nipples through this shirt?"

She looks down. "Don't change a thing. You'll find a boyfriend by the end of the night with those things."

I just want to go in, get warm, and hang out with the guys. I don't want to think about the future or college. I don't want to think about Winston. I don't care if anyone checks out of my legs or my nipples.

Inside, the smell of stale beer and body odor hits me pretty hard. While I'd like to turn around as soon as possible and bolt, Emma pulls me forward into the crowd. I can't believe this many people showed up. I recognize most of them—the cop in the corner, the taxi driver taking a shot, the fairy with a purple wig, dancing. The fairy is Katie Morris.

But no one says hello to me. Do they recognize me? Was I ever important at Burlington?

Emma hooks her arm with mine and keeps guiding me forward. She moves her way through the warm bodies so confidently that you'd think she used to go to school with these people.

"Told you. You've got *assets*," Emma whispers.

"Huh?"

"People are looking," she adds.

I glance up. I've been transported to another universe, a universe where I'm not just one of the guys—I'm feminine and sexy. Weird. As Emma and I make our way into the living room, interested eyes dart from my neck to my hips to the cow garter tied around my thigh and then back again. Totally self-conscious, I hike up the tank top to decrease my cleavage.

Emma softly pinches my elbow. "You look great."

In the living room, music blares and bodies pulse and dance. Oddly, I find Emma's words encouraging. I raise my chin, bubbling with a bit of confidence. A game of beer pong takes up the center of the room beside the stone fireplace, the same fireplace where I roasted hot dogs with Loch, Ollie, and Cowboy last winter. A crowd forms around the beer pong table, cheering and placing bets on the two vampires versus two werewolves.

Ollie plays the part of unofficial referee, cradling a crystal glass filled with brown liquid. He's dressed in a puffy lime green coat and black snow pants with a pair of matching goggles on his head. He leans against his sleek, dark snowboard and smoothly sips his drink.

When he looks over, I wave like an idiot because I haven't seen him in over a month. His hair keeps getting longer. Ollie waves back, smiling, and raises his glass to me. He then wraps his arm around a werewolf's neck and cracks a joke. The werewolf laughs. I squint. Who is the werewolf? I don't recognize him. It would appear Ollie has made a new friend.

How could we let so much time go by without hanging out? What have I missed?

Without Champ, I fear we're losing each other. Champ is the thread holding us together. If we stop believing in him, wouldn't we stop believing in each other?

The space in my heart grows wider. I stare at my feet and lose my breath for a minute, until Emma cheerfully asks, "So where's my date?"

Thank God for the mission. I need the distraction. I search the crowd for Loch, but don't see him. "Follow me," I say, taking Emma's hand.

We head down the front hallway to the back of the house. The farther we get from the living room, the quieter it gets. Soon we arrive at the closed door to the study.

"Loch isn't a fan of huge crowds," I say. "He could be hiding."

Inside the study, we find Cowboy lounging in a tired leather chair, surrounded by walls of books. He's curled up with a textbook open on his lap. He hasn't worn a Halloween costume since sixth grade, when he dressed as a cowboy, the birth of his nickname. Tonight's no exception. He wears jeans and flannel. Nothing fancy.

I smile. "Hey, man. You're here."

He looks up, grinning. "Hey. What are you supposed to be?"

I twirl, still high off the confidence boost from Emma. "A cow."

"A *sexy* cow," Emma adds.

Cowboy's eyes shift to Emma. "Who are you?"

I smack my forehead. "Where are my cow manners?"

I introduce them. Emma waves hello, and Cowboy gives her a nod. He returns his attention to what I can now see is a chemistry textbook.

"And what are you supposed to be?" Emma asks. She's just so *friendly* and *cheerful*. I wish I could be more like that.

"Myself," Cowboy says. "That's hard enough."

"You do realize this is a party," I tease. "Not a study session?"

"Just getting a head start on my chemistry midterm," Cowboy says, adjusting the book on his lap.

I perch on the armrest. "You wouldn't happen to be avoiding a purple fairy, would you?"

His jaw tightens. "Why would you say that?"

Gently, I close his chemistry book and say, "Because. Chemistry is a breeze for you."

No one studies harder than Cowboy, not even me, but he's got natural smarts. Loch and Ollie were always satisfied with average grades, but Cowboy and I shared a common interest in achieving something a little more, a desire I developed because of my dad. When I was in middle school, Dad rewarded my good grades with these cute Tweety Bird stickers that I'd keep in a pocket-sized notebook under my mattress. I loved going to sleep each night knowing they were there, safe and sound, little rewards from my father.

"You saw her." Cowboy stands up, all jittery now. "She looks amazing."

"Please. Just talk to her," I beg. "You'll feel so much better."

Cowboy runs his fingers through his hair. "You might as well tell me to fly. Both impossibilities."

"So who's the girl we're talking about?" Emma asks.

"Katie Morris," I explain. "She's nice, actually. Super-smart. First in our class." I shake my head, embarrassed. "Burlington's class, I mean. Cowboy's second. I have this theory that they have a secret competitive thing going on."

Cowboy's cheeks bloom red. "Unspoken, unfortunately."

"Come on." I stand up and grab his wrist, attempting to pull him to the door. "Go bump into her."

He pulls back. "Maybe in an hour. I need to do this reading first. Reading relaxes me." With that, he sinks back into the armchair and reopens the chemistry textbook. I don't have time for this.

I sigh, brushing a loose hair from my eye, and turn to Emma. "Let's find your date."

Back in the living room, among the loud music and many curious eyes, I land on a kind and familiar pair. My pulse quickens. I lead Emma to the kitchen doorway. Loch's leaning against the frame with vague disinterest. He holds a red paper cup in his hand as he surveys my costume.

"I'm a cow!" I shout. "See? I have a cow bell and everything!"

Loch says nothing. Just sips from his beer. He would've loved my original costume. Embarrassed, I fidget with the stupid garter thing on my thigh. Now the costume feels stupid. Why did I let Emma talk me into this?

Emma clears her throat. "What's your costume?" she asks him.

"A UVM freshmen," he replies, gesturing to his gray University of Vermont T-shirt and torn jeans.

Emma laughs. "That's so lazy!"

Loch spills a drop of beer on his lake monster shoes, but doesn't seem to care. I'm surprised he doesn't howl for a paper towel. Is he buzzed or something? No, but he looks tired. Must be all those work hours.

"Can you believe all this?" I ask. "Ollie? Throwing a party?"

"I know, right? Our little Ollie is blossoming, I guess," Loch jokes, perking up a bit.

"He moves into this gigantic house and suddenly he's a party god," I add. Ollie used to live on Newbury

Lane with the rest of us, but a year ago his parents inherited a large sum of money from an obscure relative.

Someone comes up from behind and wraps an arm around my shoulders. The arm feels slick and puffy. I turn to see Ollie grinning at me, his small, straight teeth shimmering, his breath smelling of whiskey.

He slaps my back and says, "McRib! Thanks for coming! Who is your beautiful friend?"

Emma shouts her name over the music, adjusting her cat ears. "Are you supposed to be Shaun White?"

Ollie grins and sways and holds his stomach. His eyelids get heavy. I study him. I don't know Drunk Ollie. Drunk Ollie is a stranger.

"Are you okay?" I shout over the music.

"Better than ever!" He laughs harshly. I don't believe him. His laugh is too forced and artificial. Ollie hiccups, gesturing to the crowd. "People have been curious about my new house. Just dying to see the place. So...here we are."

"Yes." I step back. He reeks of alcohol. "Here we are."

He places his hand on my shoulder. "Remember that time we mooned Principal Rogers?" He advances toward me and raises his voice, pointing at my face. "That stupid prank ruined my life," he spits. "My parents think I don't take anything seriously now. Goodbye, snowboarding dream! Thank you, McRib!"

He sways, sways, sways. Well then. When alcohol is involved, the truth comes out. My stomach rolls over and my heart drops and I don't know what to say. That dumb prank ruined my life, too. Loch looks at me, sympathy in his eyes. Why do I get the feeling this isn't the first time Ollie has blamed me for his punishment?

Ollie stumbles off, waving at someone across the room. I stand there a moment, stunned, hurt, guilty. Ollie *has* been avoiding me. He's been lying, making up excuses not to hunt. On purpose. I'd been too distracted to pick up on it until now.

"Hey," Loch says, gently touching my hip. "Don't listen to him, okay? He's going through some stuff with his parents. It's not about you."

"Whatever." I grind my teeth and watch Ollie laughing with a group of vampires across the room. My chest tightens. "I don't care."

"Hold this for a second?" Loch hands me his full plastic cup and bends down to tie his shoe.

Foamy beer sloshes inside the cup. Ollie's now talking to Cowboy, who looks nervous, sick. He drinks from a crystal glass full of what looks to be whiskey. Ollie points to Katie Morris. She's standing just a few feet from them, her back turned, her purple wings bobbing as she dances.

My body warms and my stomach twists. I fight back tears. So much is shifting and I can't figure out a way to stop it.

I drink all of Loch's beer and let out a big belch.

Loch stands, impressed. "Nice one," he says.

I wipe my mouth and hand him the empty cup.

He steps toward me and touches my hip again. "You feeling okay?" he whispers. "I know Ollie said some things—"

"Peachy," I interrupt. "Come on. We've got a job to do tonight."

Emma leans into Loch. She adjusts her crooked cat ears again. "Thanks so much for helping me,

Micah. I don't know how much Toni told you, but this means a lot to me."

Loch looks as if he wants to have a serious talk with me but then asks, "So where's the boyfriend?"

Emma scans the crowd. Her glossy lips fall into a pinched frown.

"You sure he's coming?" I ask, beer churning in my belly. I probably should've eaten something.

"Kevin likes to pretend he has better things to do than show up anywhere on time," Emma explains. "Right now, he's probably sitting at home, watching the clock, re-doing his hair a million times. God, he lives like five minutes away, too." She applies another layer of lip gloss. "He wouldn't miss a public school party for the world though. Just wait. He's coming."

As she continues to search the sea of monsters and fairies and vampires for her ex-boyfriend, Loch whispers in my ear again, "I don't have to kiss her, do I? Lipstick doesn't go with my costume."

I shake my head. "No kissing."

Loch's eyebrows raise. "That a request or an order?"

I fumble for a response but come up blank. I look away. I can't tell him that I don't like the idea of him kissing Emma. He might read too far into that response. He is my *platonic* friend. But I still think that's crossing a line. What that line means exactly, I don't know, but the thought of Loch and Emma kissing makes me nauseous. This is why I don't usually drink.

Emma digs her nails into my shoulder. "He's here," she says. "He's here. Oh, Lord. Oh, Lord. He looks good. He looks so freaking good."

Focus, Toni. I try to guess which boy could be Kevin. The skeleton by the keg? The robot doing the robot over by the beer pong table? The tree chugging a beer?

Emma disappears before I can ask. Loch clears his throat and steps to the side, revealing Emma cowering behind his tall frame.

"He looks so, so good," she repeats, trembling. "I don't know if I can keep my cool. I want to go over there and *kiss him so bad*."

Loch hides his smile by scratching his nose.

I touch Emma's elbow. "Which one is he?" I can do this. I can be a good friend to a girl. I think I'm doing this right.

"King of the Jungle," she says. "Six o'clock."

I have no idea what she means by six o'clock, but there's a guy dressed as Tarzan pumping beer from the keg in the corner. The foam overflows, splattering his leopard-printed loin cloth, the rest dripping onto the carpet. Tarzan—I mean Kevin—shrugs and walks away from the spillage. His skin is smeared with orange bronzer and grease coats his messy brown hair.

I've been staring a beat too long considering a loin cloth is involved here, but it's difficult to imagine Emma Elizabeth Swanson with that guy. I would picture her with a James Bond, someone smooth and cool or something. But, hey, I guess we've all got our reasons for falling in love with a particular person.

I clap once and pull myself together. "Okay!" I announce. "It's show time!"

. . . .

A few minutes later, Tarzan/Kevin (who smells like beer and spicy body lotion) is drooling over my cleavage, which means he's not looking at Emma and Loch. I adjust my tank top again, but this doesn't avert his attention. I try not to sneeze as I sip my fresh beer.

"Do you believe in lake monsters?" I ask.

"Huh?" he shouts over the pounding music, his eyes glued to my chest.

"There's a guy over there obsessed with lake monsters," I shout. "He's the UVM student, dancing with the black cat? They make an adorable couple, don't they?"

A ping of jealousy hits my gut. *They do make an adorable couple.* I'm starting to get a really, really bad feeling about this. Like maybe I should've insisted on Ollie or Cowboy taking this fake date.

Kevin finishes off his beer and refills it. He's barely left the keg since he arrived. I don't know how much longer I can keep this up. I feel like I'm talking to a brick wall.

Why does Emma like this guy? Maybe if I tell her that he won't stop staring at my chest, she'll see the error of her ways. But she might hate me for saying something like that.

As I take another drink, Emma turns her body and grinds into Loch as the music blares. She swings her hips, flips her hair, and does an excellent job of pretending she isn't being watched. Loch dances beside her, moving his hands toward her waist, then away again, like he can't decide if he's allowed to touch her.

Kevin moves his stare across the room and finally lands on Emma. His voice betrays nothing as he says, "I know that girl."

"Oh!" I mock surprise. "I hope she's just a friend because she's looking super-cozy with that UVM guy."

As I say this, Loch places his hand on Emma's neck, pulling her toward him as he whispers in her ear. Whatever insecurity Loch was displaying before has melted away. My blood runs cold.

His lips are close to her skin. His fingers in her hair. Her eyes locked with his, her small body folding into him like a missing puzzle piece.

"Do you know that guy or something?" Kevin asks, scratching at his loin cloth.

"I thought I did." The music is too loud. It's cutting into me. My head is throbbing.

"I used to date that girl," he says. "One word: clingy. I feel like I should warn him or something." Kevin finishes another drink and tosses the empty cup to the floor. "I need some fresh air. You coming?"

I turn around and face the wall. I can't watch this. Not sure what my problem is because they're just pretending. And we planned this. *I* planned this. Even if they aren't pretending, this isn't a big deal. Loch doesn't belong to me. He's a friend. He's *Loch.*

But I don't want them doing whatever it is that they're doing.

Adrenaline (or perhaps alcohol) rushes to my head. I need to do something. Anything to pull them apart. A diversion! I stand on an empty chair, which wobbles under my weight. These high heels make me terribly unsteady. I'd better make this quick. A few eyes move my way, but the entire room listens when I raise my cup into the air and shout, "Everybody drink and MOOOO!"

Surprisingly, a series of *moos* echoes throughout the house. Small moos. Loud moos. Drunk moos. People cheer. I'm a hit! The music roars.

In the crowd, I spot Ollie. He's leaning against the wall, his eyes closed, ready to fall asleep. Why does he want to go to snowboarding camp anyway? Why would he want to leave us the summer before college? Doesn't matter. He's unhappy. His unhappiness needs to be fixed. I raise my cup in his direction. I got him into hot water with his parents. I can get him out. Somehow.

I spot Cowboy and Katie in the corner. She's talking to him, smiling, asking him questions. Cowboy shrugs and nods and shrugs and nods, his face as red as a tomato, until Katie gets bored trying. She waves goodbye and moves across the room to talk to someone who will actually talk back. I raise my cup to Cowboy and vow to help him, too. I don't know how or if that's possible. But I will try.

So maybe this year won't be about Champ. So what? It can be about helping each other instead. Growing *together*. As long we're tight as always, it doesn't matter. I just don't want to lose these guys.

After I finish my beer, I feel myself falling, falling, falling. The chair whips out from beneath my boots. I'm spinning through the air until soft hands wrap around my waist and bring me upright again. Soft, vanilla-scented hands.

My cheek presses against his chest. All I can see are the letters on his shirt. I run my fingers over the stubble along his chin and the light freckles on his left earlobe.

"Damn, Toni. You're already drunk?" Loch's giant arm drapes over me.

"Did he see? Did he see?" Emma asks. Her cat ears are crooked again as she searches the party for Kevin.

"He saw," I say, wrapping my arm around Loch's waist. "He said he needed air. You know what that means..."

"It worked!" As Emma bounces up and down, her cat ears fly off her head. "He wants me back! He's upset!"

"It could mean that he needed some air," Loch adds calmly. "It's starting to smell rank in here."

Emma kisses my cheek and grabs my hand. She pulls me away from the comfort of Loch. No, I don't want to leave him. Not yet.

"I gotta see the look on his adorable face," she says.

As she pulls me through the crowd, cigarette smoke settles into my hair. Gross. Outside, the cold air whips across the fields in soft bursts. A clan of vampires hangs out on the front lawn, smoking and laughing, and a drunk green fairy pretends to fly across the grass. An annoyed carrot watches her from a distance, checking her watch.

"I don't see him," Emma whines.

Loch appears—I love it when he just *appears*— and hands me a bottle of water. "Here," he says. "You look thirsty."

I lean my head on his shoulder as I drink. When did I get so tired? He wraps his arm around me again, and I close my eyes, drifting away until the sound of someone barfing grabs my attention. Someone to my right is puking on a beautiful white rose bush. When the culprit reveals himself—loin cloth and all—a gasp escapes Emma's glossy lips.

"Emma," Kevin slurs. "Hey..."

It happens quickly. Emma grabs Loch's face and presses her lips to his. For some reason, I expect him to back away, explain that he doesn't like her like that, but Loch accepts the kiss. Kevin shouts something. Someone, somewhere, laughs. A white deafening noise sounds in my ears as I bend over, my stomach flipping.

My turn to barf.

ten

· · · · · · · · · · · · · · · · ·

THE NEXT DAY, I RETURN TO MY usual beauty routine—low ponytail, washed face, maybe some ChapStick—but I do adopt one change from Emma's Movie Makeover. I stick with the hairspray she gave me, only because I like the citrus-y smell of it. But my face remains lip gloss-free. After a night of pretending to be someone else, everything at Winston clicks back into place. Or so I think.

The second I step out of my car on Monday, fidgeting with my basketball shorts, Lemon walks straight up to me and says, "I need a fake date with Micah!"

I fall against my car door in shock. "Huh?" The group sessions aren't improving my speech skills.

Emma approaches, her spotless white coat wrapped around her, hair flying about in every direction. The day is windy, bitter. "I hope you don't mind," she says. "I told Lemon about what you did for me this weekend. Kevin has called twelve times since the party. *Twelve.*"

Lemon places her hands on her hips. "I. Need. Micah. NOW."

"Whoa, whoa, whoa." I pull my coat sleeves over my hands. "I don't pimp out my friends. He was doing me a favor, that's all. His body isn't for that."

Lemon makes a face, kind of like she's sucking on, well, a lemon. "GROSS. I need him as a cover. I'm not interested in his *body*."

I look to Emma. She explains. "Lemon's parents don't approve of her sexuality."

"My parents are *impossible*," Lemon says. "They refuse to let me see my girlfriend. They keep me on lockdown, but if I had a boy to go out with, they may be more lenient. Ecstatic, probably. They would let me stay out all night long if they thought I was with a boy."

As we walk to the main building, Lemon's high heels scratch against the pavement. I can't believe another Winston girl is actually speaking to me. I move my heavy book bag to my other shoulder and say, "I'll check to see if he's available."

"I'll pay a ridiculous amount of money," Lemon says.

How much is ridiculous? But I don't ask. This is too weird. I'm not selling Loch. I'm not even sure that first round was successful. It was just a mess. Literally.

"Good to know," I reply with a nod.

Lemon's black bob bounces with shine as she trots along and grabs my wrist, her pink nails digging into my skin. "Please. You don't know how much I need this. Any boy will do. Emma says you know lots of guys. Guys who aren't assholes. I need help. Have you ever been in love?"

Her question catches me off-guard, like I've just been called on in class but I haven't really been listening. I respond with another oh-so-eloquent, "Huh?"

"Have you ever been in love?" she repeats.

"What does that have to do with anything?" *Love.* The word alone makes me queasy. Aren't we all too busy and stressed out to be in love anyway?

Emma and Lemon exchange a look, and then Emma answers for me. "She's never been in love."

We're inside now, pushing through the crowd. As my book bag slams into various shoulders, I mumble apologies under my breath, annoyed. Of course I've never been in love. Who has time for that? I feel like I'm late for class. I pick up the pace. Or maybe I just want to get away from this conversation.

"Okay. MONEY," Lemon says. "Not everyone understands the nature of love, but everybody gets the nature of money. Name your price, Tonya."

"It's Toni," I correct.

Emma falls back a step, hiding behind a false quiet persona.

"I need a boy for next Friday night," Lemon continues. "A boy who can be mature about my relationship. Which means he won't ask to watch us kiss or anything stupid like that. Oh, and he should also have a car. He should know how to say a complete sentence. He should also have some manners because my parents will have to meet him."

As I open my locker and drop my book bag on the floor, Lemon slides something into my palm. A large wad of cash. I look at her, perplexed. The desperation behind her green eyes is sort of disturbing.

"I can't take this." I try to hand the cash back, but Lemon folds her hands behind her back and shakes her head. Across the hall, I catch Shauna Hamilton glaring at me. She looks suspicious. I hide the money behind the locker door, praying no one sees it and labels me a drug dealer. Or a guy dealer.

"That should get me one reliable guy for Friday night," Lemon says. I open my mouth to protest, but Lemon interjects in an unsteady voice that shuts me up. "Please, Toni."

I press my business book against my chest, pondering her offer. I don't know if I can get her what she wants. Loch will probably be working Friday. But—Ollie. Cowboy. They might be available. I don't want to admit this to Lemon or anyone, but I'm not as dude-savvy as I once was. I think the plaid skirt is scaring them away this year.

Instead, I tell her I'll do my best, and that seems to be good enough for her. She hugs me before skipping down the hallway, singing a love song I don't recognize as her black bob disappears into the thinning crowd.

I adjust my basketball shorts again. What am I getting myself into?

Emma tries to slink away, but I grab the strap of her bag, holding her in place. "Not so fast," I say. "I didn't know I was starting a service here."

"I'm not the only girl around here who could use a dependable guy," Emma says, pulling her hair back into a sleek ponytail. "Some of us need a trustworthy platonic male. I wouldn't be a good friend if I didn't tell Lemon how you helped me."

I let go, close my locker, and lean against the cold metal, sighing. "I'm glad you're back with Kevin. You look happy." She really does. A subtle glow oozes from her cleansed pores.

"I'm not back with Kevin." She smooths a loose hair.

"I'm confused." I make a face. "How did I help you then?"

"You made him realize his mistake," Emma says, examining her nails. "But I won't take him back right away. Nope. He needs to suffer."

Her ponytail flaps behind her as she disappears around the corner. I stare at the money in my hand. I still don't know about this. After several moments, the first bell rings. I tuck the cash inside my book and hurry off to class.

. . . .

After lunch, I settle into a bathroom stall, close the door, and lean against the brick wall, feeling the weight of the money in my palm. I count it. Twice. Lemon handed me $200 to rent my best friend on Friday night. Just to pick her up, chat up her parents for a few minutes, and then drop her off later. As easy and simple as a chauffeur service.

$200.

I remember what Emma said. About other girls needing my help. How many Winston girls needed a fake date? How much would they pay for one?

345 girls at Winston. Approximately 30 Friday nights in a school year. Based on Lemon's $200 fee for each Friday night date, that's a $10,345 profit for the year. If I provide a second or third guy for another date that same night, that number triples. Maybe a young lady would need to rent a boy for a fake study date on a Tuesday or something.

Bam.

Another $200.

A semester's tuition at UVM is something like $27,000, including room and board. I looked it up when he told me about his situation. Loch could save cash by living at home for the year, but I doubt he would want to do that. Plus, I could charge more. If demand increases and supply remains unchanged, the price for goods will increase.

There's a demand.

I've got the goods.

I know three trustworthy gentlemen for the job. Well, maybe not exactly *gentlemen*, but I could work on that. Help them become whoever they need to be for a particular evening.

No sex stuff. That I want to be clear on. Just friends helping friends with money. What could be the harm in that?

I run my fingertips over the bills, folding them before sliding them into my sock. I smile, pull out my phone, and text the guys. If cash won't get us all back together, nothing will.

eleven

. . . .

A WEEK LATER, THE GUYS AND I ARE
together again. At last! All four of us! We're watching
Monday Night Football in the Garrys' basement. It's
not the monster hunt I had proposed—Ollie and
Cowboy didn't want to miss the game—but I'll take
what I can get.

The New England Patriots (Boo! Hiss! Boo!) are
playing the Indianapolis Colts (Yay! Yeah! Woo!).
I'm the only one rooting for the Colts. My dad was
a huge Colts fan and spent a large chunk of his
childhood in Indiana. Some of my earliest memories
involve my dad, football, and a giant mound of
nachos. A picture of me sitting on Dad's shoulders,
my arms raised, both of us dressed in Colts' gear,
sits on the mantel in the living room. A thin layer of
dust covers it now because Mom often skips over it
when she cleans. I think she's afraid to look at it too
closely, like she might get sucked into the past and
forget about her new life with Brian.

During halftime, I propose my business plan
to the guys. The Colts are winning (naturally)
so they're all in a bit of a bad mood, but I hope to
change that.

"Gentlemen! I have gathered you here today for a very specific purpose," I announce. I stand on an overturned trash can as the basement buzzes with subdued chatter and random belches.

Loch shifts his weight on the crumb-filled couch. "Finally!" he says. "Get to the *money* you mentioned. Don't make me sit through more football."

Cowboy is hunched in a brown armchair in the corner, happily flipping through his American History textbook, waiting for halftime to be over. Ollie is slouched beside Loch on the couch, sipping a Mountain Dew. Some dribbles down his chin as he stares at the television. He won't look at me and keeps checking his watch every five minutes. I get it. He's still mad. This will fix it, though. This plan will make everything better again.

I need all of them in on this, not just Loch, although he will benefit the most. If I can get all three involved, we can bring in more money. Plus, this is something we can do together. Life can be like old times again. We can bridge the divide.

"It also involves *women*," I add. All eyes on me. I smile, struggling to keep my balance as the trash can wiggles beneath my weight. "I need you, gentlemen. The girls at Winston need you."

"Again. You mentioned *money*," Loch says, impatient.

"Emma isn't the only girl at my new school in need of a fake date," I continue. "Winston girls don't have much opportunity to forge male friendships. They've had boyfriends, sure, but no one they can really trust. Boys, according to them, have very bad intentions. They've never known the benefits of a platonic relationship with the opposite sex or the favors that may come with such friendships."

Ollie raises his hand. "I have bad intentions. Very. Bad. Intentions."

I point to him and say, "You want to fall in love, Ollie. It's obvious from the stash of romantic comedies you keep under your bed."

"So what are the Winston girls like?" Cowboy asks.

"Giving up on Katie Morris so soon?" Ollie reaches into a bag of chips and stuffs his face.

Cowboy reddens. Again. "I bored her at your party, man. She couldn't get away from me fast enough."

"That can be fixed," I say. "She'll come around."

Cowboy shrugs and focuses on the textbook in his lap. Poor Cowboy. He's just too shy. If he could open up a little more, Katie would absolutely give him a chance. They've got a lot in common. I need to figure out a way to help him grow some confidence.

"These Winston girls are super-intelligent," I say. "Ambitious." *Intimidating. Scary. Terrifying.* "They just need guys," I continue, keeping those thoughts to myself. "Guys they can use in platonic ways."

"Use?" Loch asks. "Like how?"

"To make a boyfriend jealous. To piss off the parents. To please the parents. Whatever. You will become an alibi," I say. "You will become a false door. Your job is to be a trustworthy gentleman and hide the truth. I would like to allow them access to three *dependable* guys. We'll split your date fees down the middle, so you each get paid for the time you put in. No pooling tips."

Loch frowns and scratches his stubble. "This sounds like an escort service."

"It's not an escort service," I say, folding my hands. "There will be no exchange of fluids. This is a platonic and disease-free service. It will be no different than renting a car. Or a tuxedo."

Loch raises his hand. "I've had sex in my car. While wearing a tuxedo."

Cowboy groans. "Do you have to remind us every day?"

"Pretty sure this is the first time I've brought it up," Loch says with a shrug.

After the reminder that Loch is the only non-virgin in the room, the trash can tips over, sending me flying forward. I land on my elbows with a giant thud. "Damn," I mutter as Ollie bursts into laughter.

He stands and claps. "Nice one! So elegant!"

Asshole. I feel someone's hand on my back. Loch helps me to my feet, checking my elbows for rug burn. I think he asks me something, but all I can hear is Ollie's irritating laughter. I kick the trash can, and it slams against the wall with a huge *clank.* Ollie's laughter stops.

"It's not funny!" My cheeks burn. "Would you even care if I legitimately hurt myself?"

Ollie's voice raises, drowning out the TV. "Do you even care that I can't go to snowboarding camp in Colorado because of you?"

The room is quiet. Too quiet. I suck in air, trembling. So I haven't been forgiven. Clearly. I talk slow. "I'm sorry you have to pay for your camp, Ollie. That sucks big time. It was a stupid prank, but I doubt it's the sole reason you're in trouble with your parents."

"She's trying to help us make money," Loch says, resting his hand on Ollie's shoulder. Ollie steps away, glaring at me. "Money you could put toward the camp. Didn't you listen to anything she said?"

"Did *you* listen? It sounds like a disaster waiting to happen," Ollie spits. "Of course you would defend her."

Loch clenches his jaw. Ollie looks away. Sips his soda. Sulks. This feels deeper than snowboarding camp. Am I missing something here? Why is Ollie so disappointed that he'll be stuck here for the summer? We're here. That should mean something.

"Game's back on," Cowboy says, closing his textbook. He hunches over, looking uncomfortable.

"I'm going home," Ollie says, pulling at his ear. "I just remembered. I have to help Jason with something."

When Ollie stands, I step in front of him, puffing my chest out as if this will somehow make me taller or meaner or somehow more acceptable to him. He acts like we're inconveniences. Like we don't matter. Like he'd always rather be somewhere else. That's starting to piss me off.

I poke him in the chest. "Challenge."

"You're delusional," Ollie says, waving his hand in my face. "And stuck in sixth grade." He moves past me, headed for the stairs.

"*Chicken*," I whisper.

Ollie glares at me, his nostrils flaring. Ha. No matter how much he wants to move on, to grow up, to go to some stupid camp across the country, there are still some things about him that remain the same. He can't turn down a Challenge. Hasn't been able to since sixth grade.

"Can we chill out?" Cowboy says, wedging himself between Ollie and me.

"Hey," Loch says. "Can we talk more about the business? The money—"

"Fine," Ollie interrupts, our eyes still locked. "Challenge accepted, McRib."

. . . .

A few minutes later, the football game is forgotten, and the gathering has moved to Loch's driveway. I dribble a basketball between my legs. Excitement and dread settles into my joints. The fall air nips at my bare knees. Loch and Cowboy lean against the garage door, watching with twin looks of horror.

I won the coin toss.

My ball.

Ollie stands beneath the goal, fake-yawning as I dribble and shoot.

Nothing but net.

He yawns again, bouncing the ball across the pavement as I lean forward, prepared to block him. "You can't beat me," he says. "I don't want to humiliate a girl."

"I'm not a girl!" It's one of those statements that sounds stupid about a second after it spills out.

Ollie shoots. He scores. He gloats. I want to punch him in the face. I picture him rubbing his stomach against the Dunkin' Donuts window weeks ago, joking around, somehow pretending we were still friends. He's become so *dismissive* of me.

Whatever.

I just need to take this guy out.

I go in for a simple layup, but Ollie jumps as the ball flies through the air, blocking my shot. I smell the sour cream and onion chips on his breath and scramble to rebound the ball. I dribble away from the net.

"You can't make that shot," Ollie taunts. "You never make that shot, McRib."

I plant my feet, growl, and shoot from the three-point line. The ball spins through the air and hits the backboard with a subtle clunk. The ball settles around the rim, but then flops over the side.

"I told you!" Ollie cheers.

As he laughs and rebounds the ball, anger courses through me. So I'm not good enough anymore, huh?

I barrel into Ollie's gut like a bull, and we both go flying through the air, landing on the concrete with grunts. My chin scraps the pavement, but I don't care, even as I taste blood. The ball pops loose and rolls into the grass. Ollie scrambles to his feet.

"You're crazy!" he shouts. "When are you gonna grow up, *Tonya?*"

Tonya?! Ouch. Not even Mom calls me that when she's pissed. Out of breath, Ollie examines a bloody scrape on his hand. I rub my chin, but my hands won't stop shaking. I really need to punch something. Loch and Cowboy stare in disbelief, but I don't care what they think. I kick the basketball across the yard and hurry across the lawn to my house where I can feel alienated in a more familiar way.

. . . .

Later that night, I'm sitting in my driveway with a pile of colorful sidewalk chalk stacked beside me. I shiver. The hood of my sweatshirt over my head, I draw a lake monster on the cement. The long neck, the small head, the round body, the black tail against blue water. I trace that tail over and over again until it's a thick tunnel of darkness.

The smell of chalk reminds me of Dad. He should be sitting across from me, adding to the picture, making it more beautiful and unique. He was such a good artist. I pause, short of breath, and close my eyes for a moment.

When I open them, there's a blue ice pack in front of my face. Loch plops down across from me and dangles the ice pack like a treat. I take it and press it across my wounded chin, which stings. I add rain clouds above the lake monster.

"We're in," Loch says. "All of us."

"Huh?" If I responded like that at Winston, I'd feel like a prize moron. But with Loch, it feels okay to be not-so-eloquent.

"Your business," he says, pulling the sleeves of his sweatshirt over his hands. "People use each other anyway. Might as well get paid for it. For fake dates. Or whatever."

I drop the chalk. "How do I know Ollie's not going to mess this up? These girls are my peers."

"He hates to admit it, but he does need the money," Loch says. "Cowboy does, too. He thinks the way to the heart of Katie Morris is planning an epic prom night for her."

I hesitate, doubting all of this. I thought the guys would immediately be excited about the business, but the showdown with Ollie proved otherwise. Maybe there's too much resentment to be working together. And I'm hurt they would discuss the business without me. It was my idea. Why leave me out?

"I don't know," I say, biting my bottom lip. "Maybe we should forget it."

Loch scoots closer and asks, "What are you so afraid of, Toni?"

I'm afraid my friends are all leaving me behind. I'm afraid they don't accept me anymore. I'm afraid of becoming the girl hung out to dry. I'm afraid to be different from them. I'm afraid that, without them, I'll become unrecognizable to myself. Of course I say none of this.

"Ollie's just trying to move on," Loch adds. "I wouldn't take it too personally."

"Move on from what though? A lifetime of friendship?" My voices rises. I swallow the lump in my throat. "Who would want to move on from that?"

"Yeah. I don't know." Loch fidgets with his shoelaces. I color the rain clouds blue, fighting back tears. Loch picks up a piece of chalk and adds a bright yellow sun above my drawing of Champ. We sit like that, coloring, until my hands grow numb.

Brian's voice cuts through the silence. "Toni? What are you doing out here? It's late." He stands underneath the porch light, the brim of his baseball cap shadowing his face.

I wave. "I'll be right in."

Brian lingers. Watches. Cracks his knuckles. I think about what he said about Loch being my boyfriend. I wave again, irritated, and he finally goes back inside.

Loch and I stand, surrounded by dark sky. My breath is a puff of white fog between us. The lawns around us are crunchy and yellowed, tipped with frost.

"So are we open for business?" Loch asks, hopeful. His features appear soft against the night, his wide face a complex system of lines and grooves. He scratches his chin again. I realize that Mom's right, Loch has developed a classic movie star chin. He's like a tall scruffy gentleman come to escort me to a ball or something. I step back, shivering, although I'm not so sure it's from the cold anymore. Without this new venture, there's a real possibility we could all drift away from each other. I can't lose my boys. I just can't.

"Open for business," I say with a nervous smile.

twelve

. . . .

TURNS OUT LOCH HAS TO WORK ON
the night Lemon requested. He just isn't comfortable
quitting his Teddy Bear Factory job until the fake
date market has been tested. I don't blame him.
And Cowboy has plans with his dad, but at least he
isn't studying. So that leaves Ollie to jumpstart the
business. Terrific.

I'm still the new girl at Winston, which colors me
an outcast for most people there, so I need a female
liaison to arrange the dates, even though they aren't
really dates. They are what they are: lies. Who better
for the liaison job than Emma Elizabeth Swanson?

When I approach her with the business plan at
lunch, she agrees to help, jumping up and down with
excitement, and sticks by my side for the rest of the
week. Such clinginess would normally irritate me,
but I must admit the female camaraderie feels good.
And she welcomes me with open arms. I've never
had that before.

Mom nearly faints when Emma follows me in
the door after school on Friday, various junk food in
tow. Mom's eyes light up. "Emma! How nice to see
you again!"

Emma throws out a cool "Hey, Mrs. Richards" before dumping her stack of potato chips, Junior Mints, and Dr. Pepper on the counter. Mom and Emma chat for a few minutes about the nutritional value of Dr. Pepper—both agree it should be a food group—before I have to drag Emma and her mountain of food to my room for preparations.

On the way up the stairs, we run into Brian. "Whoa," he says, waving his hands in surrender. "Watch out. Teenage girls on the loose."

I hate it when he says stuff like that. Like being a teenager and being a girl automatically labels me crazy, insane, and dangerous. Emma offers up a hello, but I drag her by the wrist to my room, ignoring Brian. Only after my door is closed and locked do I feel relaxed enough to let out a belch. I plop down on my bed, my head aching from another week of Winston homework. Emma gives me a look. And then she burps so loud I think the window might shatter.

I stare in shock.

"What? Don't let the manicure fool you," she says. "I can be totally disgusting and love it."

I laugh. "Well, that was a good one."

She proudly raises her chin and pops open a Dr. Pepper. "Thank you kindly. So." She slumps down beside me. "What's the plan this time around?"

I fill her in on my semi-plan, which isn't much, but I figure it's best to start simple.

Ollie will need some guidance. I'm not sure he understands what being a gentleman means. So we'll go over to his house first to make sure he dresses in attire that conservative parents will love. And then we will send him on his way and wait. If Lemon approves of the product we provide her, the $200 will be dished out to the appropriate employees. Those employees being Ollie, Emma, and myself for this round. I want to give Loch my share, but I know he won't accept it unless he earned it. We'll just keep things even. Fair. Simple.

"Am I crazy for doing this?" I stuff a handful of Junior Mints into my mouth.

"Maybe. Maybe not." Emma loosens her ponytail. "Thanks by the way."

"For what?" Not like I've done anything yet. I should probably be thanking her. The look on Mom's face when I walked through the door with Emma was priceless.

Emma shrugs. "For including me."

I'm surprised. She has plenty of friends at Winston. Doesn't she?

"I wouldn't have any customers if it weren't for you," I say, trying to hide my smile and keep my cool. This mushy friendship stuff is too weird. "Thank *you*."

I think we're having a moment. Maybe. I don't know. It's hard to tell.

Time for another belch.

Suddenly, Emma gasps. "Oh! We should make a website! We could make it *pink*!"

"Not a bad idea." I crack open a soda. "Except for the color choice."

"What do you have against pink?" She makes a face and straightens a cardboard movie poster leaning against my bed. *No Country for Old Men.*

"Pink is too girlie," I reply.

Emma's delicate features scrunch up when she frowns. "You say *girlie* like that's a bad thing."

In my universe, *girlie* feels like a term thrown around to express distaste for something. A color.

A movie. A book. That's too *girlie*. Quit being so *girlie*. Even terms like *chick flick* or *chick lit* somehow suggest *not good*.

As Emma wiggles out of her plaid skirt and slips on a pair of jeans, she says, "'We've begun to raise daughters more like sons...but few have the courage to raise our sons more like our daughters.' Gloria Steinem said that. Think about it."

I sigh. "What?"

"Being feminine does not equal less than, Toni," Emma says. "You're allowed to embrace your womanhood if you want to."

I tie my hair into a low ponytail, considering this. She's right. Why should *girlie* have such a negative connotation anyway?

"Embrace my womanhood." I nod. "That's on my to-do list."

. . . .

Emma and I arrive on Ollie's doorstep an hour before he's scheduled to appear at Lemon's house. As Emma rings the door bell, I glance at the rose bushes lining the front of the house, remembering the Halloween party, remembering the Emma/Loch kiss. My stomach twists. Probably because I ate too much junk food.

The success of the business rests on tonight. I will do everything in my power to keep Ollie from screwing this up. He opens the door wearing plaid pajama pants and a black T-shirt, his curly hair sticking out in every direction. He scratches his big ears, his eyes heavy with sleep. What appears to be toothpaste decorates the corner of his mouth.

I'm glad we came. We're needed.

He grumbles as we head to his room, about as happy to see me as I am to see him. He mutters a hello to Emma. We follow him down the hallway. His mom waves from the kitchen, where she's hunched over a computer, piles of papers surrounding her. She's a divorce attorney. Works a ton.

Ollie's room is bright and cluttered. Snowboards hang on the neon green walls, and a huge pile of laundry is stacked on his bed. He saves *everything*. Tickets to baseball games from years ago. Stuffed animals with mystery stains on them. Boxes stuffed full of old school papers and assignments dating back to seventh grade.

For a boy determined to "move on," he sure has trouble letting go of stuff, but I don't point this out. No fighting. Tonight's about business.

Emma walks around the room, checking out various objects as if she's touring a museum. Empty chip bags accenting his oak desk. The unmade blue bedspread. A giant rubber band ball on the floor.

"What are you planning to wear, Ollie?" I ask.

Ollie spins around, presenting himself. "I hope I'm not overdressed."

Emma begins to shuffle hangers around in the closet. Her tongue sticks out the side of her mouth as she inspects everything. "Jeez. Got enough T-shirts?" she asks.

"You can't look like a slob," I say. "You're the first impression of *Toni Valentine's Rent-a-Gent Service*. First impressions can make or break a new venture."

Ollie turns his ear toward me. "Um...*what* service?"

"Every business needs a name," I say, blushing. I like the name, but Ollie has a way of making me feel stupid. I hate that.

"I think it's catchy," Emma says. She pulls out a navy blazer and matching tie from the closet. "Here. This is conservative." She tosses the blazer to Ollie. He catches it.

"Why can't I be myself?" He inspects the blazer like it's road kill.

"You aren't being paid to be yourself," I say. "You're being paid to be a polite Republican gentleman. Who would never stick old chewing gum underneath his desk."

Ollie tugs at his ear. Emma, curious, checks out the bottom of his desk. Her shiny hair flips as she bends over. She straightens, smiling. "Quite a collection you've got there."

"I don't have time to clean." Ollie turns away, nervously scratching the back of his neck. "Can we just get this over with so I can get paid?"

Emma returns to the closet and holds up a white shirt and a pair of khaki pants. "These are perfect," she says. "Now go change."

Ollie takes the clothes, grumbles under his breath again, and disappears into his bathroom. When he shuts the door, Emma and I exchange a look, both shaking our heads.

"Is he always like that?" she whispers.

"He's undergoing some changes." *Plus, he sort of hates me right now.*

Distracted, I check my watch. Forty-five minutes until Ollie is expected at Lemon's front door, prepared to schmooze her parents. He'll need at least twenty minutes to drive across town.

I bang on the bathroom door. "We don't have all night!"

A muffled "shut up!" sounds through the door. I flip off the door with both hands. Emma opens a drawer on Ollie's desk and shuffles through the junk inside.

"What are you doing?" I whisper.

"Snooping." She opens the next drawer, humming softly.

"Why?" I think back to when I left her alone in my room while I changed into my Halloween costume. Did she snoop through my stuff, too?

"I'm curious." Emma tosses a bouncy ball in the air and places it back in the drawer. "We should know everything we can about our employees, don't you think?"

"Ollie's a good guy," I say. "Mostly."

Emma's eyes widen when she opens the bottom drawer. "Bingo," she says, dangling a black notebook between her fingers. It doesn't look familiar.

"What is that?" I ask, approaching.

She flips through the pages and says, "Ollie's thoughts. For the taking." When the bathroom door squeaks open, she slams the notebook shut and tucks the journal in the back of her jeans as she stands up. Is she crazy? Ollie's going to flip out if he catches her going through his private stuff like that. Another thought: Ollie has a *journal*?

He walks out of the bathroom with his arms stretched to the side. "I look like a freak," he says with a sour expression.

In reality, he doesn't look too bad. The shirt is wrinkled around the bottom, but all he needs to do is tuck that in to hide it. His tie hangs to the side and his hair appears like wisps of black smoke atop his head. The toothpaste is still on the corner of his mouth. Emma gets to work smoothing out the rough edges, starting with the tie.

"I tied it right," he says. "I'm not an idiot."

"Let me do my work." Emma stands an inch from his face.

Ollie looks away, his cheeks reddening. This is more the Ollie I know, not the one at the party. Ollie's sort of nervous around girls. When Emma unbuttons the khakis, Ollie jumps back, startled.

"What are you doing?" he stammers. "I don't move *that* fast..."

Emma giggles. "Just tuck in your shirt, okay?"

Ollie sighs and tucks in the shirt. Emma circles him. She smooths the blazer around the shoulders, picks off a piece of lint, and attempts to flatten his hair.

"I want my money now," he says.

"You'll get your cut when the date is complete," I say, losing patience. "If Lemon isn't happy with your performance, she will get a full refund. No one gets paid yet. This is a *team* effort."

As Ollie yanks at the tie, Emma slaps his hand away, straightening it again.

"What if she falls in love with me?" Ollie glances at Emma.

I smirk. "You're not her type."

Emma disappears into the bathroom for a moment and returns with a tissue. She wipes away the toothpaste on Ollie's mouth. "I'm not a kid!" he whines.

"Are you sure? You kind of act like one," she says, smiling. Ollie just stares at her, speechless. Good. Someone who can shut him up.

I clap once and say, "It's time! Here we go! *Rent-a-Gent* is officially in business!"

Ollie grabs his keys. "I'm only doing this for money to go to Colorado. You know. To leave this place."

He stomps out the door. I stand there, annoyed, until Emma whispers, "Like you wouldn't want to know what's going on inside his head?" She dangles the journal in front of my face.

"Put it back," I whisper. "He'll notice that's missing."

"Not in this mess. Besides, this one's full. It's old." She slides the journal into the back of her jeans and saunters out of the room. I follow, too exhausted to protest. As we watch the red VW Bug pull out of the driveway, Emma and I exchange nervous glances.

Now we wait.

thirteen

· · · · · · · · · · · · · · · · · ·

HOURS LATER, MY STOMACH ACHES from laughing so hard, my nails glitter with pink, and my hair rests in dainty waves over the shoulders of my *Mario Brothers* T-shirt. All side-effects from hanging out with Emma Elizabeth Swanson. A warning label should come with this girl.

My feet folded underneath me, I sit on my bedroom floor and lean against my desk chair. I nervously toss my phone from hand to hand. A clump of Junior Mints is stuck to the roof of my mouth.

"This must be a good sign," Emma says, checking her watch. "It's almost midnight. No bad news. Yet." She's sprawled on her back across my black comforter, her head hanging over the edge as she looks at my room upside down. The ends of her hair tickle the floor and the collar of her pale green cotton pajamas brushes her cheeks.

After sending him off like a mother waving her kid off to prom, there has been no word from Ollie. Waiting is agony, and I keep picturing him yelling at me. *"When are you gonna grow up, Tonya?"*

I pull my knees to my chest and rest my scratched chin on them.

"We should have check-in times," I say, locking away the resentment toward Ollie. For now. "We need a text or something letting us know that all is well in Fake Date Land. What if he got kidnapped or something? What if Lemon got kidnapped?"

"Please. This is Vermont." Emma tosses a Junior Mint into the air and catches it with her mouth. Impressive that she doesn't choke. "Something tells me Ollie can take care of himself. He may not have time to text. He's got to be alert and prepared for anything. Lemon's gonna be too distracted to call. Hey, is that his real name? Ollie?"

"Luke." Again, I think of the four names scratched into the wooden dock. I lift my head up. "Ollie's a nickname. We all have them."

Emma turns on her belly. "We?"

"Oh. My friends..." *Can I still call them that?* "Ollie, Cowboy, Loch, and McRib. The kids of Newbury Lane. Well, we used to be anyway."

The pink drains from her face as Emma flips right side up again. "I want a nickname. I've never had one."

"Not even when you were a kid?" I dig my toes into the carpet.

She shakes her head. "Nope."

"Well, what do you want to be called?" I tilt my head.

"You can't give *yourself* a nickname." Emma sighs dramatically. "Someone else has to choose it for you or it doesn't count."

As I'm about to suggest Peach or Princess, the bedroom door creaks open and my gut jerks. Loch mentioned he might stop by after work. His shift ended an hour ago.

Not that I'm keeping track of him or anything.

Four black paws stalk into the room. Tom Brady the cat enters with an air of pride, his chin raised high, his tail gracefully moving back and forth as he walks. He stops, gives me a look, and jumps on the bed. He curls up next to Emma.

"Hey there, pretty kitty." Emma runs her hand down Brady's back. The cat looks at me with slit eyes as he purrs. He makes no attempt to bite Emma. In fact, he rubs his head along her hand, putting on quite the love-show.

"The old jealousy tactic," a voice says from the doorway.

Loch crosses his arms across his white button-down shirt. He smiles as he kicks off his shoes, grabs a bag of chips, and sits down beside me. I'm so, so happy he's here. I resist the urge to hug him. He offers me the bag of chips. I stuff a handful into my mouth. My palms are slick with sweat, but I can't figure out why. Is Loch the cause? Makes no sense. He's the most familiar and stable presence in my life. He shouldn't conjure nerves.

Emma sits up, disturbing Tom Brady's resting place. The cat curls up on my pillow. Great. I can look forward to cat hair in my face later. Emma runs her fingers through her hair, straightens her pajamas, and bounces off the bed. She lands with a thud on the pale pink carpet. She raises her index finger and says, "I'll be right back. Bathroom." She's out the door and down the hall before anyone can respond.

Loch's eyes move to my nails. "Did I interrupt a magical girl ritual?"

I sit on my hands, hiding the evidence. "I know nothing of magical girl rituals. This is a business meeting."

Loch shifts his weight, pressing his shoulder against mine. I don't move. I don't want to move. The air warms like cider on a stove. Loch wiggles his toes. He's wearing one black sock and one white sock. "How did Ollie's fake date go?" he asks.

"Still going." The chair wobbles behind me as I move my feet. My heels tingle with the promise of sleep. Loch catches the chair before it topples over.

As I'm about to thank him, Emma reappears as quickly as she vanished, dressed in a pair of jeans and a black blouse. Hair perfect. Lips glossed. "Opening night is a smashing success, Micah," she says, strutting into the room. "*Toni Valentine's Rent-a-Gent Service* is off to a good start."

"Catchy name." He stares at her *for way too long.* "No need to get dressed for me."

Is he checking her out?

No.

Yes.

Maybe.

"Vanity is futile here, Emma. It's just *Loch,*" I say, attempting to sound casual and normal despite my disgusting palm sweat.

Loch slugs me on the shoulder. I steal the bag of potato chips, but he snatches it back. I punch him in the shoulder this time, nearly breaking my hand. I might as well have punched a brick wall. Loch grins victoriously. I pout, too nervous to continue. He gives me a what's-with-you look.

Emma flops back down on the bed. Tom Brady opens his eyes, annoyed again. One more disturbance and he will leave.

"I had to at least put on a bra," Emma says.

Loch almost chokes on a potato chip. His neck reddens. I seize the opportunity and chant, "Bra. Bra. Bra. Bra. Bra."

"Stop it!" He presses his hands to his ears.

"What'd I do?" Emma asks, mortified.

I laugh and explain. "Certain words make Loch uncomfortable. Bra. Tampon. Pianist."

"Pianist?" Emma lounges on her side, laughing. She twirls a strand of honey hair around her index finger.

"I can't explain it." Loch shakes his head and wipes his greasy hands on his jeans. "I have no control over the physical reactions that take place when I hear certain terms. It's a mystery. Anyway, I thought this was a business meeting. Ollie. Date. Money? Remember? *Money?*"

Emma shrugs. "No news is good news."

"We don't know that." I turn to Loch. "No word from Ollie. Or Lemon. Nada."

"Do you think they got kidnapped?" Loch asks.

"Do people get kidnapped around here or something?" Emma sits up. "Is this, like, a real concern?"

Something vibrates. I check my phone, but it's not producing the sound. Loch munches on some chips, unconcerned because he rarely uses his cell. He prefers to remain eternally disconnected, as nature intended. He once told me he only uses it to text me. I wipe my sweaty palm on the carpet.

Emma scrambles to snatch her phone from the floor and flips it open. Her expression changes from bubbly to stricken. She looks at me. "It's him."

"Ollie?" I straighten up, tense. This could be it. The beginning or the end of the business.

She shakes her head. "Kevin. I'll, um, be right back."

Emma hurries to the hallway and closes the bedroom door behind her. Loch slumps against my desk, rubbing his neck. "Kevin," he says. "The boyfriend."

"The ex-boyfriend," I correct, licking chip grease from my fingers.

He nods. "As it should be."

Why do you care about Emma's ex-boyfriend? I cringe. "Why's that good?"

"The guy's an ass," Loch says with a shrug. "She can do better."

Again, the image of Emma and Loch kissing at Ollie's party flashes in my head. Each time, I swear it gets more vivid. Her lips. His lips. Together. I push the image away and fidget with the string on my sweatpants.

I need to chill out. Change like this can be good. Change doesn't mean losing my best friend to a pretty new friend with perfect hair.

Emma's muffled voice floats through the doorway. She sounds calm and controlled, like she's scolding a five-year-old.

I decide to ask, instead of torturing myself with possibilities. The imagination is far worse than anything in reality. The words drop out slow, like dripping honey, but taste bitter, not sweet.

"So do you want to date Emma or something?" I stretch out my legs and wiggle my feet.

Loch searches the bag for the tasty whole chips, skipping the crumbles, which are my favorite. He chomps down on a chip. I can't stop wiggling my feet. He's the slowest eater on the planet.

"Well, I should move on from She-Who-Shall-Not-Be-Named," he says. "And Emma's cute."

The word *cute* settles into my head like a bird's nest. It won't leave and seems to keep multiplying, growing louder and louder in my head. Of course I want Loch to move on from She-Who-Shall-Not-Be-Named, but is Emma the best rebound? Emma is sweet but also a bit intense. He needs someone dependable, comfortable, and predictable. Someone who won't play games.

"You shouldn't rush anything." I say, praying he doesn't start asking me details about Emma. What's her favorite color? What's her favorite flower? Does she have plans this weekend? I can play the role of matchmaker for fake dates. Not real ones. Fake is safer. I can control fake.

"Listen." Loch places the bag of chips on my cluttered desk. "I want to thank you. So: thank you."

I fidget with my phone, grateful for the change in subject. "For what?"

"For being so cool about my situation." He frowns. "The guys have been giving me a hard time for working so much. I think they're both pissed about it."

I don't know what to say. Maybe I'm not the only one alienated from the group because of circumstances out of my control.

Emma returns, brushing a strand of honey hair from her eye. "I have news," she says, breathless.

"Are you back with Kevin?" I ask. *Please say yes. If you're back with Kevin, Loch can't date you. If Loch can't date you, life remains simple and familiar.*

"Forget about Kevin." She waves her hand. "Lemon texted me."

My heart jumps up my throat. I accidentally bump Loch's elbow. He slumps farther to the floor, inches away from resting his head on my shoulder.

Did Ollie screw up? Did he freak out Lemon's parents? Did he ruin her chances of leaving her house again? Did he forever taint me as the new girl with poisonous public school friends? Will I be tortured at school for this? Will this ruin my chances at college? Will this ruin my whole life?

A splendid little smile spreads across Emma's glossed lips. "She wants to book him for the rest of the year," she says. "We're officially in business, Toni Valentine."

For a moment, I thinks she's joking. But when she starts jumping around the room, squealing, I join her, surprised at my own brand of hyper. Ollie didn't screw this up! Woohoo! Loch chills on the floor, applauding like a rich gentleman. I spin around the room and fall onto my bed, composing myself as I remember who I am.

I don't squeal. I don't giggle. I don't spin around the room with unharnessed joy.

Tom Brady the cat jumps up from the pillow, turns his nose to the air, and scurries out of the room as I settle down and clap like a gentleman, too.

fourteen

·················

"DO YOU HAVE PLANS FOR Christmas, Tonya?" Mrs. Kemper asks.

This is the last group session before winter break, and all I can think about is which boy I should choose for my latest client, Carrie Sanders, a girl at my lunch table who needs to prove to her older sister that the imaginary boyfriend she invented does, in fact, exist. Loch is booked through the New Year. It's a toss-up between Cowboy and Ollie.

"Family. Dinner. The usual," I reply, remembering to cross my ankles as I sink lower into the arm chair. Flames crackle in the fireplace. We each hold a mug of warm cider, a special treat from Mrs. Kemper today. I don't mention that I hate Christmas because Dad's not here anymore. The holiday gives me hives, but I don't say that because I don't want to deal with the sympathy.

Thanks to Lemon's glowing recommendation, business has picked up over the last few weeks. Word of mouth is a powerful thing. By Thanksgiving, *Toni Valentine's Rent-a-Gent Service* was officially in business. To start, we're employing Loch, Ollie, and Cowboy, but we may need more guys down the road.

One critique for Ollie: Don't fall asleep while waiting in the car again. We need updates so we know that no one's been kidnapped. Other than that, the guy did good on his date. He told Lemon's parents everything they wanted to hear. He harbored Yale ambitions. He respected Lemon. He would have her home at a decent hour. After five minutes with him, Lemon's parents trusted Ollie enough to keep their daughter out past curfew, as long as she checked in with them on the hour. Brian would never trust a teenage boy he had just met like that. He barely trusts Loch.

"Ryan hates the holidays," Shauna says.

"Wonderful," Mrs. Kemper says, rubbing her temples as Shauna continues talking about the love of her life.

Something tells me the administration would not approve of *Rent-a-Gent*. They wouldn't care that our business helps needy souls hide behind the safety of false doors, giving them permission to pursue their passions. I'm thinking about making that our slogan.

Emma set her marketing plan into motion. She created a gorgeous and simple website, which shows a picture of a boy, but only his torso is visible. He wears a black tuxedo, his large hands straightening his bow tie in a very James Bond-like gesture. All that's shown of his face is a wide scruffy chin.

Okay. I have to admit, Loch looked damn good in that tuxedo during the photo shoot.

Beneath the photo, written in *girlie* scripted letters: *Pick a gentleman. Any gentleman.*

That's it. No email. No address. No contact name. There's power in simplicity. There's power in the illusion of exclusivity. There's power in Emma Elizabeth Swanson. She e-mails the web address to our classmates. If they're curious about the website, and what it could mean, they talk to Emma.

Now that he's raking in some cash, Ollie seems slightly less pissed at me, although our conversations are strictly business now. Still, I'm holding out hope he'll forgive me soon. Cowboy hasn't fake-dated yet. Which is why I'd like to choose him for Carrie. I've offered him a few job opportunities, all of which he turned down because of some lame excuse. He had to study. He had to catch up on some sleep. He had to entertain his dad on a lonely Saturday night.

The other day, I marched over to his house and flat-out asked him if he wanted in or not. No pressure, but I needed to know. "Yeah," he said, leaning in his doorway, biting his bottom lip. "I want in. Really."

He wouldn't look me in the eye though. It occurred to me that maybe he was as intimidated by Winston girls as I was, but I didn't push the issue.

"For those of you who haven't heard back from colleges yet, don't worry. It's still early," Mrs. Kemper says as Shauna finally breaks from her story.

Mrs. Kemper likes to steer the conversation toward *the future*. Winston girls, I've come to learn over the last few months, are bred to look forward, never back, unless reading the past will somehow assist in brightening *the future*.

I'm the only one in group without a clear vision of the path ahead. After her undergraduate degree, Emma will attend law school, likely Harvard, where she will specialize in cases involving stem-cell research. Her plans are *that* specific. Shauna plans to attend Stanford, after which she will enroll in the Teach for America program, devoting her life to improving the educational system in this country. Lemon is poised to discover the next great acne cream or wrinkle cream or something equally profitable.

I have no idea what I want to be. Maybe I'll attend UVM and spend weekends (and probably most week nights) watching monster movies with Loch. Or maybe I'll end up at Purdue, navigating a new world on my own. I don't know. It never occurred to me that I should be devastated by this piece of the unknown before.

The future just means moving further away from the past and all that lives there.

Just as my muscles tense up, bracing for the College Question, Mrs. Kemper announces the end of session by saying, "Have a safe and happy Christmas break!"

As I head to the parking lot with Emma, I long to forget about exams and the future and the unknown path stretching before me. Emma's presence has become an odd comfort, like an over-sized sock that continually scrunches up around the toes. I realize that, yeah, she's more than a business partner. She's my friend.

Emma scrolls through her phone, keeping up with my hurried strides. "Hey, I need to ask you something. Something unrelated to the business," she says.

"Shoot." I realize that we've passed Emma's car, but she keeps walking with me.

Her voice lowers to almost a whisper. "Would you be terribly offended if I went out with Micah?"

I stop walking and turn to face her. The wind blows strands of my citrus-flavored hair into my mouth. I spit them out and manage to mumble, "Huh?"

Emma raises her hands, palms out. "Never mind. That's why I checked. Girl code."

My brain stops functioning for about two seconds. Just as I'm about to write myself off as catatonic, it switches on again. "Nothing's going on between Loch and I," I stammer. "We're just friends."

Emma reties her white scarf about a million times. "You sure about that?"

Of course I'm sure. If something more was going on between us, wouldn't I know that? Romantic love is like staring into the face of Champ. Pretty obvious. Hard to miss.

"Toni?"

"Huh?"

"You sure?" Emma tilts her head.

I shake my head, a bit dizzy. "Yes. Didn't I say that?" We reach my car. I go to lean on the hood, but somehow miss and land on my butt.

"Oh my God!" Emma cries. "Are you okay?"

I hop back up and wipe the gravel from my skirt. "So you want to go out with Loch?" I ask, blushing. "What about Kevin?"

Emma chews her bottom lip. "I don't want Kevin anymore."

"Just like that?" Seems kind of quick, considering all we went through to try and get him back for her.

"I put a lot of thought into my rejection," Emma says, folding her arms across her chest. "He sent me flowers the other day. Red roses."

I blink a few times. "The bastard."

"I liked him better when he was a jerk. Is that weird?" She tightens the white scarf around her neck. "Don't answer that. I know it's weird. I've got issues."

"Loch isn't a jerk though," I say. The opposite, in fact.

"I know." She shakes her head. "Forget I even asked, okay?"

Emma acts like she wants to say more, but she bids me farewell as she trots over to her car, the harsh winter wind zipping around her. I dump my bag onto the passenger's seat of my Maxima, on top of a wrinkled Purdue University acceptance letter. I crank the heat and rub my hands together as I wait for the car to warm up, but it never really does. I dig through the pile of random clothing in the backseat until I find an extra pair of gloves. I slip them on and zip through the parking lot, headed for home.

As I pull onto the Veteran's Memorial Highway, I can't stop thinking about what Emma asked me. My mind drifts. Emma. Loch. Girlfriend. Boyfriend. Holding hands. Curled under a blanket. Drinking hot chocolate. Laughing. Kissing...

Suddenly, a blue van whizzes by, honking. I'm about to flip him off when I realize I'm only going 25 miles an hour. The speed limit is 50. I hit the gas and curse under my breath. My brain must be mush from exams.

The more I think about the Emma/Loch kiss at Ollie's party, the more I'm convinced that the encounter was too awkward to transform into anything real between them. Sure, Emma technically shoved her tongue down Loch's throat, awkward for anyone, but it was more than the element of surprise. The lip-to-lip contact lacked a spark, a chemistry, a melting.

But maybe I missed something. At the time, I was a bit tipsy. What do I know about kissing anyway?

I've kissed two guys, an embarrassingly low number, both of which sucked.

The first was a guy at summer camp in sixth grade, a boy with dark freckles who kissed me on a dare. Gee, that made me feel special, especially when he wiped his mouth afterward and hissed like a cat before running back to his cabin. The second and more promising of the two lip-locks would be Corey Jenkins, who kissed me the summer before junior year at a pool party behind the snack stand. After which he proceeded to ignore me, which took some effort considering we had three classes together that fall.

I don't have much romantic experience, but I'm pretty sure true romance doesn't involve kissing beside vomit-drenched rose bushes at the end of a fake date designed to win back an ex-boyfriend.

I blast the heat again, hoping for some spark of warmth. The dashboard overwhelms the country music on the radio. If Emma and Loch want to go out, who am I to stop them? Maybe she's exactly what Loch needs right now. Maybe she needs Loch, too.

He's a reliable rebound from Kevin. Loch means everything he says. He would never toy with her emotions. Besides, I really don't see it going anywhere *serious*. People should be concentrating on college applications this year. And business and money, for those of us dabbling in that world.

But a relationship? What's the point? Emma's Harvard-bound. Loch will be at UVM.

It could never work.

As I sing along to the radio in hopes of clearing my cobwebbed thoughts, a white smoke blows along the windshield. I tap the brake, hoping the mysterious fog will lift, but it only grows thicker. The engine sputters. A sad sound rises above the music. The car slows, but I'm no longer pressing the brake. I pull to the side of the road and turn off the engine. I wait a few seconds, taking deep breaths as if it will please the automobile gods and send me on my way. When I turn the key, the engine sputters again. After a single high-pitched howl, it dies.

I'm stranded halfway between Winston and home.

fifteen

· · · · · · · · · · · · · · · · ·

BEFORE CALLING MY MOTHER, I toss several curse words into the wind. I tell her where I am, about thirty minutes outside of Shelburne. She doesn't hesitate before saying, "I'm leaving now. I'll be there as soon as I can. Stay warm."

After I hang up, a ping of sadness forces its way in. I'm going to miss my mom next year. A lot. I don't want to be the whiny homesick kid in the dorms, but I probably will be, no matter where I decide to go. I glance at the Purdue acceptance letter sticking out from underneath the pile of textbooks. I wonder if my dad would be proud of me.

Honk. Honk. Honk.

I turn around and eye a familiar blue truck pulling to the side of the road. For a second I think it must be a different truck, but then Cowboy hops out, zips up his leather jacket, and trots over. I roll down my window. He rests his elbows on the door as he looks in, his cheeks flushed from the cold.

"Thought that was you," he says.

I pat the steering wheel and say, "She finally quit on me."

"Crap. I owe Ollie twenty bucks." He ruffles his short hair. When Cowboy smiles, his eyes crinkle and almost disappear. "I bet him this car would last until graduation."

"You and me both." I laugh. "Any idea how to fix her?"

He blows on his bare hands and rubs them together. "I could tell you to pop the hood and proceed to pretend that I know the first thing about fixing cars—that I'm all manly like that—but let's just save time, okay? I know *nothing* about cars. But I can't let you sit out here freezing. I'll give you a ride home though."

I nod, thank him, and call my mom to let her know she doesn't need to rescue me.

Once inside Cowboy's truck, I put my gloved hands to the heater. A few tattered paperbacks litter the floor at my feet, but I'm careful not to step on them. They are well-loved.

As Cowboy settles into the driver's seat, he takes a sip of his Diet Coke and then pulls us onto the road. I glance into the rearview mirror at my sad Maxima all alone on the side of the road. Broken. Abandoned. Left behind.

I swallow the lump in my throat and ask, "So what are you doing out this way?"

"Had to pick up some books I left at my dad's over the weekend," Cowboy says, blasting the heat.

Like myself, he built up extra credits at Burlington so he has free afternoons this year. If things hadn't changed, I'd be free, too. We don't speak for several minutes. The sound of the blowing hot air is loud and strong. Cowboy could sit like this for days, quiet, lost in thought, but it drives me nuts after a few minutes. I only enjoy quiet on hunts.

"So...you busy next Friday night?" I ask.

His chin twitches. "I don't know."

"There's a date open for you if you want it," I say. "A girl named Carrie needs a fake boyfriend for a few hours."

To the right, we pass a cluster of leafless trees that look like their own little island among a sea of brown fields. Above, the sky darkens, threatening to crack wide open.

"I've decided something." He takes a deep breath and places the Diet Coke back in the cup holder. "I'm going to take Katie Morris to prom. I'm going to stop being scared of her. She's too beautiful to be scared of. I want her to have the perfect evening. And I want—I hope—that evening can be with me."

"I know." I rest my head against the seat and grin.

Cowboy glances at me, confused. "Loch told you my plan, didn't he?"

"Was it a secret or something?" I turn up the heat, but it's already as high as it will go. Maybe I shouldn't have said anything.

"He tells you everything." Cowboy's forehead creases. He says it like he's accusing me or Loch of something.

"Is that bad?"

Cowboy shrugs. A few moments pass. I stare at the floor where my copy of *Moby Dick* rests, the cover bent.

"Tell me more about this Carrie girl," Cowboy says, changing the subject.

"Carrie?" I look up. Well-maintained suburban homes appear along the side of the road. "I've only spoken to her a few times. She's an approachable girl though. She smiles a lot. A good sign. Emma vouches for her."

"Approachable. Girl." Cowboy sighs. "Two words that don't make sense together."

"I'm a girl, Cowboy." I shrug. "You talk to me."

He leans forward, curls his fingers around the steering wheel, and says, "That's different. You're not *really* a girl. Not in the same way." He pauses. "I'm digging a hole here, aren't I?"

I laugh, but I'm not sure what he means. Maybe he means I'm not the type of girl to make a boy nervous. I'd like to be the type of girl to make a boy nervous.

"Look, I get it," I say. "Winston girls are different. Most have been groomed since conception to be perfect."

"It's not only Winston girls." He blushes and fidgets with the collar of his leather jacket. "How am I supposed to act? What do I say? Where do I put my hands? I won't put my hands on her ever. I would never do that."

I sit back, studying him. His pale face is shaded a dark shade of crimson. Like always. So this is why he's been avoiding the business. It has nothing to do with me. He's really anxious.

Cowboy's never dated anyone before, but I assumed it was because he was holding out for Katie Morris. Plus, he was always so focused on his grades, on earning a scholarship for college, that a girlfriend wasn't a priority. And I could relate. Maybe he wants to be part of the business for more than the money. Maybe he wants to learn how to talk to Katie.

"I have no idea how to act like a gentleman," Cowboy continues. We're off the highway now, bouncing down a clunky back road. We pass the Dunkin' Donuts. "I can't, like, *charm*."

I wave my hand. "You're totally charming."

"Right," he snorts.

I rub my hands together, finally able to feel them again. "You need to grow some confidence, that's all. Be yourself."

"I hate that whole 'be yourself' message." He sighs. "Easy to say when yourself is interesting."

"Remember that time in fourth grade when you stuffed three French fries up your nose? That's the very definition of interesting." Now that I think about it, Cowboy was a lot more daring even in middle school. Freshmen year, he folded into his shell.

Cowboy laughs. "Okay. I'll lead with that story when I ask Katie out. She'll love it."

I shuffle my feet, careful not to hit a book. "You're giving me a ride home. You stopped on the side of the road to help me. Very gentlemanly of you."

Cowboy stares hard at the road. We don't speak again until we reach Newbury Lane, and the winter sky has brightened, now ripped with stripes of gold. Cowboy parks the truck in my driveway. The engine's still running when he turns to me, fidgeting with the zipper on his jacket.

"I will go on that fake date with Carrie," he says with the enthusiasm of someone who has volunteered to go into a war zone. He blinks several times.

"You sure?" I ask slowly.

"I can't give Katie Morris her perfect evening if I'm broke." His voice is unsteady.

I reach for the door handle. "You'll be great, Cowboy."

He raises his voice. "I'd like some tips!"

I pause, one foot out the door. "Tips?"

"On how to be a gentleman," he explains. "How to talk to these girls."

"You don't really need—"

"Please." He leans forward and closes his eyes tight. "I can't go off to school next year paralyzed like this." He opens his eyes and looks at me, pleading.

I can't say no to that. I want the childhood Cowboy back, the daring boy who would stuff French fries up his nose. I nod. "We'll meet here beforehand. We'll talk it through."

He smiles, but his eyes don't crinkle this time. "Thanks, McRib."

As I hop from the truck, he calls out again. I stop, and he hands over my worn copy of *Moby Dick*. "Thanks for lending it to me," he adds. "Sorry it took me so long to get it back to you."

I tuck the book into my bag. "Later, Cowboy."

I watch the blue truck drive to the end of the street, to Cowboy's ranch brick home at the end. I exhale, relieved. The Carrie date is officially booked. Plus, things feel good with Cowboy. He'll be okay. He can do this.

"Finally get your book back?" a voice asks.

Loch stands in his driveway, basketball in hand. He dribbles a few times, his chin painted with dark winter stubble. I make my way over, elated to see him. After I drop my book bag on the ground, he passes the ball to me. I shoot an easy layup, raise my hands in the air, and cheer.

We play for some time, passing the ball back and forth, taking turns shooting. I tell him about my broken Maxima and how Cowboy came along at the right moment. He tells me how some kid threw up in the Teddy Bear gift shop the other day and about his plans to search the lake for Champ again. Finally. Someone wants to continue to hunt. I'm all in.

"I've got a good feeling about finding him this time," Loch says. "When the weather warms, he'll want to come to the surface. He's done hiding. I know it."

I should tell him about what Emma asked me earlier. That she wants to date him. People like to hear those things, even if he isn't interested. She's nice. She's funny. She's sweet. He should be, at the very least, flattered.

Now, Toni. Tell him now about her NOW.

I pass the ball back and smooth out my skirt. My knees are freezing. The sun's gone down now. "My mom's probably freaking out about now. Later, Loch."

Loch palms the ball and steps toward me, but stops. He smiles softly. "See you around, Toni."

sixteen

SATURDAY NIGHT. THE NIGHT OF
Cowboy's fake-date debut. Emma's kicking my ass
in *Mario Kart* when the doorbell rings. I peer out the
front window. Cowboy's waiting on my front porch,
wiping sweat from his forehead despite the chilly
air. Beneath his leather jacket, he wears a navy blue
button-down and skinny black tie paired with black
pants and shiny dress shoes. His sandy-colored hair
is neatly combed, and his pale skin is spotted with
nervous splotches of red.

Behind him, Ollie stuffs his hands into the front
pockets of his puffy green coat. His curly hair is a
mess, his jeans skinny and black. His sneakers are
a stark neon blue. All shiny new clothes I've never
seen him wear before.

When I open the door, Ollie nods and says,
"McRib."

I let them both inside. As Cowboy walks past
me, I detect the stinging scent of cologne. I wiggle
my nose and hold back a sneeze.

"You look nice, Cowboy," Emma says. She sits
on the bottom step, sipping a Dr. Pepper. Her eyes

move to Ollie for a moment, but quickly return to Cowboy.

"The tie's not too much?" Cowboy asks.

"It's perfect. Very gentleman-like." Emma rises. "Ollie could learn a thing or two from you."

"Hey, I did my job, didn't I?" Ollie shrugs and wipes his sneakers on the floor mat. He looks up at Emma again, but she's already leading us into the living room.

Mom is upstairs folding laundry, her favorite activity. No joke. Now there's a passion I won't inherit. When we enter the living room, Brian closes the Ben Franklin biography he's been reading and sits up. Emma and I's game of *Mario Kart* is paused on the TV.

"Greetings!" he says, way too loud. "What are you fine upstanding teenagers up to this evening? No trouble, I hope."

"Cowboy's got a date," I say. Not a *total* lie. "We're helping him prepare."

"A date, huh? This I know something about." Brian cracks his knuckles. "Who's the girl?"

"Her name is Carrie," Cowboy says. "She smiles a lot, apparently."

"She goes to Winston," Ollie adds, sliding off his coat. He wears a button-down purple shirt. Now that I take a closer look at him, his curls are unusually tidy. Is he dressed up for something? He's not booked tonight.

The way Ollie says *Winston* suggests Carrie might be a handful or something. I narrow my eyes.

Brian stands and nods. "Ah. Toni could help with that. She knows those Winston gals."

I wouldn't say I *know* them. "Yeah, I'm trying to help him get ready," I say. "So…"

I wait for Brian to leave. He gets the hint right away this time. He warns us to stay out of trouble again because, you know, we're teenagers, trouble is what we do, and then goes upstairs.

"Your stepdad is super nice," Emma says.

"Yeah, I guess." I cringe. Brian is nice—too nice sometimes—and I never know how to react to all of that hyper-niceness. For some reason, it makes me uncomfortable. Probably because there's something wrong with me.

Ollie glances at the TV. "Aw, *Mario Kart*. Wait. Who's Peach? She's the worst."

I blush. "She's actually not so bad."

He points at me, amazed. "You *chose* Peach?"

"Okay!" Emma announces, circling Cowboy. She's in work mode. "He looks good to me, Toni."

"Oh, come on," Ollie interjects, done teasing me regarding my video game choices, it seems. "There must be something you can improve. The guy's not perfect."

"You're so right." Emma picks a tiny piece of lint from Cowboy's shoulder and giggles. "There. *Now* he's perfect, Luke."

Ollie shakes his head, but smiles. His earlobes are bright red. As Emma paces the room, her hair bounces. Ollie leans against the wall by the fireplace and watches her.

"What if I don't know what to say during this thing?" Cowboy asks, panicked. "There's like a 100 percent chance of that happening."

I take Cowboy's elbow and lead him to the couch. Together, we sit down. "Just breathe," I tell him calmly.

"I'll text you topics to bring up if the conversation lulls." Emma speaks quickly. "But DO NOT check your texts in front of her sister or her parents. That's not gentlemanly. Just excuse yourself to go to the bathroom and text me if things get too quiet. When you return to the table, start the new conversation with whatever line I give you."

"It isn't really like me to start a conversation..." Cowboy fidgets with his tie.

I pat him on the back. "That's the beauty of this, man. You don't need to be you. You're George, Carrie Sanders's boyfriend for the last six months. George *would* start a conversation. Did you go over the George facts I emailed you?"

Cowboy rubs the back of his neck and nods. "She sure went into detail about this imaginary person."

Emma stops pacing for a moment. "George's favorite food?" she asks.

"Peanut butter," Cowboy replies.

"Favorite movie?"

"*Titanic.*"

"I hate that movie with a white passion," Emma says, shaking her head. "You ever seen *Road House?* Now that's a classic."

Ollie says, "It's okay, but *Ghost* is a better Swayze movie."

Emma looks at Ollie like he's just grown a second head or something. After a few moments, she smiles. "I almost forgot about that one."

"Hello? Not the time to discuss ancient movies!" Cowboy waves his arms. "It's almost time to go, and I'm not feeling any better about this whole thing!"

I rest my hands on Cowboy's shoulders and look him straight in the eye. "All will be fine."

Cowboy sighs. His breath is minty. "I can't do this. I can't..."

"Katie Morris," Ollie says. "You want to give her the perfect night, right? Just remind yourself this is all for her."

Cowboy doesn't need money to give Katie Morris the perfect evening. If he could practice talking to new people, he may be able to win her over through conversation. He can be charming. When he talks.

Cowboy rises and wipes his palms on his knees. Ollie crosses the room and slaps Cowboy on the back. "You're getting paid to go out with a beautiful girl," he says. "With no obligation to call her again."

Emma snorts and smooths out her pristine white jacket. "You're so full of it."

Ollie points to himself and smirks. "You speaking to moi?"

"You're the only one full of shit around here, aren't you?" Her eyebrows raise. "You would call five seconds after the date ended. Don't pretend you wouldn't."

"How do you know what I would or wouldn't do?" Ollie asks. His lips curl slightly, like he's holding back a smile. Are they flirting?

Emma inspects her nails and then looks to me, a bit frazzled. The only other time I've seen that look was during finals weeks. "What time is it? A gentleman is never late."

I glance at my phone. "Time to go. Ready, Cowboy? Saddle up."

Cowboy lowers onto the couch again. He puts his head between his knees, trying to catch his breath. When I see him like that, I want to call the whole thing off. His anxiety is much worse than I thought, and I don't want to torture the guy.

But then he lifts his head with a determined expression and says, "I'm ready. Let's do this."

. . . .

It's after midnight. Emma and I are shivering in Cowboy's driveway, awaiting his return. The light above the garage falls over us in a pale wave. The neighborhood is quiet. Eerie. I pull my black snow cap down over my ears and jump up and down to keep from freezing. Emma texts someone on her phone, smiling to herself. Maybe she's chatting with Kevin again. I don't ask.

Cowboy texted me about twenty minutes ago, but his message was simple: *Done. On way.* I'm not sure how to decipher that. He could be saving the good news to tell us in person. Or he could be saving the bad news. I hope the fake date went well, more for Cowboy's sake than for the business.

A pair of headlights appear around the corner, followed by the clunky sound of Cowboy's old truck. Emma looks up and slips her phone into her coat pocket, flushed. As the truck pulls into the driveway, Emma skips toward it and swings open the driver's door before the engine's even off.

"Can I park first?" Cowboy asks, irritated.

Emma backs off. The driver's door hangs open. "Of course, of course," she breathes. "Please do."

Cowboy grumbles, shifts the truck into park, and cuts the engine. He hesitates before climbing out, his breath a puff of fog. It's too dark to read his face, but when he slams the door shut, I get a bad feeling.

"Welcome back!" Emma exclaims way too loudly.

"Quiet," Cowboy says softly, moving past us. "You'll wake the neighbors."

Emma shoots me a look. I better handle this. I take a deep breath and follow Cowboy to the front door while Emma hangs back.

When we reach the porch, Cowboy pulls out his house key. Gently, I ask, "So? How was it?"

He smiles, but it's forced. "It went very well," he states. His voice is monotone. "Everyone bought it. I was George the whole night."

"Really?" I touch his elbow. "Because if things didn't go as planned—"

"Better than planned." He concentrates on turning the key in the lock. "It was perfect."

"Feel better about Katie Morris then?" I'm having a hard time reading him. Is he mad about something else? Or is he lying to me? "You got in some good practice—"

Again, he cuts me off. "I'm really tired, McRib. It's exhausting pretending to be someone you're not. But everything's cool. Don't worry. Your business is safe."

He opens the door, tells me goodnight, and disappears inside. The porch light clicks off. I stand in darkness for a few moments until I hear the sound of Emma's approaching high heels.

"Well? Are we still in business?" she whispers.

"I think so," I say with uncertainty. I should knock on the door. Force Cowboy to talk. But Emma slaps me on the back and giggles with excitement. I don't want to ruin her mood. Together we walk back to my house for a night of junk food and manicures.

Maybe Cowboy is just tired. I hope.

. . . .

Monday at school, Winston girls actually say hello to me. They ask how I'm doing. I get invited to some parties. Suddenly, I'm *known*. I am no longer New Girl with the romantic name. I'm a powerful business woman. I'm a woman with connections.

I've decided to give Cowboy some space for now, but I still don't know what happened on his fake date. I haven't heard from Carrie though, so I assume things were at the very least satisfactory. I'm running late this morning so by the time I stop at my locker, the hallway is almost empty. As the last bell rings, I curse and start jogging. Suddenly, the bathroom door swings open. I startle and drop my books.

A black high heel steps on my French book as I reach to pick it up, pinning it to the floor. I'm surprised to see Carrie Sanders staring down at me. Her silky black hair falls into her face. The weird thing is she's not smiling.

"Can we talk?" She doesn't move her heel from my book.

I stand, dread creeping in. My heart is already pounding. "What's up?"

"I want my money back," she spits, pressing her books to her chest. Her face is filled with fury.

I blink a few times. "Cowboy said the date went great."

"Your weird friend made things worse." She rolls her eyes. "My sister is never going to let me live this down."

"First of all, he's not weird," I reply, trying to keep my cool. "Second of all, what happened?"

"You know, I didn't ask for much." She digs her heel into my book. "A boy who didn't swear. A boy who would answer some simple questions. A boy who would pretend to be George. But George *talks*. Your guy spoke eleven words all night! I counted! And one of those was *shit*."

I groan. "Um..." I don't know what to say. I knew something was off with Cowboy, but I chose to leave it alone. "What were the other ten words?"

Carrie glares. "I. Am. Not. Really. George. My. Name. Is. Justin. Sorry."

I lean back like the wind just got knocked out of me. "Oh."

"*Yeah*," she hisses. "*Oh*."

"I'm sorry," I stammer. "Full refund. Of course."

My cheeks burn from embarrassment as Carrie follows me to my locker. I pop it open and dig through my bag for the cash. Cowboy must've been too paralyzed to text Emma or I for help because he never did. Foolishly, I thought that had been a good sign. I thought he had everything under control. Why did I let him go on that stupid date?

Carrie tucks the cash I give her into her sock and says, "You must think we're just pathetic girls with too much money, huh?"

Before I can respond, she walks away, her black heels clicking against the floor. I stand there a moment, shaking. And here I thought I might be accepted by these girls. I'm the pathetic one.

. . . .

After school, I stop over at Cowboy's to demand an explanation. His mom lets me in. She has dark circles underneath her eyes, and she's wearing a blue bathrobe. According to Cowboy, she's been depressed since the divorce. She doesn't say much to me.

Cowboy and Ollie are in the basement, playing a game of *Mario Kart*. The glow from the TV provides most of the light. There's no furniture so they both sit on the carpet, which still smells new. Cowboy's dad planned to create a massive entertainment center down here, but that didn't happen before he moved out. All that remains is fresh paint, new carpet, and an old television set.

I stand at the bottom of the steps and watch them, hurt they would perform this after-school ritual without Loch and I. Ollie finally acknowledges me with a "McRib."

"Hey." I swallow my hurt and sit down beside Ollie. Cowboy won't look at me. His eyes are glued to the television. "I think you know why I'm here," I tell him.

Cowboy drops the controller. "I'm sorry!" he exclaims. "I just couldn't be her fake boyfriend!"

"Should've booked moi," Ollie says. He keeps playing.

"What went wrong?" I look to Cowboy. Waiting.

"I should've said no." Cowboy shakes his head. He's red again. "I'm sorry. I thought I could do it. I thought it would be good practice for me or something." He pauses. Frowns. "I was wrong."

"These girls think I'm taking advantage of them now," I say, my voice unsteady. "That I'm making fun of them or something."

"Aren't you taking advantage of them?" Ollie pauses the game and stuffs a handful of chips into his mouth.

One of the Guys

I can't believe he would even suggest that. Of course I'm not taking advantage of them. "I'm providing a service."

"Why do you care what they think of you anyway?" Ollie smacks his lips. "You're going off to college next year. It's not like you have history with them or anything."

I sigh and pick at the pale blue carpet. "I just care, okay?"

"A riveting answer," Ollie replies. He smacks Cowboy on the arm. "Come on, man. It's no fun to beat you unless you try."

Cowboy picks up his controller. The two continue the game as if I'm not even there. For a few minutes, I watch them, but I can't pay attention. My mind is elsewhere. I never felt worthy of Winston. From the start, the whole thing felt like a mistake. It was this place where I was dropped because of one stupid prank gone wrong. I could never live up to Winston Girl Standards. Could never be one of them. Could never learn to embrace my womanhood or whatever. If I did, that would set me further apart from the guys. As I watch Ollie and Cowboy play, I realize that there's nothing I can do about that. It's happening anyway.

I stand and narrow my eyes at each of them. But they're oblivious to subtle girl anger. So I leave.

seventeen

· · · · · · · · · · · · · · · · · ·

COWBOY'S OUT. LOCH AND OLLIE don't have the time to keep up with the demands of the service alone. We need more dudes. Emma and I acquire two new recruits over the next few weeks. The first being Ollie's older brother Jason, who recently decided to "take a break" from college. Jason's got a lot of free time, plus he's trustworthy. The second is Henry Gardner from Burlington High, who moved here last year from Alabama. At one time, I thought Henry might become part of our group, but he eventually fell into a different crowd. He's sweet with a cute Southern accent. Bonus.

The day before Christmas, I lounge on my bedroom floor and work on my latest marketing ploy. Gentleman brochures. Winston girls interested in the service will now receive a profile of a boy, similar to the way a college would provide a brochure for a potential student. Included with each brochure: a photo of the boy, his schedule, and any special talents (tailored to fit client needs, of course). Not only do these iron out scheduling conflicts, but it practically guarantees customer satisfaction. The girls will pick the guy, rather than Emma and I scrambling to find a decent match.

A slant of rare winter sunlight creeps through the blinds and shines across the photos of the guys surrounding me. As I stare at the photo of Loch in a tux, I fidget with the string on my oversized black sweatpants. He looks really, really good in the photo. It's ridiculous.

To disguise the profiles, I place them inside a college envelope. I match each boy with a school that best represents what he has to offer for a particular date.

Ollie = Yale University
Loch = Purdue University
Jason = University of Vermont
Henry = Mississippi State

I pry my eyes from Loch's picture and stuff his profile into a Purdue envelope. Too bad there's still a handful of those photos on the floor. He's everywhere. Looking at me with that subtle grin. When there's a knock on my door, I shove everything underneath my bed and pop open my laptop. Mom walks in, her fuzzy slippers scratching against the carpet. She shouts, "Merry Christmas!"

"Christmas arrives tomorrow," I say, my heart pounding. She'd almost caught me. "Check your Kitty Claus calendar again."

She plays with the string on her sweatpants. Same as I do. "Come downstairs," she squeaks. "Your present arrived early, College Girl."

"I need to pass high school before you can call me that."

"Oh, come on. You've been accepted to your top college choices," she says, reaching down to play with my hair. "Doesn't that mean you can, I don't know, slack off for the rest of the year?"

I laugh. "Oh, Mother. You crack me up. There's no such thing as slacking off at Winston. No matter the circumstances." Which reminds me, English homework awaits.

She tugs at my wrist. The woman can't hold still. "I have to show you something! Please come downstairs? Humor an old woman?"

I sigh and stand up, zipping up my Colts sweatshirt. I throw her a funny look. "You've clearly had too many Dr. Peppers today."

Now I'm shivering in the driveway, snow seeping into my slippers, staring at a silver Ford Focus with a giant red bow on the hood. Mom, behind me, rests her hands on my shoulders. I can feel her excitement through her fingers.

Brian dangles a pair of keys in front of my face. Stunned, I take them. The keys feel cold in my palm.

"Merry Christmas." He smiles and adjusts his Patriots ball cap.

I look past him, at the car. "What, um, is that exactly?"

"That would be your new car," Mom says, rubbing her hands together for warmth.

I stare at the keys. I stare at the car. I stare at the keys again. This must be what shock feels like. I can't move. I can't say anything.

"Say something," Mom whispers in my ear. "Say thank you, at least."

"Check out the interior," Brian says. He opens the driver's door. "It's got that new car smell. Nothing like it."

I finally speak. "I don't understand. Where's the Maxima?"

Mom laughs. "*This* is your car now. Your shiny pretty new car."

"I thought the Maxima was getting fixed." A lump rises in my throat. The Maxima belonged to Dad. The Maxima belonged to me. It was an extension of me. It had my dirty clothes in the backseat. It had my fast food wrappers on the floor.

Mom moves over to Brian and curls her arm around his waist. I hate it when they do the semi-PDA thing. "Brian thought you needed a new car," she says. "I agreed."

"You need something reliable," Brian adds, rubbing his hands together. "Something new. Especially for school next year. We can't send you out of state without a car."

I understand how I should react. The same way I *should* have reacted the moment my mother told me I would be attending The Winston Academy for Girls. I should be overwhelmed with gratitude, screaming to the heavens, begging to take the new wheels for a spin. I should be showering Brian with hugs and thanks and general words of endearment.

But I don't feel that way. Not even a little.

The keys clatter to the ground. Mom says something, but I don't hear her. The wind picks up. Brian says something nice, I think, but I block out his voice and run across the lawn, my slippers flopping with each step over the frozen ground. Mom's voice returns, loud and pissed. "Toni Valentine! Get back here!"

I round the corner and slide into Loch's basement window as the tears start to flow.

. . . .

I lean against the back of the yellow couch and pull my knees to my chest. I don't know why Mom hasn't tried dragging me home yet. She knows where I am: the same place I went after I discovered I'd be attending Winston. The same place where I took refuge after I learned that my father's motorcycle had skidded off the highway, crushing him beneath it.

Something new. Brian's words. Something reliable. Unlike a motorcycle or an old car or an old life or a dead father. I hear footsteps. For a moment, I worry that I might disrupt another one of Amy's freshmen parties. But it's Loch who scoots in next to me. He offers me a bowl of Snickers ice cream and balances a second bowl on his knees. I pick at the ice cream with the spoon, but I don't feel like eating. Loch doesn't say anything. His silence suggests he already knows what happened.

"What kind of person is ungrateful for a new car?" I ask, shaking my head. "I suck so bad."

Loch yanks at his shoelaces. "You don't suck. Your outrage isn't about the car. Not directly."

The ice cream in my bowl appears melty, warm. "Enlighten me, doctor."

"This is about replacement." Loch steals a bite of my ice cream. He's already scarfed down his bowl. "Brian can't replace your dad. I doubt he's even trying to."

"I know that." Mom tells me all the time that Brian will never replace my dad. Not as a father.

Not as a husband. Her relationship with Brian is different. *Something new.*

"I liked my old car," I say. "My old car was familiar and smelled like sweat and dirty socks. I hate new car smell. It's too artificial. It's not life. My old car smelled like life. This *is* about the car, Loch. Not some deep-seeded psychological hurt concerning my father's death and my mother's ability to move on while I, apparently, can't."

Loch pauses. "Guess I shouldn't major in psychology next year."

"Listen to me." I set the bowl down. Loch picks it up and begins eating. No food goes to waste around him. "God, I'm complaining about a new car while you have to work your butt off to pay for college next year. Why do you put up with me?"

Loch scratches his stubble and looks away. His neck reddens. "I have my reasons."

"I could sell the car for you," I suggest. "That should take care of the first year tuition and books and housing *easy.*"

"You should probably apologize to your mom first." He smiles. A kind smile, not full of pity. "And to Brian. I know you want to."

I sigh. He's right. The sleeve of his navy blue sweater dips into his ice cream. He doesn't notice. "I knew you were going to say that," I tell him, wiping the ice cream from his sweater with my thumb.

"It's better than walking around with awkward tension in your house." He takes the last bite of his ice cream and scoots closer. I stare at the spot where his shoulder touches my shoulder. My body warms.

"Can you do me a favor?" I ask, looking up at him. I resist the urge to touch his stubble.

"Anything." He leans in, his dark eyes full of shimmer and sweetness.

"Drive me somewhere?"

A flash of disappointment falls across his face. When he scoots away from me, I touch my burning shoulder. He gathers up the ice cream bowls. Soon the disappointment gives away to a smile.

"Naturally," he says.

. . . .

I kneel on frozen ground and run my fingers over the glistening tombstone. Loch's bundled in his old puffy jacket and ripped snow cap. I hum a Tim McGraw song, my breath intertwining with the wind, and try to remember what my dad looked like. Dark chin-length hair pulled back by a bandana. Clean-shaven. Thin face. Tall. Funny. Wild. Gray eyes that matched mine.

About once a month, Mom brings out fresh flowers to the grave. A fresh red rose decorates the grave now, but sometimes there's a new bandana laid beside the stone. A blue one this time. But I don't know who brings them.

"The mystery visitor strikes again," I say, standing up. I want to hold his hand, but I'm afraid of the signal that might send. Besides, I'm about to cry. Embarrassing.

Despite my attempts at blocking them, the tears arrive. I turn away from Loch and wipe my cheeks with my gloves. I confess to my father's tombstone.

"It wasn't about the car." My voice wavers so I make this confession quick. "With every change that takes place—a new school, a new friend, a new car, whatever—I feel like my dad becomes more *smudged*. Blurry. I'm afraid I'm forgetting him, Loch. Like the memory of him is swept away in a current I can't follow."

Loch squeezes my shoulder. His touch sends shivers down my spine. "I'm here, Toni."

But sometimes I feel Loch slipping away, too. Maybe that's what bothers me so much about his kiss with Emma. When he kissed her, something changed. And change moves me further away from my dad. He wouldn't know me as a Winston Girl, as a lady embracing her girlie side, learning how to express her feelings. Dad just knew me as Toni, his little tomboy with skinned knees.

"Promise nothing will change with us." I turn to Loch and wipe snot on my coat sleeve. Gross. "No matter what happens next year."

"What might happen next year?" he asks, tilting his head. There's worry in his voice. "We've got a plan, right? You? Me? UVM?"

I don't know how to tell him about Purdue. It's not like I've made an official decision yet, so I decide to avoid the topic.

"Just promise nothing will change," I repeat, stepping toward him. "Please?"

Loch looks at his feet and kicks loose dirt with the tips of his shoes. The monster drawn on them has begun to fade. He's quiet for a few moments. But then he says, "Yeah, I promise."

eighteen

·················

AT HOME, I SPUTTER AN APOLOGY
to Brian and my mom. I mean every word. It's a
small miracle they don't take away the new car. I'm
grateful for it, really, and Brian shouldn't have to
suffer because of my issues. He's trying to bond, I
guess, but as much as I hate to push our relationship
into stereotypical stepparent territory, he still
irritates me. Maybe that will fade with time. Maybe
not.

I ring in the new year with Mom and Loch, who
decided to take tonight off from fake-dating. He's
earned it. We watch Christmas movies that Mom
and I can't let go of for the season. Loch tolerates
our choices, but I can tell by his occasional sighs
that he'd much rather be watching a monster movie.

A timid snow falls outside as I curl up on the
couch with a bowl of popcorn, stealing glances at
Loch across the room. He's sprawled in the armchair,
zoned out. I wonder if he's growing a beard because
his stubble is darker than usual. When he looks at
me, I look away.

Before I know it, I'm back at Winston. The
atmosphere feels fresh and rebooted. New shoes

hit the wooden floors as the overhead lights bounce off the plethora of freshly highlighted hair. I tap my nails—which are painted a dark blue thanks to Emma—against my books as I navigate the halls. I wear my hair down today, sleek and straight, a new look for the new year. Why not, right? Perhaps it's a small step to embracing a different side of myself. *My womanhood.* Nah. It's just hair.

An excitement swarms through the masses as the next step in our lives grows closer. This is it. Last semester. A nervous energy sizzles for those waiting to hear back from colleges. Emma's no exception.

"If I don't get into Harvard, my life plan is ruined," she tells me as soon as we walk into the building. It's become routine for her to greet me in the parking lot, cell phone out and ready for *Rent-a-Gent* business. Today, however, other worries plague her mind.

"Then you'll just make a new life plan," I say.

"You don't understand, Toni." She steps to the right to avoid running into a girl who has stopped to tie her shoe. Emma quickly moves back in step with me. Doesn't miss a beat. "There's one plan. Harvard."

"You're good." I wave my hand. We pass Carrie Sanders going the other direction. Her smile vanishes the moment she sees me. "You got into Princeton. I wouldn't be surprised if you took over the world one day." I mean that. Emma is a force.

"But you need a Harvard degree to take over the world." Emma covers her mouth and burps so softly that only I can hear it. I laugh. She cracks me up. "Thank Whatever-Higher-Power-Watching -Over-Human-Existence that I've got *the business* to distract me from my crumbling future," she continues. "Which reminds me. A potential new client tapped me last night."

I accept Emma's change of subject. She shouldn't be so wound up this early in the day. Harvard will accept her, and she'll proceed to do amazing things with her life and her path will always glow. She really will be fine. More than fine. I wish she could believe that.

Others may end up living on Newbury Lane forever, riding the course of indecision. And by others, I mean me. I haven't decided which college to attend. Purdue. UVM. Purdue. UVM. Indiana. Vermont. Indiana. Vermont. Both have brutal winters. The decision has become a back-and-forth whirlwind of choking uncertainty where certainty once lived. Sometimes I wake up in the middle of the night, layered in sweat, gasping for air, freaking out about choosing wrong or disappointing someone, even if that someone is myself.

"A new client," I say, pushing my own issues out of my mind. I pop open my locker. Emma leans against the one adjacent to it. "I'm intrigued."

"Brace yourself." Emma squints at me. "This is shocking news."

"Nothing shocks me anymore," I say. "I witnessed Ollie dressed as a gentleman for no good reason, remember?"

"Luke. Yes. I remember." Emma blushes. She runs her fingertips over her lips and stares at the floor, as if enveloped inside a lovely dream.

Playfully, I knock on her forehead. "Hello? Earth to Emma?"

She looks up, shakes her head. "Sorry. Business."

I finish swapping out my books and close my locker. The noise in the hallway has subsided. When

Emma reveals the name of our latest client, I almost choke. I must have heard wrong.

"Shauna Hamilton," Emma repeats, her voice low.

This must be a mistake. "Doesn't she have a real linen-scented boyfriend in Connecticut?"

"*Indeed.*" Emma gasps as if this is a horrible scandal.

"What does she need us for? Her life is perfection," I say, pressing my books to my chest. Shauna Hamilton uses group sessions to brag about her life.

"That's the other problem." Emma grimaces. "She wouldn't tell me why she needed to rent a guy. She just sent me a text, wanting to know if what Lemon told her was true, that we provide, you know, dependable guys for PG-rated use. I told her yes and asked her the basic questions, like I always do, but she never replied back."

Just a few girls lingering in the halls now. We should really get to class. "Maybe she wants to make Ryan jealous or something?" I ask. Could be anyone's guess. I just don't get Shauna.

"Maybe. She is a rich mystery, but we can't discriminate." Emma holds up her phone. "I marked her on the client list. Code name: Linen."

I laugh. "I'm curious as to where that one will lead. I bet she's a pain in the ass to please."

As we head down the hall, I try to imagine a girl like Shauna Hamilton in need of a false door. But Emma's right. We don't discriminate. We're lucky to be in business at all after the Carrie Sanders debacle. And Jason and Henry have been doing well. Each have completed a handful of fake dates. If we turn down Shauna, she might set out to destroy what we've got going.

As I bid Emma farewell, she blows an air kiss into oblivion. I wish I could be like that, full of ladylike poise, shaded like honey, but it doesn't matter whether I cross my ankles or not. I'm doomed to carry myself with clumsiness, a trait I inherited from my mother. Better than inheriting her love of laundry though.

I'm surprised how easily I fall back into the Winston routine. Once overwhelmed by it all, I slip through the hours without an inkling of a panic attack. Overall, the day is pleasant. That is, until Emma beckons me into the second floor bathroom after lunch.

"What is it?" I sniff at the strong lemon scent rising from the waxed tile.

"In about two seconds, Shauna Hamilton is going to walk through that door," Emma whispers.

"Are you psychic now?" I joke. "I hope you put that on your Harvard application. Impressive."

"Her text said to meet her here or *else*. Do you think she'll tell the faculty about the business?" Emma's voice raises an octave.

I know little about Shauna or her true motives. She's been nothing more than a minor character in my life until this point, a distraction during group sessions. Partly because of the fact that I don't want to hear more about linen-scented Ryan. Partly because she looks at me like I'm a wad of gum stuck to the bottom of her shoe.

What could Shauna possibly gain by outing the service to the faculty? What punishment would we endure? Is it illegal to run a legit fake-date service? Could I be sentenced to jail? Would this ruin Emma's chances of getting into Harvard? Would this ruin my future? Would Loch get in trouble? Would we have to return the money we've made?

For a few seconds, I see everything crumble.

My new friendship with Emma.

My old friendship with Loch.

My time with the guys.

My future.

My freedom.

My life.

The bathroom door swings open. Emma presses her lips together as Shauna strolls in, a folded envelope dangling from her right hand.

"Good afternoon," she says, plastering on a fake smile. I've never noticed before, but she has a pair of those "invisible" braces on her bottom teeth.

"This isn't how this works." I gather up some courage. "You can't just—"

Shauna slams the envelope down on the sparkling sink and says, "I want this guy."

I glance at the envelope. Purdue University. Loch. She wants Loch. Anger bubbles in my chest. He's not for her. Real or not.

"Purdue is a good school." I grind my teeth. "They have an excellent engineering program."

"I know about your service." Shauna folds her arms over her chest. "Everyone does. Don't play games."

I shrug. "Who's playing?"

Shauna stares me down so hard it's like she's trying to stop my heart with her mind. I sigh and check each stall for spies. Emma kicks in the doors with her heels to double-check and then stands guard by the door, nervously checking her phone.

I speak slowly. "Think of my service like Fight Club, Hamilton. First rule: don't talk about it. Especially on school grounds."

"What's Fight Club?" she scoffs. Her teeth, I notice, are slightly yellowed.

"Well, I could show you." I roll up the sleeves of my navy sweater, but Emma throws me a warning look. So I compose myself.

"This is an emergency," Shauna says, her voice rising. "I don't have time to play your games."

"Why should I make an exception for you?" I ask, beyond annoyed.

Shauna tightens her jaw and scratches her elbow. Her words come out flaked, uncertain. "Do you know who my father is? He's the top attorney in the state. If I tell him that you, Toni Valentine, are running an escort service for Winston girls, he'll have you thrown in jail for a super-long time. Don't mess with me."

Wow. The nerve of this girl. Emma gasps and watches me, waiting for my reaction. Here we are. Our fears manifested under the blossoming lights of a pristine lemon-scented bathroom.

"I don't respond well to threats." I fake-smile. My face is starting to hurt.

Shauna tosses her red curls. "I'll pay extra. I can't make it through the rest of the day without this settled. I need to know that I've booked my rental for next weekend."

I look to Emma, who shrugs and rubs her fingers together to indicate money, money, money. I would very much like to turn Shauna Hamilton away, but I'll hear her out. I'm reasonable.

"Keep your voice low. And speak of this to no one, understand? I don't need everyone thinking I'm prone to exceptions."

Shauna sighs with relief and lowers her voice to a whisper. "Ryan, my boyfriend, promised that he would come to my family's annual skiing trip, but now he can't. He bailed. Something about his dad having surgery or something. I need a boy there. Desperately."

I'm almost rendered speechless. "Is his dad okay?"

Shauna gives me a strange look. "Oh, he's fine. It's a routine procedure or whatever. No big deal. Can you provide the Purdue guy for the weekend or not?"

"The service only provides platonic dates," I say.

Footsteps outside. We all shut up. When the footsteps fade, Emma opens the door and peers outside. After a moment, she closes the door and gives a thumbs-up. All clear. Still, we better hurry this up.

"Like I need to pay for real romance," Shauna whispers, rolling her eyes. "We go skiing every year with the Mayhews, a vile family I've been forced to interact with all my life because my mom happened to be in the same sorority as Mrs. Mayhew. Ben, the Mayhew son, is completely obsessed with me. If I don't have a guy there, even a guy just pretending to be my boyfriend, he will not leave me alone for more than two seconds. He's relentless and pathetic and annoying. It will be hell without someone there to discourage his advances. I need a shield."

I ask, "For the entire weekend?"

"Saturday through Sunday. One night. Name your price," she adds. Her voice is panicky.

"We've never booked an overnight engagement before." Emma types on her phone, taking notes.

"Skiing." I rub my chin with my index finger. "You'll want Yale. Our Yale guy is an impressive snowboarder."

Shauna roughly points at the Purdue envelope. "No, I want this guy. He's the cutest."

I pick at my thumb. "I just don't know if he's the best choice here..."

"I'll pay anything." Shauna's voice grows louder. "I need the cutest guy possible."

Anything? She'll pay anything? The first year's tuition at UVM for Loch perhaps? But Ollie's clearly the better choice for this date. How can I convince Shauna? She wants what she wants. I need to discuss this with Emma. Alone.

"Leave your number with Emma," I say. "We'll be in touch. In the meantime, it's best not to talk to me. We don't want the faculty growing suspicious."

Plus, I don't enjoy conversing with you. At all.

Shauna blurts out, "I'll give you two thousand dollars."

Now I *am* rendered speechless. Did she say *thousand*? Emma's blue eyes widen with joy. Discussion over. I clap my hands and rub them together and say, "Consider it done then."

. . . .

I realize my mistake as I'm driving home. Before agreeing to the weekend date, I should've checked with Loch. He's scheduled to work next Saturday. Crap.

Ten minutes from home, I give Loch a call and decide to butter him up before presenting the job. He hates calling in sick, but maybe two *thousand* bucks could persuade him.

He answers on the second ring with a muffled hello.

"Hey," I say. My mood immediately lifts knowing he's on the other end of the line. "You. Me. Monster movie tonight?"

"Sounds like you've had the kind of day I've had," he replies, sighing so deeply into the phone I can practically smell the cinnamon gum on his breath. "My turn to pick the movie."

"Like you'd ever let me forget."

I smile all the way home.

First I stop by my house to grab a Mountain Dew from the fridge and sputter a quick hello to Brian (hey, I'm trying here). Outside, a light snow cakes the tips of dead grass with white. When I slip through the Garrys' basement window, Loch is already waiting for me on the couch, dressed in a hoodie and oversized sweatpants. He grins. Just looking at him makes me all comfy.

About halfway through *King Kong,* I present Shauna's request, minus her threat to send me to jail (minor detail). I lead in with the money. At first, Loch looks excited, but when I finally take a breath and let him respond, he says, "Hell, no."

"Perhaps you didn't hear me," I say, moving my feet underneath me. "Two. Thousand. Bucks."

Loch scratches his stubble. If it's always itching him, I wonder why he doesn't just shave. Probably for the same reason I would sometimes go a week or two without shaving my legs. Before I had to wear a skirt everyday, that is. Laziness.

"There's clearly something wrong with someone who can spare that kind of money for a fake boyfriend," he says. "What's wrong with her? Is she a serial killer or something?"

I think a moment. It's a reasonable question. I shake my head. "You should see her nails. One can't be a serial killer with a perfect manicure all the time."

Loch stretches and yawns, the couch cushion lowering under his weight, pushing him closer to me. A creamy darkness sifts through the basement window. The lights are off, and the flickering images of the television fall over us. We watch the movie for a bit.

"I hate this part," I say, fidgeting with my socks. The characters onscreen chain up King Kong. It's so sad, the way they take him away from everything's he ever known. I bury my face in the warmth of Loch's shoulder, breathing in the cotton-y scent of his sweatshirt. "You know this movie makes me cry, Loch."

"You look extra-nice today," Loch whispers. The TV goes silent. "I like your hair. It smells like citrus."

For a moment, I close my eyes and allow those words to warm me. *You smell like vanilla and it's the most delicious, wonderful smell ever.* Then I remember myself and squirm and move away from the comfort of his shoulder. As I sit up, my cheek brushes against his stubble. I swear my body temperature rises another degree or two. I scoot to the other end of the couch and clear my throat, unsure what the heck just happened there.

"No changing the subject," I say with a forced chuckle.

Loch shifts like a cat trying to find the perfect resting spot. "I will do this job on one condition," he says.

Politely, I cross my legs, hoping this makes me feel more business-y. Because this is business. "Name it."

He responds with a symmetrical smile. Suddenly it feels like I'm about to be pulled into something I won't be able to climb out of.

nineteen

· · · · · · · · · · · · · · · · · ·

LOCH'S ONE CONDITION IS THE
reason why I'm lugging Shauna Hamilton's suitcase
from her parents' giant SUV among snow-crusted
woods and towering mountains. My modest duffel
bag rests somewhere beneath Shauna's designer
luggage, which is probably worth more than all of
my possessions combined. I almost drop it, but a
pair of hands reach from behind to grab the handle.

Loch whispers, "What does she have in here? A
dead body?" His breath tickles my skin. I hide my
smile.

"Darn," Shauna shouts as she hops out of the car.
Her furry snow boots land on the gravel driveway.
"The Mayhews aren't here yet. *Shucks.*"

"Drop the sarcasm," Mrs. Hamilton singsongs,
throwing her arm around Shauna's shoulder.
"Sarcasm is not for ladies."

On the outside, Mrs. Hamilton resembles an older
replica of Shauna. Red hair. Light freckles. The jagged
gestures of a dictator. However, there's a softness in
her that's lacking in her daughter. I wonder if it's
true what they say about girls eventually becoming

their mothers. Perhaps that softness will emerge from Shauna after graduation.

"OH! MY! GOD! I think I just stepped in rabbit shit!" Shauna hops around as she tries to get a look at the bottom of her shoe. Birds scatter from a nearby tree, the peaceful quiet broken by her shrill screams.

Then again, maybe not. Maybe Shauna will always be Shauna.

Mr. Hamilton, a jolly man with slicked-back hair and long sideburns, moves in next to Loch. "Atta boy," Mr. Hamilton says, gesturing to the bags in Loch's arms. "Never let a lady carry her own bag."

Mr. Hamilton walks ahead to the cabin, snow crunching beneath his boots. He deliberately leaves the bags for his daughter's new "boyfriend" to drag inside. Loch gives me a You-Owe-Me-Forever-Look, marking the tenth one since we left Shelburne two hours ago.

It's true. I owe him, but I'm working off my debt. I'm renting myself out this weekend, too. Believe me, I'd much rather be at home watching *Family Guy* reruns.

To pull off the illusion, Shauna's parents need to believe that Loch and Shauna are really an item. The last-minute boyfriend swap must occur often in Shauna's world because her parents accepted it without question. They treat Loch like he's just another one of Shauna's boyfriends to deal with for a weekend, soon to be out of their privileged lives for good.

I, on the other hand, am welcomed with stifling enthusiasm that reeks of familiarity.

"I am so thrilled that Shauna made a female friend this year," Mrs. Hamilton whispers as she leads me up the walkway to the cabin. She hooks her arm in mine, as if we are dear friends in a Jane Austen novel. "You may not have noticed, but Shauna can be rather intimidating to other girls. It's a jealousy thing, unfortunately. It's nice to see a secure young lady like yourself handle her."

I look up at the cabin and my breath catches. Camping for the Hamilton family translates to a state-of-the-art cabin complete with cable, Internet, and a hot tub on the balcony. Inside, dead animals hang on the walls above a glistening wooden floor. The scent of pine drifts everywhere.

I stare at the giant deer head above the stone fireplace until Shauna rips me from my reverie. She taps my shoulder and whispers, "I'm not paying you to just stand there."

Right. I'm on the job.

Shauna isn't thrilled about my attendance this weekend. I think she wanted Loch all to herself, like most girls would, but Loch wouldn't come without me. His sick way of torturing me, I guess. Because I have to be here, Shauna puts me to good use though. She insists I make her look good, popular, and lovely. That I tell stories to her parents about her glory at Winston. This required homework, of course, since making up such massive lies on the spot would be challenging. On the drive up, I told stories of Shauna's imaginary kindness and admiration throughout the halls of Winston, laying it on pretty thick.

While Shauna blabs on about her imaginary relationship to her parents in the kitchen, I check out the various rooms in the cabin. There's a freaking movie theater in the basement! I run my fingers over the leather seats, excited to curl up with a cup of warm cider and watch a flick later. There are *some* perks to this job.

A few minutes later, I find Shauna and Loch organizing the luggage in a Western-themed bedroom upstairs. I notice that my bag is resting next to Shauna's luggage. I stare at my duffel. I stare at the mound of pink suitcases. Horror settles into my chest.

"There's my roommate," Shauna crows, smiling.

I look at Loch, who appears rather amused by the situation. "And where are you sleeping?" I ask.

"Had to insist on my own room," he says, tucking his hands into the front pockets of his jeans. "I'm a terrible snorer."

"Such a liar." *I'm the snorer.* Loch sleeps like the dead.

"Isn't that my job though?" Loch asks. "To lie?"

"It's just one night," Shauna says in a low voice. She glances at the open doorway, nervous. "I'm not thrilled either, Toni. If I sleep alone, Ben could sneak into my room."

"Have you considered pressing charges against this guy?" I ask. "This sounds like more than an annoying crush."

Shauna sighs and slips out of her sophisticated yellow jacket. "Okay. Maybe he doesn't sneak into my room, but he probably thinks about it. My parents won't let me sleep in the same room as my boyfriend anyway, real or fake. We have to make them believe you and I are, like, close. The best of girlfriends. Remember?"

She's right. It's all part of the act. *Two. Thousand. Dollars.* I repeat the number in my head to hold onto my slipping sanity. This will all be over soon, and Loch will be one step closer to attending UVM next year.

As Loch exits the room, he squeezes my shoulder. "Remember," he whispers. "Serial killers can't have perfect nails."

"Bra. Bra. Bra. Pianist," I whisper back.

He tenses, reddens, and goes down the hall to his bedroom. Shauna rolls up the sleeves of her black sweater and begins to unpack. She checks her phone every two seconds. "Ryan said he would keep in touch," she says, tossing her phone on the bed in frustration. "Nothing for the last hour. Not one word. Not even an emoji. Sometimes I don't understand him at all."

I mumble something in reply and slink into the hallway. I find Loch in his room, staring out the window at the beautiful cluster of snow-covered trees surrounding the cabin. I keep my voice low just in case Shauna's parents venture upstairs.

"What did you tell the boss to get off work for the weekend?" I sit down on the bed next to his unpacked bag. "Chicken pox? The flu? A broken heart?" Loch looks at me, frowning. I continue, "Ebola? Malaria? The plague? Vampirism?"

"I quit."

"You what?" I accidentally shout it. I press my hand over my mouth, as if that will somehow reverse the noise.

"The boss wouldn't let me take any more time off." Loch wipes his hand over his buzzed hair. "I made a choice. The hours sucked anyway."

A sick feeling settles into my gut. "Well," I say softly. "Good."

He tugs at the bottom of his sweatshirt. "Think I made the right decision?"

I brighten. Of course he made the right decision. I hope. "You're the most popular product we've got,

Loch. There's a waiting list a mile long for you," I say with confidence. "Now you'll have time to go on more dates and bring in more money. No more teddy bears."

"Wait—there's a waiting list?" He turns away from the window.

I shrug and fidget with the zipper on his duffel bag. "Winston girls think you're adorable."

"You're a Winston girl." He sits beside me on the bed. The springs squeak. "You think I'm adorable?"

I blush and shove my hands into the pocket of my hoodie. I glance at his wide, scruffy chin. "Duh."

Loch scratches that stubble and turns to me, accidentally bumping my knee with his. I squirm a little. Is it warm in here?

"Toni, I..." He doesn't finish. He jumps up because Shauna appears in the doorway, her chest heaving. She gasps for air, leaning against the frame.

"You two can't be sneaking around together like this," she shout-whispers. "If Micah is going to be alone with anyone in a bedroom, it should be me."

"Relax," I tell her. "Nothing's going on."

I look to Loch to back me up on that, but he gazes out the window again, clasping his hands behind his back. Silent.

"I don't give a rat's ass about your love life, Toni Valentine," Shauna hisses. "But I do want what my deposit promises me. Your business would never survive another incident like Carrie Sanders. Understand?"

"We're doing what you asked." I stand, fidgeting with the string on my sweatpants. "I told your parents that you pulled me out of my darkest depression and inspired me to apply to Ivy League schools. That lie alone was worth your deposit."

"Look, in about five seconds, the job is about to get a whole lot worse," Shauna says.

Downstairs, a door slams and there's a huge roar of laughter. Someone snorts. There's some type of singing. Loch and I exchange a glance. Shauna cringes. The Mayhews have arrived. It's showtime.

twenty

....

THE FIRST THING I NOTICE about Ben Mayhew is his blatant disrespect for personal space. When Shauna introduces me as her dear friend from school, Ben wraps his wire-like arms around my shoulders until my face is stuffed into his puffed-out coat. The second thing I notice about Ben Mayhew is that he smells like cigarettes. I gag at the strong scent. When he releases me from his grasp, I hide behind Loch. I don't like smelling or touching strangers.

Shauna wraps her arm around Loch's waist and yanks away my security blanket. "Ben, darling, this is my boyfriend Micah Garry," she says. Is she really speaking in a faux-British accent? I think she is a little bit. Wow. "I'm in love with him. He's totally in love with me. We'll probably get married someday."

My jaw drops. There are no words. Loch keeps a straight face. I'm impressed.

Ben scans Loch as if assessing a new car and says, "'Sup?"

Loch outstretches his arms. "Oh, come on. Let's hug, man."

As a horrified look forms on Ben's face, Loch envelops him into an enormous bear hug. I bite the inside of my cheek to keep from laughing. Ben's narrow face gets lost in Loch's massive arms. The hug holds a beat too long before Ben manages to squeeze away. He straightens his coat, tries to keep his cool.

Ben's an interesting-looking guy. It's like someone pinched his body from head to toe. Everything from his nose to his arms to his ears appears narrow and smashed. He walks with an unpracticed swagger, and his shaggy brown hair falls over his eyes in kinky waves.

I brace myself for another act of Shauna's performance, but the front door swings open. Mrs. Hamilton and a woman I presume to be Mrs. Mayhew enter the living room. They kick bags along the way. Loch hurries to help with their luggage.

"The roads were fine on the way up," Mrs. Mayhew says, breathing heavy. "But there's supposed to be a huge snow storm tonight."

"I hope not," Mrs. Hamilton replies. "But I came prepared if we get stuck here for a few days."

"Special cider?" Mrs. Mayhew giggles. Mrs. Hamilton nods and laughs.

Stuck here? For a few days? Please no. Mrs. Mayhew shakes my hand and introduces herself. She looks nothing like her son. Yellow hair, huge teeth, robust-nature. When the polite chatter dies down, Mrs. Mayhew looks at me and asks, "Will you be attending Yale with Shauna next year, Toni?"

The question catches me off-guard. I came prepared to talk about Shauna and her imaginary golden life at Winston, but not myself. I scratch the back of my neck, nervous. *Lie, Toni. Just lie. This is what you do now. LIE.*

"Of course she is," Shauna interjects. She bundles her red curls into a messy bun. "We plan to be roommates."

"Thank goodness," Mrs. Mayhew exclaims. "It will be so nice knowing your roommate. My freshmen year was a disaster because of mine. I swear she never bathed."

I don't want to attend Yale with Shauna, not even in an imaginary world. Loch senses my annoyance and nudges my elbow. I keep my mouth shut.

After everyone gets settled, Mr. Hamilton announces that it's time to hit the slopes. Shauna and Loch load up the ski gear while I check my phone for messages. Emma's latest nugget of encouragement: *KA-CHING!* The reminder makes me feel a little better, but I'm still counting the minutes until this weekend trip is over.

On the ride to the slopes, Shauna sits smashed between Loch and I in the backseat of the Hamiltons' SUV. I notice that her knee touches his knee. The whole way. *Is that touching necessary?* Ben's in the front passenger's seat so he can't see back here. So there's no need for the knee-on-knee contact. I grind my teeth and stare out the window at the mountains.

At the cozy ski lodge, the group splits into advanced and beginner. I slide myself into the beginner category to keep an eye on Shauna and Loch. I can't remember the last time I went skiing anyway. My dad used to take me when I was younger, but I was never any good. Shauna is advanced, but she makes a point of saying over and over, "I don't want to leave my boyfriend." And Ben doesn't want to leave Shauna.

So we're stuck as a foursome.

We grab a late lunch from the lodge cafeteria and find a table among the red-cheeked snowboarders. I sit beside a sullen Ben as he picks at the cheese on his pizza. I eat two slices before Shauna scoots closer to Loch and kisses his cheek. Well. I'm full.

"Micah's a genius," Shauna says, resting her head on Loch's shoulder as she speaks to Ben. "He's going to be a doctor."

Ben sniffs and stuffs a string of cheese into his mouth. I lean forward and play with the silver tab on my Mountain Dew can. "Oh, yes. Micah is intelligent," I say. "And ambitious. He's going to be a world-famous proctologist someday. Isn't that right, Micah?"

Loch nearly spits out his Coke.

"What's that?" Ben asks, rasping out the longest sentence I've heard him speak thus far. His voice is low, rough. A smoker's voice.

"It's a doctor who basically stares at—" I begin to explain, but Shauna cuts me short.

"I'm exhausted," she says with a yawn. "Micah and I were up late last night."

Shauna proceeds to nibble on Loch's left earlobe. I pop the tab from the Mountain Dew can so hard that the empty can tips over. A string of cheese dangles from Ben's chin as he looks away. I feel sorry for him. He's in love, a condition I imagine isn't easy. He can't help the way he feels. He can't help who he is. Shauna's laying it on pretty thick. *Too* thick.

"Ben, you wanna hit the slopes?" I ask.

He brightens and nods, jumping up. As we toss away our trash, I glance over to see Loch watching me. He looks stricken, a victim left behind with the lioness. I feel bad abandoning him, but this is part of the job. I sure don't want to sit there and watch Shauna nibble on his ear like it's candy. She should back off once Ben is out the door.

Eager for the cold air, I hurry outside. Ben leans against the ski rack and sighs. "Man, that sucked," he says, pinching his thin nose.

"Yeah." I peek through the window. Shauna is sitting alone at the table now, scrolling through her phone. Frowning. Good. I don't see Loch anywhere. I feel better now that they're away from each other.

Ben leans toward me. I can smell the cigarette smoke on his jacket. "We have to break them up."

"Excuse me?" I pull on a pair of gloves.

"Oh, come on," Ben says, smiling. "You want him. I want her. We have to break them up."

"First of all, I do not want him," I say with confidence. "He's Shauna's boyfriend." I pause. I feel like throwing up, just saying that. "Second of all, that sounds like the plot to an awful romantic comedy."

Ben shuffles his feet. "You stare at him like you want him."

I force a smile. "Do you want to ski down the big hill or what?"

"I don't know." He turns around and looks up at the mountains. "I'm a beginner."

I slap his back. "You shouldn't let labels deter you from doing exciting things, Ben."

He turns to look at me. Shrugs. "What the hell," he says. "If I die, at least I don't have to watch Shauna chew on some other guy's ear again."

Amen to that.

. . . .

As I gaze down the slope of track-stamped snow, it dawns on me that I have no clue what I'm doing. I can handle a ball or a pool stick or a video controller. I have general faith in my athletic abilities, but my confidence wavers when Ben gives a thumbs-up, snaps on his goggles, and takes off down the hill, letting out a howl of excitement. His skis cut through the snow with ease. Within seconds, his silver puffy jacket is a blur.

Beginner? Either Ben's very modest or he lowered my expectations on purpose to impress me. Or he's a liar. Like the rest of us.

My stomach flips more times than the snowboarders spinning through the air. I think about Ollie and how much he would love this. People whiz by me one by one like it's no big deal to dive down a mountain. *How does Ollie do this? WHY does Ollie do this?*

I'm frozen. I imagine living up here forever. I could attend Purdue by mail. I could send my assignments down with snowboarders. I could be the girl living on the impossible mountain with an unknown path ahead of her.

"Just relax." A hand lands on my shoulder. I meet Loch's kind eyes. "Don't think about it so much, Toni."

"How did...?" I clear my throat, which is very dry. "How did you get up here so fast?"

"You've been standing up here for thirty minutes. Ben said you looked ready to hurl. His word, not mine. *Hurl.*"

I lie, embarrassed. "I think I ate a bad slice of pizza."

Pink splotches Loch's cheeks. He scratches the black whiskers along his chin with his glove. "If you think about it too much, fear will take over and you won't do anything," he says. "That's my general life theory."

"Is it too late to do the bunny hill?" I joke.

Loch jabs me in the shoulder. "We'll go together, Toni. I won't leave your side."

I don't really want to be the girl who lives on the scary mountain forever so I nod, prepared to take the plunge. With him by my side, I'll be okay. This won't be so bad. Together we count to three, push forward, and begin the descent.

All begins well. My legs keep steady. My shoulders straight. The cold wind blasts my cheeks. I relax and realize that I'm actually having fun. So this is why Ollie does this. This is why he wants to travel across country this summer. *The rush.* I fly. I soar. Look at me! A confident business woman mastering her fears!

When I turn to look at Loch, everything goes horribly awry. The look on Loch's face is one of pure fear. Lips pulled back in a silent scream. Jaw twisted. Eyes wild. He's seconds away from landing on his face. His large limbs twist about in every direction, grasping for something, anything to stop the inevitable crash. By some small miracle he remains on his feet, which isn't a good thing because the longer he manages to stay up, the faster he zooms down the slope.

The harder he will fall.

The ski lodge below grows larger, larger, larger. Oh, God. We're going to crash into people. We're going to hurt someone. We're going to die. Oh, God. I'm going to die a virgin. Loch isn't. Loch has lived! Why am I thinking about this right now?!

There's the ski lodge ahead. A crowd of people. Bones will be broken.

I grab Loch's hand and look him in the eye. Seconds later, he's falling forward, and I brace myself for the crash. Loch releases my hand and tumbles. A shower of snow rises to the sky as his body slides. I find my balance until I turn around to see if Loch's okay. That's when my feet fly out from underneath me and everything goes white.

twenty-one

· · · · · · · · · · · · · · · · · ·

I HOLD MY CELL AWAY FROM MY ear as my mother's frantic cries bleed through the receiver. Flames dance in the stone fireplace, brightening the dead animals hanging from the cabin walls. My legs stretched along the couch, I stare at my phone and wait for a break in Mom's panic. Finally, she takes a breath. I seize the opportunity to reassure her again.

"Mom, this isn't the first time I've broken my arm," I say. "I'm fine. I didn't even cry."

There were various swear words flying about on the ride to the hospital, but no tears. This break isn't nearly as bad as when I broke my arm in the sixth grade jumping off the tool shed in Cowboy's backyard. Because Ollie dared me to. This incident is also less humiliating.

"You need to come home," Mom replies between sobs. "I want my only baby home now."

I'd much rather be curled up beside Mom with a large bowl of popcorn right now, watching a seasonally inappropriate movie like *Christmas Vacation* or *Home Alone*, but alas, that heavenly scenario is not in the cards tonight.

"There's a winter storm." I glance out the cabin window. Thick snowflakes plummet to the ground in a cluster of rage. "It's too dangerous to come home tonight. This is your responsible teenage daughter speaking. Tell Brian I said that."

Mom sighs into the phone. "I shouldn't have let you go in the first place."

Twenty minutes later, she calms down after I promise a thousand times to call the minute we leave tomorrow morning. She tells me that she loves me and I tell her that I love her and I hang up with a huge guilt pit in my stomach.

"I shouldn't have told her," I tell Loch. He sits across from me in a moose-themed arm chair. He lowers the *Vermont Monsters* book he's reading.

"You did the right thing." He raises the hood of his gray sweatshirt over his ears. "I bet you twenty bucks she'll have pumpkin pie waiting for you when you get home."

"I'll take that bet." I scribble on my white cast with a black marker. I draw a stick-figure skiing down a steep hill. The skier has wings, one of which is broken.

Shauna's parents felt awful about the accident. Both were in freak-out mode the whole time. At the hospital, Mr. Hamilton kept telling me that a lawsuit wouldn't be a good idea, as if I were considering such an option as my arm twisted in an unnatural way. I assured him I didn't plan on suing anyone until I was at least thirty, but he didn't find that funny.

The adult gang went to bed an hour ago, but I can't sleep. I like watching the snow drop onto the ground like a thousand tiny white bullets. I like Loch near me. I like the quiet, which is now interrupted by the sound of Shauna's pink slippers scraping across the floor. She enters the living room dressed in a red silk bathrobe. Where do you even buy something like that? She balances three large mugs of steaming something and sets them on the coffee table.

"A nice treat after a hard day's work," she whispers.

Shauna plops down in the deer-themed chair next to Loch, sighs, and takes a drink from her mug. She looks at me like she wants to say something. I'm really not in the mood for confrontation. Ben's been in the shower for thirty minutes. I'm actually starting to worry he may have passed out from the pain of his unrequited love. I'll give him another ten minutes before I send Shauna in to check on him.

I take a large gulp from the mug. "Yum. What is this?" I ask, bringing the cup to my lips for seconds.

"It's my mom's special cider," Shauna replies, adjusting her robe.

Loch drinks and coughs. "Rum. That's rum. And maybe a teaspoon of cider."

I set the mug on the coffee table and push it away. "I probably shouldn't mix that with the pain medication."

"Toni Valentine. Always so responsible," Shauna says with a smile. "Who would guess that you run the business that you do."

"What business?" Ben appears like a freaking ghost, drying his hair with a towel. He's wearing gray sweatpants and a white tank top. Shauna realizes her slip-up and stumbles for an explanation, but she comes up with nothing more than a few strange gurgling sounds.

"Toni teaches a pole-dancing class," Loch chimes in. I glare at him. Seriously? A subtle smile forms on his lips.

"No kidding?" Ben asks, stepping further into the room. "Let's see some moves, Toni."

I continue to draw on my cast. "Can't."

"She's shy." Loch sighs and sets his book on the coffee table. He's so teasing me.

"I'm not shy," I reply. "If you want to see my moves, you've got to pay. Like everybody else."

Ben leans against the wall and folds his arms across his chest. "Can we get a free sample? Every good business gives a free sample."

I continue to scribble on my cast, tired, a little cranky. I'm earning every penny for this job, that's for sure. "I don't think so."

"Spoken like a true *chicken*," Loch says. I stop drawing and look up. Loch's eyes glimmer with mischief. With that indirect dare, I'm on my feet. I yank at the bottom of my *Mario Brothers* T-shirt and move to the center of the room. Ben claps, Shauna appears horrified, and Loch's expression is hidden behind his mug of special cider. He doesn't think I'll actually do this. Well, *watch me*.

"I need a pole," I say. I run a hand through my hair, unsure how to proceed.

"Is this really going to happen?" Shauna sounds disgusted.

"I was kidding, Toni. You don't have to do this," Loch says. He gives me a warning look. Like maybe I should sit down. Take it easy.

I spot a walking stick among the wall decor. I lift it from the wall and return to my place in the center of the room. The jagged stick comes up to my waist. I set it in front of me, lean on it with my good hand, and stick my butt out. The pain medication wipes away any self-consciousness.

"Holy crap. This is going to be good." Ben sinks into the couch and kicks up his feet.

"I need music," I announce.

Ben whips out his phone, presses a few buttons, and the living room fills with the sounds of a sexy-slow rendition of The Ronettes' "Be My Baby."

I give him a look. "Really? This is what you listen to?"

"Let me guess," Ben says, rolling his eyes. "You thought I liked rap or something? Well, consider yourself corrected."

I feel Loch watching me. As my body bursts with heat, I realize it's now or never. I can be sexy. I can totally do this.

"This is a little move I like to call Getting in Touch With Your Womanhood." I slide down the walking stick, slow and seductive, as the soft melody rises.

Ben's eyes grow wide. Shauna snorts and drinks her cider. My hips move to the music. I dance around the stick, leaning into it, using it for balance and a focal point. Soon I lose myself in the soft sound of guitar strings. My hair falls over my face, cloaking me from the watching eyes. Everything fades into the background. I am alone with heartache.

When the song ends, I expect laughter and jokes—the works. Maybe even a new nickname. But I lift my head, brush the hair from my eyes, and greet a stunned audience.

Shauna's jaw hangs open. "I am totally taking your class."

"Can I have your number?" Ben asks, dead-serious.

"See." I straighten up. Catch my breath. "I'm not a *chicken*."

I place the walking stick back on the wall and return to my seat. Loch leans forward, rubbing his forehead as if he has a bad headache. He finishes off the mug of special cider and moves on to my cup, drinking quickly.

We chat for a while, mostly about my accident, until Shauna announces she's ready to go to sleep. Ben retires soon after, leaving Loch and I alone with the crackling fire. He hasn't spoken since the pole-dancing demonstration. My eyelids feel heavy. I continue doodling on my cast.

"Why did you start the business, Toni?" Loch asks. His voice is almost a whisper. "You don't need the money that bad."

I flip the black marker around in my palm. It's a reasonable question, but I hesitate in revealing the truth. "I don't know," I say. "Boredom?"

He adjusts his socks—one black, one white again—and leans against the armrest. "I thought your cure for boredom was mooning principals."

"Look where that landed me." I sigh, sinking further into the couch. "I don't know. I wish I could say I wanted to help people. The truth is I wanted a way to tie my old life to my new one. I felt like my life was floating away or something."

Loch moves to the couch and rolls a large furry blanket over both of us. "I told you before," he says. "I'm not going anywhere."

Blushing, I pull the blanket to my chin and smile. Loch takes the marker from my hand and writes something on my cast. The room is dark, lit moment-to-moment by the flickering fireplace. I lean into him and breathe in the scent of cider and vanilla. I wiggle my toes. When he's finished writing, he sets the marker on the coffee table. As his hand moves to my knee, the fire creaks and moans and pours heat over every inch of me. He leans closer, closer. His rum cider forgotten.

I wonder why the world doesn't shake from my heartbeat. The pounding behind my curved bones is so freaking loud. Loud enough to send an avalanche racing down the mountain, encasing us in this moment like the lovers of Pompeii. My right foot rubs against his sock as I shift my weight. The promise he made at my father's grave feels as fragile as the embers rising into the chimney. My head buzzes with lost thoughts and insane possibilities for my path ahead. *Our* path. I read what he wrote on my cast in his sloppy boy-handwriting: *My sincerest apologies.*

I look up. Before his lips link with mine, Loch adds, "I have to break the promise I made. About avoiding, you know, change between us?"

Of course I remember the promise. But when he kisses me, I forget everything. I forget lake monsters. I forget names scratched into wooden docks. I forget Winston. I float away.

Loch pulls back, keeping close, and whispers, "Maybe we shouldn't do this here."

I mumble something that isn't a word and study the dark hairs along his movie star chin. *Holy crap. I just kissed Loch.* I jump up, practically gasping for air. The blanket falls loose from my shoulders.

"I better get to my room," I blurt. "Goodnight." As I bolt for the exit, I slam my knee into the coffee table. "Ack!"

Loch stands, concerned. "You okay?" he asks. His dark eyes are so freaking distracting.

I step back, making sure he doesn't get too close. My knee throbs. "Yep. I'm good. Later."

"Goodnight, Toni," he says.

But I don't look at him. I just give a stupid wave and limp off to my room. My knee seriously hurts. Quickly, I close the door and climb into my bed and pull the covers over my face. *Okay, heart. You can calm down any minute now.* I lay there for some time, staring at the ceiling. My arm itches beneath my cast. My knee aches. But I don't care about any of the pain. I just replay the kiss over and over until sleep grabs hold and shoves me under.

twenty-two

······················

THE NEXT MORNING, I WAKE UP to the sound of clanging pans, sizzling eggs, and running water. My head feels like a stone too heavy to lift. But I sit up, groggy, and try to itch underneath my cast. I lift the covers and study my bruised knee. Ouch. Not sure I can handle another injury on this trip. Barefoot, I pad to the kitchen, which is full of busy bodies. I peer into the living room and examine the couch. There it is. The scene of the crime.

Cider.

Warmth.

Fire.

Lips.

Stubble rubbing my cheek.

His hand on my skin.

"Good morning, Tonya," Mrs. Hamilton shouts over the counter, flipping a pancake. "How you feeling today?"

I groan, suddenly very aware that these people are admiring my bedhead. I shuffle into the kitchen and ask as casually as my voice will allow, "Where's Micah?"

Mrs. Hamilton flips another pancake. "Shauna took him to the lake to go ice-fishing early this morning."

My stomach jerks. *He's with Shauna?*

"Ben went along with them," Mrs. Mayhew adds. "No one wanted to wake you. How's that arm?"

I look at the words on my cast. The shape of each letter. The meaning hidden behind them. *My sincerest apologies.*

I swallow hard. "Everything's great. Thank you for asking."

. . . .

An hour later, I wait on the couch with my packed duffel bag at my feet. The rest of the luggage rests by the door, along with a nervous Mrs. Mayhew, who keeps glancing out the window.

"They should be back by now," she says.

"They probably caught a fish," Mr. Hamilton says, fiddling with his phone. "My Shauna always catches something. We'll leave as soon as they get back."

I call my mother to tell her about the slight delay. She takes it surprisingly well. While we wait, I play a game of Go Fish with Shauna's parents and Mrs. Mayhew, but I can't concentrate on anything other than the taste of Micah's mouth. I wonder if Shauna is kissing that mouth right now. *Ugh.* I slam the cards down.

"Don't be a sore loser, Toni," Mrs. Hamilton huffs, gathering up the cards.

Is that what I am? A sore loser? Did I lose him? I pace the room, a bundle of nerves. I shouldn't care. Micah doesn't belong to me. He's still on the job.

He's paid to pretend. Things went too far last night, but it isn't too late to set things back the way they've always been. Kissing ruins friendships.

I can't afford to lose Micah.

But.

That *stubble*. That *mouth*.

Footsteps sound outside the door. It sounds like someone kicking snow off their boots. Seconds later, the door opens, revealing a stunned-looking Micah wrapped tightly in his black jacket and fluffy black scarf. His pink cheeks burst against the white background behind him.

My stomach does this thing I can't describe. Yep. There he is. Stunning.

"Thank the Lord!" Mrs. Mayhew exclaims, shuffling the deck of cards. "We were about to send out a rescue crew. Where's Ben? Shauna?"

"Out back." Micah's shoulders are stiff. He avoids eye contact with anyone.

Mr. Hamilton claps. "She catch something?"

"Uh. Yeah." Micah clears his throat. "She caught something. If you can call it catching."

Mr. Hamilton checks his phone. "We should hit the road. But first I must see what darling Shauna has brought us!"

He exits through the back door, which slams behind him. Mrs. Hamilton sighs and gathers up the cards. Mrs. Mayhew slips on her coat and joins the party around back, giddy to see Shauna's "catch." Whatever that means.

Micah hurries over and whispers to me. "You sure that girl's not a serial killer?"

He's close. Too close. His fingers brush my elbow, and my elbow ignites. This is enough to drive me insane within a matter of days.

"Huh?" I'm distracted by his rough edges. The fact that he can light me on fire.

When Mrs. Hamilton approaches us, I panic and spin around and pretend to be going somewhere very important, but I end up walking straight into the wall. Boom.

"Oh my God!" Mrs. Hamilton exclaims. "Toni? Are you all right?"

I hold my aching nose. Ouch. Ouch. Ouch. I give a stupid smile. "Must be the pain meds," I say. "Making me kind of loopy."

Mrs. Hamilton touches my shoulder. "Please be careful."

She shakes her head and goes outside to join the others. I slide into my coat, wiggling my hurt nose. This is just getting ridiculous. I avoid Micah and hurry to see what the others are doing, but he's right behind me. I can feel his breath on the back of my head.

"Toni," he whispers. "Whatever you do back there, don't look in the red cooler."

. . . .

The first thing I want to do is glance inside the red cooler. It rests beside the fire pit, a red dot among the snow. Mr. Hamilton peers inside it, a thrilled expression across his face.

"That's my daughter," he says with pride.

Shauna grins. "There it was, crossing the road. I didn't mean to hit it, of course, but the damage was done at just the right spot. The body's still in one piece."

Ben looks at Shauna like she's some kind of goddess. I shiver several feet away, hands stuffed into the pockets of my coat. Micah stands close enough that I can feel the heat rise from him. Will he try to kiss me again? Not now, of course. But in the future perhaps?

"Darling, we should probably load up the car," Mrs. Hamilton says.

"I want to skin it first." Shauna glares at me. "I need to change my shoes. I don't want to get blood on my boots."

Skin it?

Skin *what*?

Why is she looking at me like that?

"Do it when we get home." Mr. Hamilton pats his daughter on the back. "Put plenty of ice in there so that it holds. It's only a few hours. It should be fine. We need to get going. Tonya's mother is worried."

"Come on, Ben. Help us finish loading up the car," Mrs. Mayhew orders.

The Hamiltons and Mrs. Mayhew go back inside. Before Ben follows his mother, he looks to Shauna and says, "You're amazing. I always knew you were amazing." He beams and hurries to the cabin. Micah, eager to leave, starts to follow, but Shauna stops him.

"Let's talk business," she says, pulling out a hunting knife.

Holy crap.

My gaze moves to the cooler.

I can't stop staring at it.

Have I entered into a real-life horror movie?

Micah sighs and shoves his hands into his coat pockets. "Make this quick, Shauna."

Oh my God. I totally have.

"In case you didn't notice, Toni Valentine, Ben loves me," Shauna says. She takes a step forward. Snow crunches. "A lot. He loves me more than ever. And it's all your fault."

"You're not making any sense," I say, shaking my head. "Could be the pain medication. Could be the fact that you're just not making sense."

"Let me remind you." Shauna brushes a curl from her eye with the tip of the knife. "You. Micah. The couch. A cozy fire. Last night. Kissing. Ring any bells, Toni?"

I look at her. Oh. That.

"Ben saw you," Shauna continues. "And he knows the truth now, thanks to Micah."

"He thought I was cheating on her," Micah explains, wiping his head. "He wanted to kick my ass. He needed the truth or he would've ended up with a broken arm, too. Safety first."

Shauna sharpens the knife on a nearby rock.

"Okay." I raise my hands, trembling. "Can we just talk about this? No one needs to get hurt."

"You completely humiliated me, Toni!" Shauna slides the knife into a leather case and sets it beside the cooler. I breathe a little easier. "If you hadn't insisted on coming along, this could've worked out perfectly! Ben thinks I hired a guy to pretend to like me, and now he's more persistent than ever. He says he'll love me forever, and I don't have to pay him a cent blah blah blah. God, do you have any idea how this feels? I feel like the biggest loser in Vermont!"

"Just tell Ben that it's not true," I say, sighing. "Tell him no, Shauna."

She grumbles and tightens her yellow scarf. "He doesn't want to hear it. And now he thinks I made up Ryan, too. Thanks, Toni. Really. Why can't you two stop looking at each other like that, huh? Why can't you pretend for one weekend not to be crazy in love with each other? Is that too much to ask?"

At the same time, Micah and I reply, "We're not crazy in love with each other."

A pause.

We both point to each other and shout, "JINX!"

I laugh. I can't help it. Micah breaks into an adorable grin. Shauna just stares at us for a few moments. Shocked.

"I want my deposit back," she says. She picks up the red cooler. "All of it."

"Oh, come on," I beg. The morning sunlight slips through leafless branches, momentarily blinding me. "Micah did what he was hired to do. He gave up his weekend, his job, for you. He hugged you. *He let you lick his ear.* He earned that money."

"Micah blew the cover." Shauna shakes her head. "Which means he did not do what I paid for him to do. I want my deposit back. Every cent. I will call the police."

"The police?" I spit. "Are you serious?"

She lowers her voice. "I'll tell them all about your human-trafficking operation."

"Wait," Micah interrupts as my fingers curl into a fist. He looks to Shauna. "Forget it, okay? Have your money back. I don't want it anyway." He digs into his coat for his wallet and hands over the bundle of bills still wrapped in a pretty pink ribbon. I hate that she wrapped her money up like that. "Take it," he tells her. "It's all there."

"Micah." I touch his shoulder. *No. You need that money.* "I'll work this out."

Shauna snatches the cash from Micah's glove. "You're finished, Toni Valentine."

· · · · · · · · · · · · · · · · · ·

So the drive home is awkward. Shauna's parents pull into my driveway and bid Micah and I farewell. Shauna hops out and throws our bags in the snow. She doesn't look at either one of us as she climbs back into the car. I watch the SUV drive off, glad to be rid of her, but pissed that we had to return the money.

What a waste of a weekend. Worst of all, Micah quit his job for it. I feel so guilty for getting him involved with someone like that.

Micah hands me my bag. I take it, and my fingers graze his and my body warms. "Thanks," I say, blushing. "I'm sorry. I'll try and get the money back. At least some of it."

He scratches his scruff. "This whole thing might be too good to be true."

"Shauna Hamilton doesn't matter." I groan. "Screw her. She's crazy. I'll still make you a lot of money. Promise."

Promise. The word pulls me back to last night. The promise he broke. The kiss. Here we are now, alone in my driveway. No one around. He could kiss me again. *He could kiss me again.* My heart pounds.

"I'm thinking the business isn't a good idea," he says, swinging his bag onto his shoulder. "People are emotional, unpredictable creatures when it comes to relationships."

"I've got it under control." *Don't leave this. Please.*

Loch rubs the back of his neck. "That's the thing, Toni. You can make all the profiles and charts and schedules that you want, but you'll never be completely in control. There's an uncontrollable human element to this."

My heart drops. "Are you saying you want out like Cowboy?"

He hesitates. "I'm going to beg for my job at the Teddy Bear Factory back. If they take me, that job is my priority. This is just too risky for me right now."

I take a step back and nod. He looks at me, opens his mouth, and closes it again. He wants to say something else, I can feel it. And I want to say something else. I want to bring up the kiss, but I don't know how without sounding like an idiot. Gently, Micah touches the tip of my nose and says, "Later, Toni. No more walking into walls today, okay?"

As he steps away, I call out, "Hey, Micah?"

He stops, turns, and waits. For a second, I see hope in his eyes, but I'm pretty sure the pain medication is screwing with my head. Still. I should say something. Anything.

I ask, "What was in the cooler?"

He makes a gross-out face. "A dead rabbit."

I shudder and watch as he hurries up the walkway leading to his front door. He looks like he's running away from a bad date, and I guess he kind of is. Between Shauna nibbling on his ear and his lips crashing into mine, this was probably the worst weekend of his life.

I go inside and pretend the tears streaming down my cheeks are tears of joy to be home. Mom embraces me. She examines my arm, but I don't tell her about my other injuries. My bruised knee. My throbbing nose. My aching heart. Just when I think I might be able to forget him for a few seconds, Mom pulls out the pumpkin pie.

twenty-three

. . . .

EMMA AND I TRUDGE THROUGH
the parking lot on Monday morning, fighting the
bitter winds. I wrap my scarf around my face and
hope that she doesn't ask what happened over the
weekend. I'd prefer to silently obsess about it until
I develop an ulcer, but Emma grabs my elbow and
whispers in my ear, "What happened this weekend?"

My thoughts aren't working properly because
Micah inhabits them. He twists the words in my
head and blurs my focus. I can't think of a lie. I
don't want to lie. I mumble something in response
and unwrap the scarf as we step inside Winston. A
lost piece of paper sticks to my sneaker, but I kick it
aside and move along.

After several minutes of silence, Emma yanks me
into the bathroom and corners me by the sink. She
folds her arms over her chest and demands, "Talk."

I can't help it. I tell her everything. I need to tell
someone. When I get to the part about The Kiss, I
nearly choke on the story. I attempt to retell the tale
as casually as I can, mentioning more than once how
The Kiss was no big deal. I want someone to tell me
it was no big deal.

When I'm done, Emma blinks a few times and pulls out her lip gloss. She rubs the stick against her lips and hands me the tube. I've become oddly accustomed to sharing these types of girlie things with her but decline, my lips naked.

I swear I can still taste the cider from Micah's mouth.

Emma rubs her lips together and says, "That's a lot of information to process."

I pick at my thumbnail. Maybe she can give me some perspective. "You wanted to know what happened," I say.

Emma sighs. "Did you really pole dance?"

I blush. "It was more of a walking-stick dance."

She fidgets with her silver stud earrings. "This is serious trouble."

I groan and lean against the sink, a bit dizzy. "I knew it was a bad idea. Loch and I are friends. We shouldn't be kissing." I pause and take a deep breath. "We shouldn't start anything. I don't think we'll even be in the same state next year."

"Eh?" Emma blinks a few times.

"I would be choosing UVM for Loch, not for me," I say.

"So where do you wanna go?" Emma smiles. "Take Loch out of the equation."

I hesitate, my gut jerking. I know the answer. I think I've known since the day I got my acceptance letter, but I didn't want to admit it. Going out of state means growing apart from the guys. Now I know that's inevitable. "Purdue," I say with a nod. "I want to go where my dad went."

"Then that you shall, Toni Valentine," Emma says, resting her hand on my shoulder. I smile, relieved to make a decision, to take a leap, however terrifying. But an unsettled feeling rests in my gut. How will I tell Loch?

"Now," Emma continues, frowning. "Back to business. This is strike two against us. Shauna won't be quiet about her dissatisfaction. She's not as forgiving as Carrie." She pauses. "Does Micah want out?"

"I don't know." I shake my head. "He still needs the money. Do people care that much what Shauna thinks?"

"Let me worry about Hamilton." Emma frowns, in serious business mode. "I have texts from her, asking about the business. If anyone discovered that she used the service, she would be mortified. I'll expose her if she tries to destroy us."

I smile. Like I said. This girl should come with a warning label. "You'll take over the world someday, Emma Elizabeth Swanson."

Emma brightens. "You just worry about Micah Garry. And that kiss."

I turn to the mirror and notice red blotches forming along my collarbone. "I mentioned the whole kissing thing was nothing, didn't I?"

Emma slings her arm over my shoulder. "Welcome to the dark side, Toni Valentine."

"I'm not on the dark side," I stammer. "Wait. What dark side? Like Darth Vader?"

The last bell rings. We exit the bathroom and I re-explain how The Kiss was nothing. But I don't think Emma gets it. She just keeps nodding and smiling. As the bathroom door swings shut behind me, another paper gets stuck to my sneaker. Something about this one catches my eye. I stop and pick up the envelope and run my fingers over the Purdue logo in the corner.

"Someone's being careless with the brochures," I say, annoyed.

"I don't think it's carelessness," Emma whispers. I look at her. She stares right ahead, very still. I follow her gaze to see the blanket of white envelopes covering the empty hallway.

"Holy crap," I breathe. Panic. Pure panic. "We have to clean these up! If any of the faculty finds them..."

Mrs. Kemper appears around the corner. She picks up an envelope and opens it, curious. I'm pretty sure Emma has stopped breathing beside me. I grab her elbow, as if holding onto her might make everything okay. Mrs. Kemper's face changes from content to disturbed as she reads over Micah's profile.

"Shauna did this," Emma whispers. "I know it."

"It'll be fine," I whisper back, squeezing her elbow. "Names aren't on the profiles. Just a boy's picture. His fake hobbies. No big deal."

Mrs. Kemper looks up at us and says, "Ladies?" She marches toward us, the open envelope in hand.

"We're screwed!" Emma whisper-squeals.

"You know anything about these?" Mrs. Kemper asks.

"All of these college brochures littering the hall?" I shake my head. Try to whip out some acting skills. "Maybe someone's trying to make a statement?"

Mrs. Kemper's thick eyebrows raise. "A statement about what?"

"A statement about the pressure of choosing the right college," I ramble, scratching my collarbone. I can feel the red blotches there, giving me away. "Maybe these envelopes are supposed to represent, I don't know, the cluttered mind or something."

I run out of bullshit so I stop talking. Mrs. Kemper frowns. She's not buying it. An eternity passes. I think Emma might faint.

"You're late. Get to class, ladies," Mrs. Kemper orders.

. . . .

Later that night I open my laptop with the intention of watching a movie to clear my head, but my thoughts return to the blanket of white envelopes. I chew on the string of my hoodie, nervous. Mrs. Kemper will investigate. It's just a matter of time before the profiles are traced back to me, especially if Shauna Hamilton is questioned. This could be it. The end of the business. And Micah won't have money for UVM.

Micah. I rub my fingers over my lips and retrace his steps on my mouth. My lips are numb. My thoughts shift from Micah to Micah to Micah. I stare at the words written on my cast until the letters transform into nonsensical symbols of nothing. Words. Letters. Sentences. I inhabit a foreign world. Like Emma said, I am walking on the dark side. Everything tastes different, looks different, sounds different.

Outside my window, I hear the familiar sound of a basketball skidding across pavement. I peek through the blinds. Ollie, Cowboy, and Micah are playing basketball in the Garrys' shoveled driveway, each boy bundled up against the cold.

That's what I need. A moment of normal. Old times.

I throw on a Colts sweatshirt and head outside. Mom got the mail today, but I walk to the mailbox with purpose. I can't play with a broken arm, but I'd like to be invited over. There. Ollie spotted me. I think. Maybe not.

Snow seeps through my sneakers. I steal glances at the game. Ollie dunks the ball, cheering to the overcast skies. Cowboy rolls his eyes. I open the mailbox and gaze inside the hollow vessel. I look up and meet Micah's stare. My heart pounds.

He looks away and steals the ball from Cowboy, laughing. He misses what should've been an easy layup. Stomach churning, I make my way back to the house with my hands tucked firmly inside the front pocket of my sweatshirt. The stupid kiss. This silent treatment is all because of the kiss. It ruined everything.

"McRib!" Ollie shouts, tucking the ball under his arm. "Show us your moves!"

I try to hide my smile and relief. They're messing with me. This is how the guys operate. They tease and joke and give silly nicknames. I casually make my way over, but I want to run across the lawn and thank them for including me. Micah and Cowboy look very uncomfortable. Cowboy's the only one who looks at me. A few awkward moments pass. Why is this so weird?

"Hey, Cowboy," I say. Seems like I haven't seen him in forever. "Any progress with Katie Morris?"

He shuffles his feet. Looks down. "Still waiting for my perfect moment to open a conversation," he says. "I did get that scholarship to Johnson State. So there's that."

"Congratulations!" I say. Good for him. I hate that we've lost touch over these last few weeks, but we've both been busy. Besides, we'll have the summer to catch up. I hope. So what if he can't talk to Katie Morris anyway? He'll grow out of his painfully shy phase. Eventually.

I scratch at my cast and look at Micah, but he turns away and shoves his hands into his coat pockets. We should really talk. This is torture.

"We wanna see your moves, McRib," Ollie says, bouncing the basketball.

Thank God. A distraction. I raise my cast. "I can try one-handed," I say.

Ollie's grin grows wider. "You don't need the ball."

"Don't." Micah looks at Ollie and rubs the back of his neck. I'm not understanding something, but I try to keep my cool.

"Ollie's afraid I'll knock him over again," I joke. I shiver, not exactly dressed for snow-play. But I don't want to go back inside now.

Ollie's eyes narrow, and he licks his chapped lips. "Why didn't you choose me for the snowboarding date?"

His tone is accusing, laced with an edge of mean. I'm a little taken back, but I reply confidently, "The client chose Loch. The client gets what she wants."

"Seems to me," Ollie says, dribbling the ball, his tone dark, "that you want to help Loch earn money. So he gets more dates than any of us. All I get is Lemon."

Micah sighs. "Come on, man. Let it go."

"Not true." My voice rises. This isn't about the snowboarding date. This is about the stupid prank. He still blames me. "I want to help all of you. This is supposed to be a team effort."

Ollie dribbles the ball harder and harder until I think he might shatter the concrete. "Two thousand dollars for the weekend? That would've made a huge difference to me. This thing between you two?" He nods at Micah, then me. "It screws everything up. I'm not the only one who thinks that."

Ollie glances at Cowboy. Cowboy raises his hands in surrender. "I don't want to do this."

"Do what?" My heart thumps. What's happening here? This feels like a rebellion. An unraveling. Streetlights cast shadows across the snow. The neighborhood is cold, quiet, most everyone tucked away in their living rooms, winding down, preparing for bed. While I feel like my world with my boys is about to crack.

"You want to know why I don't go on hunts anymore?" Ollie asks. He tugs at his earlobe. "I see the way you look at Loch out on the water. We're not the same kids we were. Next year, we'll all be gone. Accept it."

My cheeks warm. *The way I look at Loch? What does that mean?* "That's why you want to spend the summer in Colorado?" I ask, trying to keep my cool. "You want to abandon us as soon as possible because it's inevitable that we change?"

Ollie frowns and dribbles the ball some more. "I'm not sure I even know you anymore."

"I'm the same person I've always been." I fidget with the string on my sweatpants. "This is about your parents. You won't stop blaming me for that dumb prank. It's not my fault you've goofed off for years, Ollie. And it's not my fault your parents are making you take some responsibility for something."

Ollie shoots the ball and misses. The ball rolls into the snow. Ollie leaves it there and blows into his bare hands, warming them. He points to the basketball goal. "Well," he says with a sinister grin. "Aren't you gonna show us your pole moves, McRib? I hear that's a new hobby of yours. See? I barely know you."

I step back, a wave of dizziness slamming into me. No one moves or talks. A gust of wind fills the silence. I look to Micah. But he's facing the garage door, his face hidden behind his gloved hands. He shakes his head over and over like that movement might fix something. It won't. What exactly did he tell them about our little trip? Ollie kicks at a clump of snow.

All of a sudden Cowboy retrieves the ball and goes in for a dunk. After he makes the shot, he moves across the driveway in calm-cool-Cowboy-mode, arms raised, trying to get some kind of applause from us. No one claps though. At least someone's trying to break this terrible awkwardness. But I don't even need to be here. Ollie says he doesn't know me anymore. Well, I don't know him either. I'm not sure I know any of these guys anymore.

I turn away from my boys—wait, they're no longer *my* boys—and march toward my house. This is the part where I say goodbye to my childhood existence. This is the part where everyone is different. No turning back. No clinging to what once was.

Behind me, his voice. "Toni! Wait! I wasn't making fun of you!"

I can't even look at Micah. I break into a jog and hurry inside. I press my back against the front door and catch my breath. I glance at my cast, at the stupid words scrawled on it, and wonder what else he told them about the trip. What else they laugh about. I am nothing more than a joke to them. A conversation piece for the basement. I am no longer one of the guys.

twenty-four

. . . .

"YOU SURE YOU WANT DO THIS?"
Emma asks. She sits at my desk and organizes rarely used Post-It notes by color. "Because you don't have to. You could just not wear them anymore."

I adjust my hoodie. "This is my way to vent. Plus they ride up my butt too much. Skirt or no skirt."

I look at my old pair of basketball shorts strewn across my bed. In my right hand I hold a pair of scissors. I take a deep breath. Time to say goodbye to things that don't work anymore. As I raise the scissors, Emma belches. I glance over my shoulder. She waves her hand and says, "Sorry. Please. Continue."

Without another thought, I cut the shorts down the middle, but the scissors get stuck on the fabric. So I attempt to tear the rest. This proves impossible with my broken arm. Emma hops up and takes one side of the shorts. I take the other. She gives me an encouraging nod.

"Ready?" she asks.

I nod. We each pull our side, and the shorts rip straight down the middle. Satisfied, I place the scissors on the bed. I plop down at my desk and gulp a Mountain Dew while Emma studies the torn shorts, perplexed. Look at that. Something I once refused to let go of torn up.

Emma's phone vibrates on the desk, and I startle. The screen lights up. I catch the name before Emma hurries over and picks it up. The text is from Ollie.

Flustered, Emma studies the screen and says, "Um, Ollie's headed over to Lemon's."

I stiffen. "Right on schedule."

Over the last few weeks, Mrs. Kemper investigated the origins of the brochures, but Winston girls know how to keep a secret. Everyone's lips are zipped, along with their wallets. Business has been slow. Nonexistent, actually. Tonight is an exception. Ollie and Micah are booked because it's Valentine's Day.

"This will blow over, Toni." Emma sighs, sitting on the bed. She swings her legs. "Whatever's going on with you guys."

"Yeah. Maybe." I look away. *It really won't. What's done is done.* I sip my soda, depressed. I miss the guys, but I'm done trying to mend those bridges. They don't see me as the tomboy with skinned knees anymore. I don't see them as the guys who would never hurt me.

"Fingers crossed all goes well tonight." Emma focuses on the business. She slides her phone into the front pocket of her jeans. Her nails are neon blue today. "Maybe *Rent-a-Gent* could get back on track."

I shrug and play a game on my cell phone. With low demand, we had to fire Henry and Jason. We saved what business was left for Ollie and Micah. *Micah.* Emma coordinates his dates now. I'm currently not speaking to him. It's weird. I'd spent the year determined to hang on to my friends and somehow lost them in the process. Ollie thinks I don't care about him. Cowboy's pulled away since his disaster fake date. And then there's Micah. Well. Things *definitely* aren't the same there.

I've been thinking about the summer we saw Champ. How we sat at the edge of that dock, legs hanging over the edge, bare feet in the water. We watched the sun go down. Crickets chirped and cicadas sang while a warm breeze floated over the water. We were sitting in silence, sharing a bag of oversized Skittles, when we saw it surface. That dark mass several feet ahead of us. That tail. Champ's tail. It had felt like magic. From that moment on, we were inseparable.

Emma's cheery voice breaks into my memory. "I have a date later," she says. "A real one."

"Don't tell me you're back with Kevin." I place my cell down and lick sugar from my lips.

Emma studies her bare feet and picks a piece of lint from her pink sweater. "New guy," she says. "Someone you know."

My stomach drops. Is she talking about Micah? After the night on the basketball court, he texted me a few times. Wanted to talk in person. I said no. I need space. It just hurts to look at him. And I *miss* looking at him. Whatever we had—whatever we were going to have—is ruined.

So maybe I should be cool with Emma dating him. I can't claim him. I should let him go. "You can date whoever you want to date, Emma." I force a smile. Cringing. "You have my blessing."

She hops up to open the blinds, and a ribbon of moonlight rushes in. Emma studies the pile of crunched papers beside my desk but restrains herself in organizing them. She sits back on my unmade bed. "Really?" she asks. "That's a huge relief."

I swallow the lump in my throat. My stomach gurgles. I dig my toes into the carpet. "Where's he taking you?" I'm grinning so hard my face hurts. "The lake?"

Emma leans back on her elbows and makes a face. "Luke hates the lake," she says. "And it's freezing."

I shake my head. "Wait—Luke?"

"Yeah." She pauses. Smiles. "Who'd you think I was talking about?"

"No one." I throw my empty soda at the trash can near the door. It hits the side but bounces in.

Emma laughs. "Micah? You thought I meant Micah? That's sweet, Toni. That you'd let me have the love of your life and all."

"He's not—" I pause. Now's a good time for a change in subject. "So Luke? Tell me more."

Please don't bring him up again. Emma senses that. "It started when I read his journal," she says.

I laugh. "You *kept* that?"

"I was curious!" she says. "I didn't expect to fall in love with his words."

Love. Love. Love. A sickening word. I move to the floor and pull my knees to my chest. I practically whisper, "You're in love with him?"

"I don't know." Emma sighs and giggles. "It's early. We've only hung out a few times. But I've got a good feeling. Have you ever read anything he's written?"

"You mean did I steal his journal and read it?" I smirk and pause. "No."

"I didn't *steal* it." Emma leans forward, twisting her hair tighter around her finger. "I returned it."

"I'm scared to even ask what he would write about," I say, opening a box of Junior Mints. Probably how much he hates me.

"He wrote a lot about that monster in Lake Champlain," she says. "Sounded like a pretty great summer for you guys."

I look down, smiling, remembering the excitement of that day. A melancholy washes over me. I open another Mountain Dew. "Well, good. You deserve to be happy, Emma."

"So do you, Toni." She picks a loose string from the sleeve of her pink sweater. "It kind of sucks sometimes, doesn't it?" She tilts her head. Her honey hair falls over the side of her face. "Being in love?"

I examine the vacuum-streaks on my pale pink carpet. Emma insisted on vacuuming when she got here. "I wouldn't know," I say with a shrug. But I totally know what she means.

"He'll be home before midnight." Emma speaks slowly, carefully, like she's breaking bad news to me. "You should go talk to him."

I know she's not referring to Ollie anymore. But I can't talk to Micah. I just can't. Whatever I say to him, he'll repeat it to Ollie and Cowboy, and I don't want to be a *joke*. Nothing feels sacred anymore. But I feel him over there, next door, his weight impossible to ignore. It pisses me off, the way he affects me.

"You know what?" I stand, as if this abrupt movement could permanently shake Micah from my mind. "I've already got plans tonight."

. . . .

I arrive at the cemetery after midnight. The harsh moonlight shines over fresh red roses scattered near tombstones. A few heart-shaped balloons blow in the wind. I park on the side of the road that cuts through the cemetery.

A miniature notebook tucked under my right arm, I navigate the graves, a familiar path. His grave is cloaked in shadow, stubbornly hiding from the Valentine moon.

"Hi, Dad," I say, kneeling on the frozen ground. I pull the hood of my coat over my ears. "Happy Valentine's Day."

Sometimes I wait for the stone to speak back to me, for a low hum or whisper, anything, but not even the wind humors me. It's a stark quiet around here, as if sound's forbidden. I lean forward and read his name again and again. I hope the letters will somehow morph into someone else's and this could all be a bad dream. Like maybe he'll walk up behind me, tell me to come home, that it's late, and he'll throw his arm over my shoulder. We'll laugh about our bad dreams because that's all it ever was—what happened to him, what happened to me, what happened to our family. A bad dream.

I wipe my nose on my sleeve, surprised to find hot tears on my skin. I thought I had mastered the art of keeping them away. I examine the rows of Tweety Bird stickers in the notebook. They're starting to fade, the once-bright yellow bird now sickly. There must be at least a hundred of them, lined up page after page, the cartoon bird smiling and then scowling and then wearing glasses, the stickers all various shapes and sizes.

Abruptly, they stop. Blank pages follow. I got too big for them, I guess. If I'd let him, Dad would have kept handing them out for every little thing I did, probably forever.

I sit like that for some time, the stickers on my lap, trying to remember why I earned each one, and then I hear crunching gravel. A pair of headlights appear on the horizon. A car moves steadily down the road. I close the notebook and stand.

"Dad, I hope you can see me," I whisper to the tombstone. "I hope you can see everything. I hope you can know the new me. And all the new mes to come. Because I don't want to stay the same forever, Dad. I want to be a girl with painted nails. A girl who can wear a skirt now and then. Well, *maybe*." I chuckle. "I want to be the college girl. The brave girl. The scared girl. The businesswoman. The engineer. The teacher. The nurse. The doctor. When we meet again—and I *know* we'll meet again—I hope you can still recognize your little tomboy with the skinned knees."

The car parks in the small lot to the right. A figure steps out and walks swiftly along the foot path toward me. I step behind a tree to hide—a strange instinct, but a part of me wonders if this is the mysterious visitor to my father's grave. The one who leaves a new bandana now and then.

I watch the tall figure navigate the foot path, half-jogging, and stop at Dad's tombstone. The clouds move, allowing the moonlight to push through for a moment, shining on the boy standing there. The boy with the scruffy chin and the wide jaw and the buzz-cut. He's wearing a suit, his tie loose and crooked.

I watch him set a red bandana on the ground. He stands for several minutes, his head bowed. And then Micah looks up and walks away. I don't move until his Honda vanishes into the darkness.

He and my dad got along well. We hadn't reached the age for romantic entanglements yet, so Micah was just the boy next door. But I didn't expect this—his special visits to my father.

A feeling—a strange, full, lovely feeling—balloons inside my chest and spreads. It's a feeling I can't shake on the drive back, no matter how loud I play country music. *Micah*. Of course he visits my dad. Even though we're not talking right now. I take the long way home and cruise along the lake. I glance over now and then, half-expecting to see Champ splashing in the water, his black tail whipping about. He must be so lonely down there. Especially tonight.

Maybe change doesn't have to mean growing apart. Maybe it can mean growing closer. I won't know unless I let Micah see the part of myself I keep hidden. Emma's right.

I gotta talk to him.

When I pull into my driveway, I see him sitting on the front porch. My heart pounds. Maybe he has the same idea I do tonight. I slam the car into park and jump out, breathless and excited. Man, I've missed him.

"Hey," I say, trying to hide my smile. I don't want to appear over eager.

I stop when Cowboy appears around the corner. Something's not right. "What's wrong?" I ask.

"It's Ollie," Cowboy says, fidgeting with the zipper on his jacket. He looks to Micah, who stands with his beautiful face scrunched and serious. "He's in trouble."

twenty-five

· · · · · · · · · · · · · · · · ·

I SINK INTO THE WORN LEATHER OF
the Honda's passenger seat and reach for the loose
thread near my knee. Nervously, I pull at it. It feels
different without Ollie here. Heat from the vents
blasts my cheeks, and I pull my coat sleeves over my
cold hands, watching the night through the window.
I ignore my pale reflection in the glass.

"Before his phone cut off, he said he was
somewhere on Lake Road," Micah says. "We'll start
looking there. Keep an eye on your phone in case he
calls."

My phone rests in my lap, but I'm still not sure
how I can help the situation—whatever that may
be, exactly. I'm here though. All I know is that Ollie
called Cowboy about thirty minutes ago, desperate
for a ride home, and Cowboy recruited Micah as
back-up.

As we drive along the shore, the headlights punch
the surface of the lake. There's so much I want to say
to Micah, I need to say, but I don't. Not with Cowboy
here, silently watching. Cowboy's quiet nature never
bothered me before, but tonight his presence feels

loud and obvious. Micah sniffs, groans, and pulls a tissue from his pocket to wipe his bright red nose.

I look at him, tugging at the seat thread. "You're not taking care of yourself."

"It's a cold." He shrugs. "It's nothing."

"In two days, you'll be imitating a corpse in your bedroom," I say. His jacket is wrinkled, his tie loose. Dark circles rest under his tired eyes.

He flips on the radio. The volume, as always, is stuck on low, but a Keith Urban song plays. He doesn't change the station, and I know that he's playing the radio for me tonight. He sniffles. "You can't predict the future," he says.

"I can predict yours." I lean back. Glance at him. "It's a gift."

He suppresses a smile. "Or a curse."

I shrug. "Or both." Maybe the way I feel about him is a gift and a curse. A gift because of the butterflies and whatnot and a curse because it means everything will change. Not just with us. Like Ollie implied, what happened with Micah and I affects the whole group.

All of a sudden, he blurts out, "I wasn't making fun of you about the dancing at the cabin, Toni. I know you don't want to hear it, but it's the truth. I was asking for some advice. That's the only reason I said anything about it."

I stare at the stick-figure I drew on my cast, my eyes shifting to his words below the drawing. I look at those words more than I care to admit. It feels nice, sitting beside him, almost like old times, except that everything beneath the surface is different. Like we're hiding a lake monster of our own beneath polite words and nervous gestures and childhood nicknames.

"Can we just focus on finding Ollie?" Cowboy asks. "He sounded drunk or something."

Micah coughs and slams on the brakes, jolting me forward. The car screeches to a halt. The seatbelt digs into my skin.

"Dude!" Cowboy yells, waving his arms.

"Sorry about that, but I think that's him." Micah points at something in the distance.

I squint through the windshield. Someone waves near the water, dancing in the headlights. A boy with curly black hair. A boy with something red smeared across his face.

"Oh my God." I get out of the car. Cowboy follows and runs ahead of me. Micah climbs out but keeps the car running. The headlights shine across the road.

Ollie stumbles toward us. He halts when he sees me and shouts, "What the hell, Cowboy? I told you to come alone!"

"I didn't bring her," Cowboy says, shaking his head. "Loch did. Dude, what happened to you?"

Ollie's injuries come into focus. Dried blood decorates his nose, and his right eye is swollen shut. A large gash slices through his eyebrow. His dirt-smeared shirt flaps in the wind, and his black pants are spotted with more blood.

"What the hell happened?" I ask, my gut twisting. Poor Ollie.

Ollie snorts. "What does it look like? *I got my ass kicked.*"

"By who?" How did Ollie end up stranded in the middle of the night, beaten to a pulp, when he's supposed to be working for Lemon tonight? Maybe he pissed off the wrong person with a snarky comment or something, but I fear this has something to do with the job. Which means this is my fault.

Ollie looks at Cowboy and then Micah. "I don't want her here, guys. She'll tell Emma. It's embarrassing."

"Let's get out here," Cowboy says, ruffling his hair.

I slide off my coat and hand it to Ollie, but he stares at it like it's a bomb. "It should fit you," I say. "Come on."

Micah adds, "Take it, man. You're turning blue."

Ollie yanks the coat from my hand and wraps it tightly around his bruised body. He leans on the guys and limps to the car while I walk behind them. A few minutes later, we're all back in the car. The heat blasts. Ollie sits in the back behind me, his head resting against the window. He doesn't kick my seat. He's very, very still.

Cowboy sighs. "Who did this?"

"I don't know," Ollie says.

"You must've seen something?" I tread carefully.

Ollie runs his battered hand through his curls. "One second I was sitting in my car, waiting for Lemon to leave her girlfriend's house so I could take her home, and the next thing I know some guy is beating the shit out of me on the road. He stuffed me into the trunk of a car that smelled like fish and then dumped me here. He wrecked my cell phone, too."

"We should go to the cops," Cowboy suggests.

"No!" Ollie protests. "No way my parents will let me go to Colorado if they know about this."

"They might notice the broken nose," I add, turning around in my seat. "And that cut above your eye looks disgusting. A trip to the hospital isn't a bad idea either."

"Thank you for the unsolicited advice," Ollie snaps. "Take me home. That's all I need."

Micah and I exchange a look. What else can we do? He shifts the car into drive and pulls onto the road. We head toward Ollie's house in silence.

Ollie doesn't keep quiet for long. "I want to be paid extra for this," he says. "This is an occupational hazard." I glance in the rearview mirror to see Ollie dab at his nose with the sleeve of his shirt, but the bleeding seems to have stopped.

"It's a dangerous business," Cowboy adds.

I wave my broken arm. "I know all about dangerous, thank you."

"We don't know if this incident is related to the job," Micah says. He turns away from me and coughs into his hand.

"Please!" Ollie cries. "The job is to lie! Maybe someone found out the truth! All I know is that this is the first time someone has punched me for no damn reason at all!"

"I'll talk to Lemon," I interject, tugging at the loose thread in the seat. "I'll figure this out."

"I can't do this anymore." Ollie shakes his head. "I quit, okay?"

I turn around. "What?"

Ollie wipes dried blood from his nose. "Cowboy was right to get out early. Do you have any idea how bat-shit crazy these Winston girls are?"

"They are pretty crazy," Cowboy says.

My cheeks burn. "Winston girls aren't crazy. They're just people. They need a break every now and then. Like everybody else."

Ollie laughs. "Like I said. *Crazy*. And you're one of them now."

"SO WHAT?" I scream. "I'M PROUD TO BE ONE OF THEM!" I point at him. "You know what? You're fired, Ollie!"

"You can't fire me!" he spits. "I already quit!"

Micah slams on the brakes, and we all slide forward. This time, I am semi-prepared, but Ollie smacks his nose against the back of my seat and cries out, "What the hell, Loch?"

"Toni's just trying to help us, man," he says.

Ollie pauses. He goes in for the kill. "She's going to Purdue next year. She tell you that? You two tell each other everything, right? You lovebirds—"

"Will you just shut *up* for once in your life?" I ask, my heart thumping. I tug harder at the thread. It pops off, loose in my palm. I stare at it to avoid looking at Micah. Emma told Ollie about my decision. I'm leaving Vermont next year. He knows, and I wasn't the one to tell him. I waited too long.

After a few moments, I find the courage to look over at Micah. He studies the steering wheel and scratches his red nose. I drop the thread to the floor. "Micah—"

Ollie throws open the door and stumbles out of the car. We aren't far from his house, but he's in bad shape.

"Someone should go after him," Cowboy says. He taps my shoulder, as if I should be the volunteer.

"Um, he hates me," I say. "You go."

"This has gotta stop," Cowboy says. "Go, Toni. Work it out."

Ugh. I climb out of the car and catch up to Ollie. Before I reach him, he says, "Back off, McRib. I'm serious."

I fall back a few steps, but I follow. Behind us, the Honda creeps along, the headlights illuminating Ollie's bruised face. Man, he looks awful.

"I'm sorry I got you in trouble with your parents," I call after him. "I'm sorry you can't go to Colorado. I'm sorry about whatever happened to you tonight."

Ollie just keeps walking. Limping. I continue to follow but stay several steps behind. I stop at the end of Ollie's driveway. When he reaches his front door, he goes inside without so much as a wave. I'll probably never see my coat again. Well, so much for working this out.

I get back in the car and close my eyes and pretend. I pretend I'm a ten-year-old girl dribbling a basketball down the center of a road. Pretty houses with emerald lawns border my path. A lake shimmers in the distance. Beneath the surface, a lake monster lurks. I'm surrounded by my three best friends. Boys who protect me. Boys who make me laugh. Boys who challenge me. Boys who make me feel big.

Moments are fossils. I dust them off. I keep them in my pocket.

I turn to Micah. "Are you done, too? Because I understand. If you are."

Of course we're talking about something larger than *Rent-a-Gent*. This is the conversation hidden beneath insults and bloody noses, beneath basketball games and monster movies. I wonder what Mrs. Kemper would advise here. Is honesty the best policy?

Micah lets out a huge sneeze and blows his nose. He keeps driving, silent. When we get to Cowboy's house, Cowboy opens the back door and says, "Well, this has been an interesting Valentine's Day."

I turn around. "Hey, Cowboy."

He pauses, halfway out the door. "Yeah?"

"You should ask Katie Morris to prom," I say. "Just ask, dude. You don't need money to win her over. Just be honest. Be yourself. Be a person. Next year, everything could be different and you may always wonder about her. Just say hello. Start there."

Cowboy stares at me blankly and then blinks a few times. His face turns red. He opens his mouth to say something, but then climbs out of the car and jogs to his front porch. I guess my advice isn't that valuable. At this point, I probably wouldn't listen to me either.

We pull into Micah's driveway, both of us quiet. I climb out of the car, weak in the knees. Maybe it's the excitement of the night, my anger, or maybe this feeling stems from something else entirely. He gets out and sets his keys on the hood of the car and slides out of his suit jacket.

"I got my job back," he says, his voice scratchy, "but I'm not done." He hands me the suit jacket. "Here. You must be freezing."

I curl my hands into the vanilla-scented sleeves. "Thanks."

It's time to go inside, time to begin the transition into a new day, but I can't bring myself to move from his driveway. The basketball hoop looms above us. This is what I wanted, to be alone with him, but now it feels strange.

He smiles. "This has been quite the violent Valentine's Day."

"*My Bloody Valentine* would be an appropriate movie choice for the evening." It sounds like an invitation, and it is. I want him to come to my room and curl up with me, but his feet don't move. The pause between words is torture. He coughs and sneezes and wipes his nose. On second thought, he should rest. Maybe this isn't the best time for this conversation.

"Congratulations, by the way," he says, scratching his nose. "On Purdue. That's great. Your dad would be psyched."

"Thank you. I..." I should explain, but I don't know how. I changed our plan without consulting him. I wish space didn't exist so everything could be in one place and we wouldn't have to separate.

"Good night, Toni Valentine." Micah sniffles and walks away, sliding his hands into his pockets. A sharp, clear thought races through my mind. A thought swimming inside my head for weeks, months, maybe even years. A terrifying, distorted, illogical, lovely, wonderful, vibrating thought.

I'm in love with my best friend. I'm in love with Micah Garry. SHIT.

twenty-six

THE FOOD COURT IS LOUD, HOT, and reeks of French fries. How I loathe the mall. A cluster of colorful bags with tissue sticking out the top fall over Emma's feet and Lemon's pink high heels. I have no idea how she walks in those things without breaking an ankle. Unlike my friends, I have just spent the last three hours pretending to inspect overpriced shoes while trying to convince myself that my recent revelation is a mistake. A side effect of some sort.

I can't be in love with Micah Garry. I'm leaving for college in the fall. Long-distance relationships don't work. Assuming Micah shares the same feelings, which, let's face it, he probably doesn't. I'm like Ben Mayhew, pining for someone who will never want me.

Lemon folds her hands in prayer-like fashion and says, "I'm sorry, Toni. I'm an idiot. No. I'm a moron."

In her maternal way, Emma pats Lemon on the back. "You couldn't have known this would happen."

Lemon smooths the ends of her black bob. "But I should've been more careful. Me and my big mouth."

"It's not your fault." I nibble on a French fry. Two tables over, a baby starts crying, and I bite the inside of my cheek to keep from screaming, too.

What happened to Ollie is my fault, not Lemon's. I keep picturing Ollie's pathetic limp and the dried blood on his face. I told Emma about it, despite Ollie's wish to keep the incident private. She's my business partner and my friend and she needed to know.

Just as I feared, *Rent-a-Gent* is responsible for Ollie's broken state.

"I had no idea that Jess's brother would go that far," Lemon continues, sipping her Diet Coke. "My girl wasn't exaggerating when she said he could act like an overprotective psycho."

Emma continues to soothe Lemon. Lemon continues to unload her guilt. I pick at my corn dog, void of appetite.

Jess, Lemon's girlfriend, was at the grocery store a few days before Ollie was hurt. Jess's older brother, Jacob, overheard Lemon talking to her parents there about Ollie. Lemon was laying it on thick at the time, going as far as to say she hoped to marry Ollie one day.

Her parents ate it up, but Jacob, who was fully aware and accepting of Lemon's real relationship, thought Lemon was cheating on his sister. That really pissed him off. His reaction could be classified as sweet if blood weren't involved. Jacob turned his anger to Ollie.

When he spotted Ollie sitting in his car outside of the house, waiting for Lemon as normal, Jacob flipped out. I hate to even think about it. Ollie could've been seriously hurt. Because of me.

Rent-a-Gent is in shambles. No Ollie. No Cowboy. No Jason. No Henry. Micah is the only boy left. And I'm freaking in love with him.

Maybe this is the way it should be. Maybe this is a wake-up call. I can't control people. I can't use people, profit or no profit. If I try, everything turns out messy and bruised. Ollie's face proves that.

On the drive home from the mall, Emma tries to raise my spirits by blasting the country station. She thinks I'm depressed because of the sorry state of the business. If only she knew.

"It's another small hiccup, Toni." She drums her fingers along the leopard-printed steering wheel cover. "We made a mistake. We kept our clients safe, but we weren't thinking about the boys. I assumed they could take care of themselves. Dumb, huh? We should give the boys fake names to protect their real identities or something. We can still do this."

"The demand isn't there anymore," I say, resting my head against the window. Emma's spotless car smells like spring air. It's nice. "Maybe it's time to end this, Emma. Really end it. It's only a matter of time before Mrs. Kemper discovers who's behind it all anyway. We should distance ourselves."

Emma presses her lips together and stares straight ahead. I think we both know this is the end. It's time to cash in our chips. We failed. Our business failed.

Admitting my feelings for Micah was difficult enough, but I don't know how to tell Emma about it. Girls share these things, I think. But talking about my *feelings* isn't my strong point.

If I say it out loud, will it lose its meaning?

Is love more powerful when it's a secret?

After Emma drops me off at home, I stare at Micah's house, my breath fogging in the cold. I would bet every cent of my *Rent-a-Gent* profits—which are currently tucked away safely beneath my mattress for a rainy day—that he is holed up in his room right now, sick as a dog. I bet he's not eating or drinking. I bet he's not taking medicine. He's like a cat. He will hide his pain until the end of time.

Inside, Mom and Brian are curled up on the couch, watching a home improvement show on TV. Their laughter floats into the kitchen as I gulp down a can of Mountain Dew. A fresh batch of Brian's incredibly mouth-watering, heavenly delicious, mini-raspberry and white chocolate whoopie pies rests on the kitchen counter.

I steal a peek into the living room. Mom and Brian remain stuck together like two melty chocolate figurines, nuzzling each other, lost in a bliss I fear I will never understand. They didn't hear me come in.

My attention returns to the whoopie pies. Unable to resist, I shove one in my mouth and scoop a few into a Tupperware container. I stuff a pack of cold medicine into my back pocket, grab a jug of orange juice from the fridge, and head next door.

I balance the orange juice on top of the Tupperware, staring at the Garrys' doorbell. For a moment, I second-guess myself. What if he doesn't want to see me? What if he pushes me away? The thought of him lying in his room, plagued by illness, alone and suffering, trumps my fears. I ring the bell.

Amy answers the door. Her cheeks are stained with blush and her lips are colored apple-red. "Oh," she says in a less-than-enthusiastic tone. "It's you."

I brighten. "Hey, kid."

Amy closes the door behind me. "Please don't call me that."

She bounces to the floor-length mirror hanging next to the coat rack, ignoring my presence. She checks herself out, smacks her lips, adjusts her red sweater, hikes up her skinny jeans. I remember a time when she dressed like me. Basketball shorts, frumpy T-shirts, old sneakers. I remember a time when comfort came first for her.

I clear my throat, opting to attempt conversation with this new stranger. "So you're almost done, huh?"

"Excuse me?" Amy looks at me through the mirror. She has his eyes, but hers lack his comfort.

"Freshman year." I smile. "In a few short months, you're done. It's the hardest year of high school, in my humble opinion. If you make it through undamaged, you're good to go."

Amy scoffs. "Maybe it was hard for you, Toni. Not me. I'm popular. Oh, and I don't belch like a man." As she huffs up the stairs, her bare feet leave prints in the carpet. I sigh and readjust the load in my arms.

"Nice," I mutter as I head down the hall to Micah's room. The house is eerily quiet. I assume his parents are out for the afternoon. They're the kind of couple that goes couch shopping every Saturday afternoon, but they never actually buy one.

When I reach his door, it feels like a trapeze artist is swinging behind my ribs. I raise my hand to knock and almost drop the jug of orange juice. I decide to set my care package on the floor. Mrs. Garry is not a fan of stains. Like mother, like son.

I yank at the bottom of my sweater and pick off a black cat fur from the sleeve before I knock. A noise sounds from behind the door, but I can't make out any words. So I turn the knob and step inside.

The first thing I notice is the pile of crumpled tissues surrounding the bed like a fortress. Organized book shelf containing monster books? Check. Dust-free television on top of an equally dust-free stand near the bed? Check. Bigfoot poster? Check.

I spot an unmoving body sprawled across the hunter green comforter, staring at the ceiling. I inch forward. "Your imitation of a corpse has improved since the last time I saw it. You legitimately look like death. I'm impressed."

Micah's mouth hangs open. A strange snarling sound escapes him as he attempts to respond. I'm surprised flies aren't buzzing in here.

"Erm," he mumbles.

I set the packet of cold medicine on the desk before bringing in the orange juice and pies from the hallway. I unscrew the cap of the orange juice and ask, "Can you sit up please?"

"Erm."

I scoot Micah into a sitting position until his head rests against the wall. His eyes look glazed, his nose red, his lips chapped. He snorts and lets out a disgusting sneeze. I jump out of the way just in time.

"You're lucky I have a fantastic immune system," I say, bringing the jug of orange juice to his lips. "Drink."

"Nngh."

I roll my eyes. "Just do it."

He takes a few sips and swallows two pills. If Micah would attempt a good night's rest every now and then, he could avoid the nasty colds. He doesn't think he's susceptible to disease. He thinks he's a machine. But he spends so much time combing the lake for legends, he's bound to run into some germs.

"When your taste buds regain functionality, there's a surprise waiting on your desk," I say, screwing the juice cap back on. I straighten the pie container so the ends are perpendicular with the desk. Just like he would want it.

I open the drawer on the TV stand and dig through the various DVDs, searching for the perfect movie.

"Hey! Don't mess with my stuff!" His voice sounds clogged as he sinks lower into his comforter, groaning.

"Oh! He speaks!" I exclaim, clutching my heart. "Relax. I'm choosing from your stash. Which means I can't go wrong."

One title catches my attention. I pop in the DVD, kick off my shoes, and scoot in next to Micah on the bed. As I slide my feet under the covers, my sock brushes against his. He doesn't move. I wonder if he can hear the sound of my heart.

"Tell me." I set a full box of tissues on his lap. "How many Academy Awards has *Ice Spiders* been nominated for? With a title like that, I imagine it sweeps all categories."

He sits up a little. "Oh, this is a classic."

I can't think about anything else other than his shoulder touching mine. We stop talking and lose ourselves in the movie. About thirty minutes later, the medicine kicks in, and his eyes start drooping. I slide out of bed, pull on my shoes, and tiptoe to the door.

"Toni?" Micah whispers from beneath the covers.
"Yeah?"

"You're pretty. And awesome." He sneezes and wipes his nose. "You know that?"

My heart pounds as I flip off the light. Oh, man. *I so love you, Micah Garry. Loch.* "You're delirious," I say. "Go to sleep."

As I watch him burrow deeper beneath the covers, I almost tell him. I should tell him. That I love him and all. It can't be that hard. Just say the words.

Maybe tomorrow.

When he'll remember.

twenty-seven

·················

THE NEXT MORNING, I WAKE WITH
Tom Brady the cat sleeping on my head. He purrs
super-loud. I move very, very slowly. All of a sudden
he hisses, digs his back claws into my forehead, and
then bolts from the room.

"AH!" I curse and sit up, clutching my head. A
faint smear of blood sticks to my palm. I groan and
check the clock. I'm already late.

I clean up the scratch and slap a Hello Kitty
bandage to my forehead, the only kind we have.
Oh, the irony. I trip a few times as I scramble into
my Winston uniform. As I comb the knots from my
hair, I glance out the window. Micah's car is still in
his driveway.

In the kitchen, I grab a Mountain Dew, hoping the
sugar will provide some extra courage. Mom enters,
wearing her scrubs, her hair pulled into a high bun.

"We need to talk," she says.

"I'm late—" I'm hoping to see Micah before he
leaves. Not sure what I'll say to him though. I just
want to see him.

"This won't take long." Her eyes rise to my
forehead. "What happened there?"

I mumble something about the cat. Uneasy, I sit down and slide the pop can from hand to hand so it makes this annoying sound across the countertop. Seconds later, Brian enters the room, and that's when I know this conversation is likely to suck. I've been ambushed.

"Brian and I would like to ask you something," Mom says, glancing at her husband for reassurance.

Brian straightens his tie and sips his coffee. I'm not sure what he does for work. Something to do with insurance, I think. Maybe I should ask him sometime. "My brother offered your mother and I his cabin this weekend," he says.

"Can't go," I interrupt. "No offense."

Brian blinks a few times, as if he's hoping to wipe me from existence with his stare. My mother leans forward and takes the pop can away from me.

"We want to go alone, sweetheart," she says.

I sit back. "Oh. What happens to me then? Are you going to throw me out on the curb next to the recycling bin?"

My mother looks to Brian again, ignoring my comment. "We know it's last minute. But we both think you're responsible enough to take care of the house while we're gone."

Maybe *she* thinks that, but Brian looks pale at the thought of leaving a (gasp!) teenage girl alone in the house. He believes a teenage girl to be the equivalent to an in-heat hyena. Like I'll stain the couch with my hormones or something.

"What do you think?" Mom asks, hopeful. "Is that something you can handle, Toni?"

Brian desperately wants to get away from me for a weekend, I can tell. Who am I to squash his dream?

I plaster on a fake smile and reply, "Sure. You can totally trust me."

Mom slides the can back over to me. "Good. We'll head out later tonight. Now go to school. Do amazing things."

I jump up and run out the door. As I rush down the driveway, I catch a glimpse of Micah's car disappearing around the corner. And then it's gone. He's gone.

. . . .

The Circle of Feelings has been silent for five minutes. The apple cider untouched. I stare at the wooden floor as if it's the most interesting thing on the planet. Emma sits across the circle from me, chewing on a strand of her hair. Her eyes are wide and bug-eyed.

Mrs. Kemper waits, a *Rent-a-Gent* envelope in her right hand.

"No one knows anything about these boy profiles?" Mrs. Kemper asks. "I find that unbelievable."

Lemon coughs but says nothing. Not even Shauna speaks. She stares at the mugs of apple cider lined up on the table before us. We're all suddenly catatonic.

Mrs. Kemper crosses her ankles. "Running a business on school property is a serious offense," she says, voice stern. "This type of operation goes against our code of conduct. Someone knows something. These profiles didn't end up in the hallway on their own."

Without thinking, I look accusingly at Shauna. Mrs. Kemper catches it. *Crap.*

"Tonya? Shauna?" She holds up the envelope. "Do either of you know about these?"

My butt itches. I look to Shauna. She looks to me. A slow sly smile appears on her lips, and then she opens her mouth to speak—

I blurt out, "I'm in love with my best friend!"

Shauna's jaw snaps shut, and everyone stares at me. Mrs. Kemper leans forward and says, "What?"

"I want to share today," I stammer. "I'm ready to share. For real."

Mr. Kemper blinks a few times. "Well. That's different. Um, go on, Tonya."

I look around the circle. At all the Winston girls staring at me. Lemon. Shauna. Emma. I've never felt so vulnerable. I wipe my sweaty palms on my skirt.

"I'm in love with my best friend," I continue. "He's my next door neighbor. This boy I've known since forever. But he doesn't know it—at least I don't think he does—and I'm afraid telling him will ruin our friendship."

"Another boy problem." Mrs. Kemper sighs and rubs her temples.

"Like maybe he doesn't see me the same way," I continue, ignoring Mrs. Kemper. It feels good to unload. "Maybe he's mad because I'm leaving Vermont for college, and I didn't tell him. I changed our plans! I feel like a total jerk for that."

"You chose a college?" Mrs. Kemper brightens. "That's wonderful, Tonya."

"Thanks." I shift my weight. "That's not really the issue I'm having, though..."

Mrs. Kemper claps her hands. "Okay," she grumbles. "I think we can cut group short for today." She holds up the white envelope. "If anyone knows anything about these brochures, anything at all, let me know. I will get to the bottom of it." She picks a stray hair from her navy blazer. "Have a good afternoon, ladies."

....

Emma follows me through the parking lot, bundled up, her honey hair full of static. "You should tell him."

"I can't. No way." I shiver, the wind bitter and mean. Anxious for warmth, I hurry toward my car. I can't wait to get home and hide in my room for a while. As I pull out my keys, Emma calls out, "Hey, Toni."

"Yeah?" I unlock my car, distracted.

"I'm not ready to give up on our business yet," she says. "That sounds crazy, right?"

I look at her. Her cheeks are bright red, her lips glossy and pink. "It's too risky to continue," I say, brushing a hair from my eye. "You heard Mrs. Kemper. Running a business on school ground is a serious offense. We need to back off. Shut it down. We're lucky no one's turned us in yet. We could be suspended or expelled or—"

"This can't be the end of it!" Emma suddenly squeals. "It can't just end like that!"

She looks panicked. Her eyes wide again. Like I just took away her car or something. Calmly, I say, "It's over, Emma. It has to be."

She flaps her arms. "Just like that?"

"Just like that." As I open the car door, she grabs my elbow, stopping me.

"We'll still hang out though, right?" she asks.

I give her a look. "Why wouldn't we?"

She sniffs, pulling at her pale pink mittens. "Sometimes I wonder if you'd be my friend if it weren't for the business."

I laugh and slug her on the shoulder with my good hand. "You're stuck with me forever, Swan."

Her nose crinkles. "Swan?"

"Could be a nickname for you," I suggest, shrugging. "You're elegant, but fierce when you need to be. Plus, you know, it ties in with your last name. Do you hate it?"

Emma thinks it over. "*Swan.* I kind of like it."

I pat her shoulder again. "We could always change it. No harm in that. Later, Swan."

Inside the car, I crank the heat and sit there a few minutes, rubbing my hands together. I watch Emma trot to her vehicle. It doesn't feel right, ending the business so abruptly. Just like that. Without any warning or goodbye. What we need is a send-off. I climb out of the car and run toward her, shouting her name. She stops and looks at me.

"You know. We should have a proper goodbye." I'm out of breath. And shape, apparently. "For the business. How does a farewell party sound? My mom and Brian have left me in charge of the house."

Emma smiles and then shrieks and hugs me so tight I can't breathe. I think I might turn blue.

"That a yes?" I laugh. She releases me and punches my shoulder. Ouch. The girl can hit.

. . . .

Later I sit drawing on my driveway, waiting for Micah's car to appear around the corner. A dust of snow remains on the grass, but the streets and sidewalks are clear. I pull the hood of my coat over my ears. The sun set twenty minutes ago. The streetlight and the moon shine down as I try to sketch a yellow bird onto the semi-wet pavement.

Finally, the Honda appears around the bend. I drop the chalk and stand, shoving my hands into my pockets. I watch him park. I watch him get out. I watch him shut the door. I watch him scratch his chin. I watch him look up at my bedroom window.

He looks down and squints into the darkness and says, "Toni?"

I wave. Like an idiot. And now he's coming over. Oh, man. *He's coming over here.*

He wears a pair of khaki pants and a white polo shirt beneath his jacket. His work uniform. His breath is a puff in the cold, and I want to catch that breath. Put it in my pocket. Save it. Man, that's so weird. Love makes me so weird.

"Hey. You okay?" he asks.

"Great. Why? Are *you* okay?" I bounce on my heels like I have to pee. I try to stop, but I can't hold still around him.

"Feeling better. Thanks to you," he says. "Those pies are incredible."

"Brian made them." It occurs to me that we're alone again. We're alone a lot. And yet we can't seem to untangle this mess.

He nods, shuffling his feet. "Another ski injury?"

I get lost in his eyes for a moment as I say, "Huh?"

He gestures to my forehead. Mortified, I cover the Hello Kitty bandage with my hand.

"That's nothing." I blush. "A feline incident."

"Stupid Tom Brady," he says.

I flex my fingers. I look at his words on my cast. *My sincerest apologies.* I think I'm in love with his handwriting, too. Again. Weird.

"Hey, um, are you available next weekend?" he asks after a few moments of silence. *Is he asking me on a date?* "It's supposed to be unseasonably warm. Champ may make an appearance."

"Next weekend?" I pretend to think because I don't want to admit that my calendar is wide open these days. "I could do that. Of course. Can't wait. Sounds awesome. Yeah. Totally. Hooray." *Hooray? I'm so lame.* "Speaking of plans, I'm having a party tomorrow night. You'll come, right?"

"A party? Here?" He makes a face. "Following in Ollie's footsteps now?"

"It's just this farewell thing for the business," I say, scratching at my cast. "We have to, um, shut down. Officially."

"Figured that was about to happen." He pushes his shoulders forward.

I feel guilty. Maybe if I had handled everything better, he could've made more money. "I'm sorry, Micah. I wanted to help you..."

He waves his hand. His adorable hand. "It's okay," he says. "I qualify for financial aid. And my grandparents can help a little. I'll still have to work a lot, but it'll happen."

I brighten. "UVM?"

"Reliable Loch." He scratches his stubble. "Never changes his plans."

"You can change them if you want to." I take a step forward. The space between us shrinks. The light above the Garrys' garage turns on. His parents must be waiting up for him.

"That's the thing," Micah says, lowering his voice. "I don't want to change them. I like where I'm headed."

I look away, flushed, and think about next year. The distance. The differences. I imagine getting what I want right now. This second. Micah saying he loves me. Maybe he does feel the same way, but he doesn't want to say it. Maybe he doesn't want to hear me say it.

I can't read his expression. He wipes his buzz-cut and steps back, widening the gap between us. "Anyway. Your party," he says. "I'll see if I can make it."

"I hope you can." I force a smile.

"Later, McRib." And then he gives a casual farewell nod. As he walks away, I open my mouth to speak, to grab his attention, but nothing comes out. Before I know it he's inside. I could go over there, knock on the door. I could text him, call, but I'm paralyzed.

McRib. I'm just McRib to him.

twenty-eight

. . . .

I *SHOULD* BE THE RESPONSIBLE teenager Brian's so certain doesn't exist, but if he assumes I'll do something bad while he and my mom are enjoying their cabin getaway, I might as well fulfill his wish. Brian loves to be right. So it's like I'm giving him a present.

When the doorbell rings, I slide down the banister and land in the foyer with a giant thud. I open the door, and Emma holds up two matching black dresses with fringe on them.

"Let the rebellion commence," she says with a smile.

After I shower, shave my legs, pluck my eyebrows, and dry my hair, Emma applies my makeup. She chats about Ollie as she coats my lips with sour-tasting gloss. The two have yet to become an official couple, but they've gone on several dates. A movie here, a dinner there. No kiss. *Yet,* Emma emphasizes. I'm happy for them. Really. Someone should be experiencing romantic success around here.

When she's done, I'm afraid to look in the mirror. The spaghetti straps of the dress dig into my shoulders. Each time I adjust them, Emma slaps my hand away. Tom Brady sits at the foot of the bed, playfully swatting at the ends of the fringe each time I walk by. If I never wear this outfit again, at least it doubles as a giant cat toy.

Emma surveys her work. "I'm so good at this, it's ridiculous."

I look in the mirror hanging on the back of my bedroom door, surprised to see a reflection of, well, myself. Mascara, shiny lips, faint blush. The girl is me, though. I don't feel foreign to myself tonight.

"Thank you." I'm trying to stay upbeat, happy, but my last encounter with Micah lurks behind my every thought and feeling. *McRib.* Never have I hated that nickname more.

Emma tosses her makeup tools into a heart-shaped bag. "So I have news. And it's not boy-related."

"Good." I sigh. "I need a boy break."

"I got into Harvard."

I spin around. "Are you serious?"

Emma nods, keeping her cool as she combs her hair and smooths the fringe on her matching dress. She starts to apply fake eyelashes as if she didn't just announce the best news in the world. I can't help it. I bounce up and down, squealing, screaming, "WHY AREN'T YOU FREAKING OUT WITH ME RIGHT NOW?"

"I'm trying to be more like you," Emma says. "Calm. Cool. Collected."

But I keep bouncing. The walls shake, and a few soda cans topple off my desk. Tom Brady gets so irritated he hops off the bed and runs from the room.

"WELL STOP IT!" I shriek. "FREAK OUT WITH ME!"

Emma laughs and joins in. It's a good thing Brian isn't here to listen to our high-pitched yelling. After a few minutes of jumping around my room like maniacs, we stop to catch our breath.

"Tonight is now the Emma-Got-Into-Harvard-So-Let's-Freaking-Celebrate Party," I say, bowing to my genius friend.

Emma pulls the final pieces of our outfits from her bag. Two pink glittering bow ties.

"I know I sound like a broken record," she says, strapping the bow tie to her neck. I do the same. "But you should tell him."

I frown and turn away. I examine the pink glitter as it sticks to my fingertips. *McRib.* A clear sign he wants me as Friend Only. Great. I'll take it. Better than nothing. So if I tell him how I feel, everything will be ruined. No. I can't say anything. Ever.

. . . .

A group of girls in fancy prom-like dresses rush into my house, giggling, and head straight for the bathroom. Boys in wrinkled suits carry silver trays of chips and cans of beer around the room like butlers. I've been too preoccupied with the shifting tides of my friendship with Micah to ask Emma about the details of the party. She planned the thing. In one day. *Who are these people?* I know maybe a handful of them. I grab a beer from a nearby tray, but I don't recognize the boy holding it. I shrug, pop open the can, and drink.

"It's a gentleman and ladies theme," Emma says, sneaking up behind me. "You like?"

"Very classy." I give a thumbs-up and watch some guy in a tuxedo chug a beer.

I adjust the bow tie around my neck and lean against the banister in the foyer. I search the crowd, but Micah is nowhere to be found.

"He's not here yet," Emma says, tapping her nails along the railing. "The second I see him, I'll find you. Promise."

She pats my back. I force a smile. When I do see Micah, I plan to bolt in the other direction. Emma goes off to mingle with the crowd, flawlessly entertaining the guests. I sip the cold beer in my hand. I stare at the front door, praying he doesn't walk through it.

The door opens. Cold air flows in.

My fingers tighten around the can. I take another sip, prepared to run, but Cowboy enters, dressed in a navy blue suit with a flannel shirt underneath. He's holding someone's hand.

The hand of Katie Morris.

Cowboy closes the door behind them, his cheeks red, of course. Despite his nerves, he's still here, with Katie Morris. Unbelievable. Katie grins and plays with the ends of her short red hair. She spots me.

"Hey, Toni!" she says.

I try not to sound too surprised. "Katie. Hey. Glad you came."

She's wearing a beautiful strapless black gown, little makeup, and a simple silver necklace. The three of us stand there for a beat too long, slowly drifting into Awkward Town.

"Hey." Cowboy looks at me. "Nice party."

"Thanks for coming." I slug his shoulder. At least Cowboy and I are still on pretty decent terms. We may be drifting apart a little, but that's okay. I've come to accept that drifting friendships happen. Nothing I can do about it. Despite my best efforts.

Cowboy clears his throat and turns to Katie. "Did I ever tell you about the time Toni mooned Principal Rogers?"

Katie laughs and shakes her head, fidgeting with her necklace. "I gotta hear this."

"Oh, you'll love this story." Cowboy smiles and leads Katie into the kitchen. Faintly, I hear him say, "So Toni had this idea last summer to prank Principal Rogers..." His voice fades into the party noise. Good for him. Moving forward. Living with no regrets.

Unlike me. I've got a ton of them.

I'll drive myself crazy staring at the door all night so I work through the crowd until I'm standing in the center of the living room-slash-dance floor. Bodies press against mine. I am the loneliest girl on the planet, even as Lemon wraps her arm around me, whiskey on her breath, and shouts, "Thank you, Toni Valentine!"

Jess appears behind her, glowing, her light hair streaked with hints of blue. Her flowing white blouse is covered in a dark stain. Whiskey, I'm guessing.

I shout, "Glad you two could make it!"

"I told them!" Lemon blurts out, slurring her words. "I told my parents that I love Jess, and if they don't like it, they can shove it!"

Lemon kisses Jess, gentle and sweet. Man, everyone's just so freaking happy tonight. It's kind of disgusting. Jess places her hand on Lemon's hip.

"We've been celebrating," Jess says. "Perhaps one of us a bit too much. I need to get this one home before things get messier."

Lemon curls into Jess and waves goodbye, totally sloshed. Another tray of beer floats by on another stranger's fingertips. I grab one and then try and mingle a bit, but I don't know most of these people and I'm just not in the mood to be super-friendly.

I want something familiar. I make my way to the staircase in search of Tom Brady, wondering where he's hiding.

Back in the foyer, I run into Lemon and Jess again. Lemon is resting her head on Jess's shoulder while she gently strokes Lemon's back. I approach, and Lemon looks up and suddenly barfs all over the banister. I stand there, shocked, as the puke drips from the wood and onto the carpet like sap. Huh. Looks like she ate nachos recently.

"Oh my God!" Jess shouts. "I am so sorry, Toni!" Lemon groans and sways. Jess leads her out the front door for some fresh air.

"STAY BACK! I WILL GET SOME PAPER TOWELS!" I announce to the grossed-out bystanders. "Please stay away from this spot, people. I don't need more..."

As if on cue, some girl throws up all over her dress. Several people scream. Without another word, I run upstairs in search of cleaning supplies before the Barf Epidemic really explodes. I pull three rolls of paper towels, two bottles of carpet cleaner, and two cans of air freshener from the linen closet at the end of the hall. Maybe it's my imagination, but I can smell the vomit from here.

Brian is going to be so pissed.

twenty-nine

· · · · · · · · · · · · · · · ·

DOWNSTAIRS, EMMA IS GUARDING
the vomit. She has pulled her hair into a ponytail.
She takes the supplies from me, spraying the air
freshener about a million times. "This is under
control," she says, nodding toward the kitchen.
"Micah's here."

I stare at the hallway leading to the kitchen like
it's a tunnel leading to a magical world. He's here.
Just a few feet away. My heart pounds, my palms
sweat. I want him to see me in my black dress and
pink bow tie and Emma's black high heels. I want
him to see that I'm not the girl next door anymore.
I feel like a womanly force poised to take over the
world with a snap of my black-painted fingernails.

The front door opens, and more strangers enter,
talking, joking, dressed up and glamorous. Suddenly,
a violent *meow* sounds, and a black furball shoots
out the door before it closes.

"Tom Brady!" I shout. "Crap!"

Outside, the cold air shocks my system. I stand
on the porch, cursing, as Tom Brady sits on the
walkway, staring at me. His yellow eyes are like
clumps of gold in the night.

"Tom." I speak slowly, carefully. I'm afraid to move. "You're not supposed to be outside. You know that."

His eyes narrow into slits, and he proceeds to lick his paw. I shiver, but if I go inside to get a coat, he'll run off. I take a deep breath and creep toward him, my heels scraping against the cement. Tom Brady looks up, glaring. I stop moving. After a second, he returns to his bath. I slip out of the heels and crouch down, steadily inching closer. I'm almost close enough to reach out and grab him when he looks up, meows, and scurries into the bushes lining the front of the house.

"Seriously?!" I yell.

"You looking for something?" a voice asks.

I turn around. Ollie is standing on the porch, dressed in a black tuxedo. A coat is draped over his right arm, and his curly hair is slicked back with shiny gel. A white bandage covers the gash in his eyebrow. His eye is still black, bruised. I feel awful just looking at him.

"Tom Brady."

"The cat, I hope." Ollie approaches, grinning. "I doubt you'll find the Patriots quarterback around here."

"The stupid creature got out," I say, sighing. "Brian will be heartbroken if I don't find him."

"Which direction did he go?"

I point to the bushes. Ollie hands over the coat, which I see is actually mine. "Thanks for lending it to me," he says.

"No problem." I pull it on, yanking the sleeves over my hands. My teeth chatter, and my bare feet are freezing. Ollie shines the light from his cell phone across the bushes. We search in silence for several minutes.

"Listen," Ollie says, pushing aside a branch for a better look. He avoids eye contact. "I'm sorry I sort of lost it with you. That wasn't cool."

I'm not sure how to move forward here. Everything feels so fragile, like one wrong move could break what little is left of my former life. "Well, I'm sorry for getting you beat up," I say.

"I chose to work for you." He pulls at his ear. "Most of the time, I had fun doing it. You were right about Winston girls though. They aren't crazy. They're just people." He pauses. "I'm not going to Colorado."

My fault. "The whole prank was a stupid idea—"

"It's okay," he interrupts. "I'm fine staying here. I had enough for the tuition. It was my choice."

"Emma have anything to do with this?" I tease.

He looks at me and smiles. I can tell that he's happy. Emma has that effect. Even though Ollie is planning to stay in Vermont now, I already know that this upcoming summer won't be like any of the others. The four of us could search the lake for Champ every day, every night, but it would be different. Because we're different.

The front door opens. Micah steps onto the porch, a black snow cap on his head. He's dressed in jeans and his GONE SQUATCHIN sweatshirt. He holds something behind his back as he hops down the steps, approaching us.

"Hey," he says. "The party's inside, you know."

"The cat's missing. You're good with animals." Ollie slaps Micah on the shoulder. "He's somewhere in the bushes. We think. I better get back inside to help Emma with that vomit."

"Such a gentleman," I say.

Ollie skips up the walkway, disappearing inside, leaving Micah and I alone in the cold.

"Sooooooo," I say, determined to fill every moment with some kind of noise. No awkward silence here. "Whatcha got there?" I try to peer around him to see whatever he's holding behind his back.

"An early birthday present." He reveals the object. A teddy bear. Not just any teddy bear.

"You've got to be kidding me," I say in awe as I examine the bear's demented mask, shredded T-shirt, and miniature chainsaw. Bits of blood sprinkle the tiny chainsaw. Adorable. "A Texas Chainsaw Massacre Teddy Bear?"

Micah laughs. "You said you wanted one."

I grin, touched, and hold the bear close to my heart. "I'll cuddle with him tonight."

Micah shoves his hands into the pouch of his hoodie. My heart sounds loud and insistent as I hold the bear close. A cold breeze blows through, rustling the bushes. I shiver. He moves forward and rubs my back to warm me. Man, his *touch*.

I lean into his chest and turn my chin upward. I just do it. I kiss him. He leans down and presses his hand firmly to my back. I fold into him. My head is a delicious fog. My knees shake, but no longer from the cold.

After a few moments, I pull away but keep close, searching his eyes. Time expands as I wait for him to say something. What does this mean? How many times can we kiss before one of us acknowledges out loud that this is more than a friendship? I mean, seriously?

"I gotta go," he whispers, looking away. "Goodnight, Toni Valentine."

"Um, goodnight." I watch as he jogs across the lawn and enters his home. Minutes later, his bedroom light turns on. I stand in place for several minutes, perplexed, examining the Texas Chainsaw Massacre Teddy Bear in my hands. I turn and head back inside, confused and excited and terrified.

Tom Brady waits on the porch, flicking his tail back and forth. He glares. When I open the front door, he trots inside, purring, like his job is done.

thirty

·················

THROUGH MY WINDSHIELD, I watch Emma jump up and down at the front entrance of Winston Academy, holding a bundle of pink balloons. A small crowd gathers around her. She spots me and waves. A balloon breaks free and disappears into the gray sky, but this doesn't damper Emma's spirits in the slightest.

I consider going around to the back entrance, but that will make things worse for me later. Emma will insist on celebrating a day I would rather skip over this year. I might as well face it. I zip up the new Purdue fleece Brian and Mom gave me this morning and head into the chilly March air.

"Happy birthday!" Emma squeals as I approach. A few girls wish me a happy birthday before heading inside. Lemon stays behind, pressing her hands into the pockets of her plaid coat, while Emma hands me the bundle of pink balloons.

"Thanks." I accept them, as if I have a choice. I eye them. "Will these fit in my locker?"

"You're supposed to carry them around with you all day," Lemon says. "For the complete humiliation effect. It's one of the many reasons I love my summertime birthday."

I struggle to get the balloons through the doorway. They float above the sea of bodies as the three of us conquer the busy hallways. Various girls wish me happy birthday as I hurry along, my cheeks burning from the attention. When I get to my locker, I attempt to shove the balloons inside. No such luck.

"Don't bother." Lemon smirks. "Emma has a back-up set in her car anyway." I can't help but laugh at this. Of course she does. Emma beams.

"I shall see you ladies at lunch," Lemon says, waving. "I am off to send romantic messages to my lovely significant other!"

After she leaves, Emma gives me a look. "So. What's the deal?"

I groan and press my head against my locker. "I still don't know what's happening!"

"Make another move!" Emma says, patting my back.

"I made the last one!" I whisper-shout.

Two weeks since the last kiss. Two weeks. Micah and I are speaking again, but that's it. We talk about Champ. We talk about horror movies. We don't talk about the kiss at the party. We don't talk about *us*.

"Well, we're going out for your birthday tonight." Emma flicks my shoulder. "We'll discuss details at lunch."

"I've got a ton of homework—"

"Nope! No protesting, Toni Valentine!" As she skips away down the hall, I shake my head and smile to myself. Thank God for her. A balloon hits me in the face as I close my locker. I sigh and drag them down the hall.

But Emma doesn't show up at lunch. When the bell rings, I start to worry. I navigate the halls, searching for her. Maybe she went home sick. But if she did, she would've texted me. Wrote an email. A letter. Sent a carrier pigeon. Something. Emma doesn't go silent.

"Toni!" Lemon waves. I wave back, moving through the crowd toward her. When I reach her, she lowers her voice. "You hear about Emma?"

I shake my head. "Is she okay?"

"She got called into Mrs. Kemper's office," Lemon says, fluffing her bob. "There was an anonymous note linking her to the business. Rumor is she got expelled."

"*What?*"

"Expelled," she repeats.

I feel sick. "That doesn't make sense. What'd the note say?"

Lemon bites at her nails. "Don't know. A lot of girls are freaking out because we don't know who else was named. Emma's the only one who's been called in so far."

The bell rings. Lemon hurries off, throwing me another worried look. I stand there a few minutes, alone in the empty hallway, shaking, my stomach twisted into a sick knot. I rush to the bathroom and splash water on my face.

This can't be happening. Not to Emma.

The rest of the day drags. I stare at clocks. I stare at my phone. I wait for my name to be called next. I text Emma about a million times, but she doesn't reply. She must hate me. I got her into this. I ruined Harvard for her. Did Shauna tell Mrs. Kemper that the business belonged to Emma? Or did Mrs.

Kemper find out about Emma's involvement some other way?

Emma *was* the liaison. She booked the clients. She was more high-profile than I was. But I can't let her take the fall for this.

After the last bell, I race to Mrs. Kemper's office and raise my hand to knock. I pause. My armpits sweat. My heart pounds. My throat goes dry. This is it. The end. No more lies.

Knock. Knock. Knock. Mrs. Kemper opens the door immediately. "Tonya," she begins.

Before she says another word, I say, "*Rent-a-Gent* was my idea, Mrs. Kemper. My business. I did it. Alone."

. . . .

Mrs. Kemper picks at a loose hair from her blazer as she glares at me from behind her desk. The curly strand seems to hit the floor with a sickening thud. I wipe my sweaty palms onto my plaid skirt. The stack of gentleman profiles sit in front of Mrs. Kemper on the desk.

"You're quite the entrepreneur," she says.

"Was," I correct. "We shut down. I will never do anything like this again. I promise."

Mrs. Kemper sighs. Shifts her weight. "This is serious, Tonya. Winston frowns upon this type of behavior. This business of yours, whether still in operation or not, is highly inappropriate."

It feels like Micah should be in the room, holding my hand, comforting me. I'm about to be expelled, and all I can think about is my best friend who is really more than my best friend but I'm not sure because we keep ignoring this thing going on between us. Despite the fear bubbling in my stomach, I do what I need to do. I'm too tired to fight anymore.

I confess everything. I start at the beginning, but I leave out any real names. If anyone needs to go down for this, it's me alone. I tell Mrs. Kemper about Micah and the Halloween party and about false doors. I explain the desperation so many of us carry for things to appear different than what they actually are. I emphasize that the service had nothing to do with sex or even friendship, but that it served as a blanket to hide behind.

"I'm sorry," I continue. Tears run down my cheeks, and I wipe a glob of snot onto my sleeve. "It was wrong. I know that now. I wanted to help a friend. I didn't want to lose him. I wish I could take it all back. I don't understand people, Mrs. Kemper. I don't understand them at all. I'm not Winston material, and I don't deserve the future this place has given me. I deserve to be expelled."

The chair squeaks as Mrs. Kemper leans back, studying me with her kind eyes. I don't know what she's thinking, and I won't begin to guess. People are wild, unpredictable creatures. You can't shove them into an envelope.

"I appreciate your honesty, Tonya, but this is simply unacceptable," Mrs. Kemper says.

I hold back a huge sob. "Am I expelled?"

"I don't have much of a choice here," she says softly. "Please wait outside while I call your mother."

. . . .

How's this for an ending: Expelled from a school that I didn't want to attend in the first place, but somehow grew to like. My childhood best friend is no longer my best friend, and now we're in some strange limbo about our relationship. My college plans are probably ruined, which means my future is ruined so I'll have to live with Brian and Mom forever.

Just when I learn to embrace change, my life comes to a screeching halt.

I wait on the bench outside Mrs. Kemper's office, tapping my sneakers against the spotless floor. I'm out there for about thirty minutes before I hear footsteps echo in the hall. I expect to see Mom, but it's Brian walking toward me, dressed in his fancy insurance-something suit.

"They called *you*?" I ask.

"Your mom did. She's stuck at work," Brian says. "This sounds serious, Toni."

I hold back more tears, humiliated. Brian sits beside me but keeps a good distance. "What happened?" he asks.

"Mom didn't tell you?"

"I want to hear it from you," he says. "Your side of the story."

This surprises me. I wipe my palms on my skirt again, nervous. "Maybe you should just talk to Mrs. Kemper."

"Toni." He loosens his tie. "I know I'm not cool or funny and, yes, I like the New England Patriots. I don't always say the right thing. I feel like a complete moron sometimes. But you can talk to me. I'd like to help you." He pauses. "You just kind of intimidate me."

"Really?" Of all the things that have happened today, this is the most shocking.

He turns toward me. The overhead light illuminates his gray hairs. "I thought you knew."

I almost laugh. "Just thought I annoyed the crap out of you."

"You? Annoying? Not even a little," he says, resting his elbows on his knees. "If I thought you were annoying, I would avoid you completely. But you know how I'm kind of around all the time? Maybe being a little too nosy? That's me. Trying to bond..."

I smile. He *is* always asking questions about my life. About Micah. About Winston. Not because he wants to replace my dad or control me or irritate me but because he wants to *bond*. I feel like a fool for not noticing it before.

So I tell him the truth. All of it. Why I started the business in the first place. My new friendship with Emma. What really happened with Micah. How Mrs. Kemper discovered the truth. When I'm done, he looks away, making this strange gurgling sound as he thinks.

"Thank you for sending me here," I add. "I'm sorry I got kicked out."

"Okay then. Wow." He stands, frowning. He takes a few deep breaths. "Sit tight. I'm going to talk to this Mrs. Kemper."

I await my fate.

thirty-one

....

THEY'VE BEEN IN THERE FOR OVER
an hour now. When I press my ear against the door,
I hear only the muffled sound of Brian's voice. He's
doing a lot of talking, but I can't make out the words.
He sounds serious though. Angry.

I lie down on the bench and think about Micah
to pass the time. Thinking about him is my favorite
pastime lately. I wonder what he's doing at this very
moment. I wonder if he's thinking about me, too. I
take out my phone and read through our texts. He
sent me several "happy birthdays" today. He must
be thinking about me. At least a little.

Does he regret the second kiss? Does he regret
the first kiss? Why has he never mentioned them?
Maybe he wants to go back to the way things were?
How long can we go on pretending like everything's
normal?

When the door opens, I jump up and my pulse
quickens. This is it. My sad ending comes to fruition.

Brian steps out first. He looks tired, worn, his
tie loosened. Mrs. Kemper follows, picking at her
blazer, and shakes Brian's hand as she says, "Have a
good afternoon, Mr. Richards."

"Again. Thank you," Brian replies in a serious tone. They obviously weren't exchanging jokes in there.

Mrs. Kemper's eyes flash to me. She doesn't say anything before she returns to her office and closes the door. Man. She can't even look at me anymore. I'm that big of a loser.

"What happened?" I ask, picking at my thumb. "She hates me, doesn't she?"

Brian zips up his fancy coat. "Follow me."

I stand there, shocked, and watch him walk down the hall. He stops, turns, and says, "Let's go, Toni."

Startled, I jog to catch up, my sneakers squeaking against the floor. As I follow Brian through the parking lot, I keep waiting for him to tell me the official news. Shouldn't he at least express how much I've disappointed my mother? The silence is killing me.

"Drive straight home," he says, twirling his keys. The wind messes with his thick, graying hair.

As he walks to his car, I yell, "What happened? How long are you going to torture me?"

He just waves. I sigh and run to my car. Happy birthday to me.

I'm expelled.

. . . .

Mom gets home about ten minutes after we do. Brian had instructed me to wait in the living room so that's what I'm doing when she walks in the door. I tap my feet against the frayed carpet as I sink farther into the couch. Brian rests silent and still in the plaid armchair across the room like a silent king.

He won't look at me. I so wouldn't mind if the couch just swallowed me up right now.

Mom takes off her red coat and slings it over the back of the couch. When she's yelling at me, I'll just focus on the cute cartoon kittens stamped all over her scrubs. She folds her arms across her chest, pacing back and forth, and glares. I look away.

"You're going to torture me as well," I say, swallowing the lump in my throat. I talk quickly. "Okay. I deserve that. I'm sorry about the whole thing. Lying is bad. Lying for money is even worse. I thought I was helping people, but I just don't know anymore."

I'm out of breath and on the verge of tears. Mom plops down beside me and pats my knee. Her look softens. "You're lucky you weren't expelled, Toni."

I blink a few times. "I *wasn't* expelled?"

Mom looks to Brian. "You didn't tell her?"

Brian shrugs. "Thought I'd let her sweat a little."

Oh my God. My life isn't ruined! A huge weight falls from my shoulders. I exhale, clutching my chest as if to console my worried heart. "I'm not expelled?" I ask. "Really? What about Emma?"

"Emma is no longer implicated in this, thanks to you. But what you did was against Winston code," Brian says. He stands and rolls up his sleeves. "So you do have detention for the rest of the year. Plus, you have to write Mrs. Kemper a thousand-word essay about your future. She said it can't include anything about boys."

Relief washes over me, but I hold back my laughter. I don't want them to think I'm not taking this seriously because I am. "I can do that," I say, nodding. "Wow. I thought I was toast."

"You were," Mom says, her voice still in lecture-mode. "Brian has excellent negotiation skills."

When I look at Brian, he just shrugs again. But he saved me. Without him, I would've been a goner. I jump off the couch and wrap my arms around his neck. He's so surprised he makes this little woof-like sound and pats my back a few times and says, "I think you're crushing my rib cage."

I pull away and apologize for the bear hug. This is sort of weird so I take a few steps back and contain myself. I don't think Brian and I have ever hugged before. Not even at the wedding.

"I know you're eighteen now, but we've got to ground you," Brian adds. There's a hint of a smile on his face.

"Duh." I've never been so happy to be grounded in my life, but I keep a straight face. I dodged a major bullet. But now I can mope about not kissing Micah anymore without feeling guilty about developing the habits of a hermit. This is the happiest punishment ever.

"Well." Mom rises and clears her throat. "I can't wait to hear more about this business of yours, Toni. But first, who wants pizza?"

The doorbell rings. We all look at each other. "Wow," I say. "Fastest pizza delivery in the world. Did you order with your mind, Mom?"

Mom finally cracks a smile and goes to answer the door. I'm left alone with Brian. My newfound hero.

"So," I say awkwardly. "Thank you."

"You're very welcome." Brian rolls his sleeves back down. Maybe the turn in our relationship feels as weird to him as it does to me.

"Pepperoni?" he asks.

Excellent timing for a subject change. "My favorite," I say.

"Toni?" Mom calls from the foyer. "You've got a visitor."

My first thought immediately jumps to him. He's come to talk things through with me. To figure our thing out together. I run my fingers through my hair, lick my lips, and skip to the door, excited to hear his voice. I hope there's more kissing.

But it's not him. It's Emma. She stands there in her Winston uniform, wringing her hands, her eyes red and puffy.

"Emma," I say, concerned. "Are you okay?"

"Hey." Her voice is soft and low. "Sorry I haven't texted you back. I've been a little freaked out. Can I come in?"

"Yeah, yeah." I step aside to let her through. She enters, close to tears. I tell Mom and Brian we need to head to my room for some serious girl discussion.

"I'll order that pizza," Mom calls up the stairs as we go.

Emma enters my room first. "Pizza," she says, shaking. She paces. "Sweet. Wish I could eat, but I feel so sick about all this."

I close the door. "It's okay, Emma."

"Shauna wrote a note saying it was us, Toni," she rambles. "The business. You and me. When Mrs. Kemper questioned me, I said nothing. Not a word. She let me go, but I'm worried she'll find more evidence and then expel me. Did she talk to you too?"

I tell her to calm down, to breathe, and then I fill her in on what happened that afternoon. How Brian saved my butt. How everything's going to be okay. How I took responsibility for the whole thing.

When I'm done, she blinks a few times, squeals, and hugs me. A lot of hugs today. This one lasts a while. Finally, Emma peels herself away and wipes a tear from her eye.

"Can I tell you something, Toni?" Her voice sounds soft, feathery.

I nod, kick off my shoes, and plop down on my bed, letting out a huge sigh. What a day. My head's still spinning.

"I've never really had a friend who was a girl before," she says. She chews on a strand of her honey hair.

"You know what?" I snort. "Me neither. Shocking, I know."

She lets out a huge belch and sits down at my desk. She kicks off her heels and scratches her neck and smiles. "Thanks."

"Thank you, Emma," I reply with a smile. "And I'm sorry I got you into this mess to begin with."

"Best mess of my life," she says, relaxing a little. "I owe you. Big time."

"Don't worry about it," I say.

I can't say I regret the business—it brought Emma into my life—but I'm glad that it's over. If the guys want to let me go, I'll just have to let them.

Later, Mom brings up the pizza. We eat in my room. I change into a pair of sweats and a long-sleeved T-shirt. I laugh so hard my stomach hurts as Emma does a spot-on imitation of Shauna bragging about linen-scented Ryan in group. Every now and then, I glance at the Texas Chainsaw Massacre Teddy Bear resting on my bed. I cuddle with it at night, which I'd never admit to anyone out loud, not even Emma. It smells like Micah. Like vanilla. There he is again. Invading my thoughts. Emma catches me staring at the bear.

"You've got to figure out this Micah thing," she says, wiping cheese from the corner of her mouth. "What if you go off to school with everything all up in the air and confusing like this?"

I sigh. "I just want to know what the heck he's thinking. If I knew what he was thinking, I could react accordingly."

Emma takes one last bite of pizza and wipes her hands together. "Just ask him. Talking about your relationship and defining it doesn't mean it has to end."

End. I hate the word. The thought of anything ending with Loch—friendship or otherwise—guts me.

Emma stands. "I gotta go." She adjusts her skirt. "My parents don't like it when I'm so far away from home on a weeknight. Like twenty minutes is *that* far away."

I nod and walk her downstairs, but my head's still swimming with thoughts of Micah and endings. Today feels so full of luck. Maybe I should march next door and tell Loch how I feel. Or maybe I've used up all my luck for a while. Maybe I shouldn't push it.

At the door, Emma thanks Mom and Brian for the pizza and then heads out with a new skip in her step. I return to my room and lie on my bed and cuddle with the Texas Chainsaw Teddy Bear. Micah. Micah. Micah. I don't want to lose him. I can't lose him. But I'm afraid that if I tell him how I'll feel, he might freak out and distance himself from me. But if I don't tell him how I feel, things will just continue to get weirder and weirder between us and we'll drift apart anyway. I'm stuck.

The doorbell rings again.

"You're popular today," Brian yells up the staircase. "It's for you, Toni!"

I just want to go to sleep at this point, but I force myself to sit up. It's then I notice that Emma forgot her pink glittery hair tie on my desk. She must've come back for it. I put it on my wrist and head downstairs. I stop on the bottom step. My heart suddenly beats louder. Faster. Fiercer. Because it's not Emma.

"Hey." Micah smiles. That smile. He's dressed in monster-hunting attire. Dark clothes. Camera dangling around his neck. Snow cap on his head. His stubble could be classified as more of a beard now. "You busy? I was thinking we could go out on the lake," he says, bouncing a little. "Search for Champ. I just got this feeling, you know? That something special could happen tonight."

Words. I should say them. I hop down that last step and glance over my shoulder at Brian and Mom huddled in the foyer.

"I'm grounded," I say. It's the last thing in the world I want to be right now. My punishment is starting to feel like a punishment.

"You're really grounded?" Micah asks, fidgeting with the camera. "On your birthday?"

"She's really grounded." Mom's standing behind me now.

"I'm really grounded," I repeat.

Brian walks up, chomping on a piece of pizza. "I don't know," he says. "It *is* her birthday."

I look at him. "Dude. You don't have to do that. You've already earned like a million gold stars from me today."

"We'll leave it up to your mother then," Brian says with a nod. He returns to the living room to watch TV.

I try to look as pitiful as possible. I widen my eyes at Mom. I slump my shoulders. I prop out my bottom lip a little. If she could hear how wild my heart is beating, maybe she would let me go.

After a moment, she sighs. "Be home before midnight," she says, pointing a finger at me. "Tomorrow, your grounding begins. No joke."

I hold in a squeal and manage a polite, controlled nod. Then I grab my coat and run out the door.

thirty-two

....

MICAH DRIVES. HIS EYES ON THE
road. Perfect posture. Silent. Focused. He looks like
he's taking a driver's test or something. I pull my
coat sleeves over my hands and then off again. I
keep looking at him, but he doesn't look at me. I hate
how uncomfortable I feel in a familiar place. This is
super weird.

I clear my throat a million times. Tell him. Don't
tell him. I don't know. Maybe I should just blurt it
out. Get it over with. Actually, I probably shouldn't
tell him while he's driving. What if that causes a
crash?

Outside, the sun is setting. Oranges and yellows
and purples streak the sky. This is the longest drive
in the history of drives. Why aren't we there yet?
I steal another glance at him. Micah doesn't move.
Just keeps staring ahead. The lake finally appears. I
relax, but only a little. I need some fresh air.

I'm out of the car before Micah shuts off the
engine. The sun slips between a cluster of dark
clouds. Pensive mountains rest in the distance. I
look around and soak this all in. I do love this place.

The serenity of it. The memories. I'll miss it next year.

Together, we walk down the dock. I jog a little to keep up with his long strides. We still don't talk, but there's a rhythm to our actions. The dock knows our footsteps.

I don't have any of my usual gear. No snacks. No camera. Just me. And Micah. All I need. The lake water shivers against the dock, and the pontoon boat bobs and sways in the water like it's drunk. Micah climbs aboard first and holds out his hand to help me on. This gesture startles me. It's new, but I go with it. I slide my hand into his, immediately jolted with heat from his touch. After I settle into my usual spot—so light-headed I might float away—I shove my hands into my pockets. The skin where he touched me aches in the most wonderful of ways.

Micah settles behind the steering wheel with ease. It's where he's most at home. I watch him. His strong jaw. His dark hair. His thick whiskers. His searching and romantic eyes. The sky darkens and a faint clap of thunder rolls in the distance. Micah examines the sky, frowning.

"Do you want to head back?" he asks. His voice. Deep and smooth. Kind and gentle. Familiar and new.

I shake my head and swallow the lump in my throat. "I think you're right," I tell him. "Something magical might happen tonight. We don't want to miss it."

He smiles softly and starts the engine. As the boat plugs along, the wind whips my hair in every direction. The sky grays. We pass sandy shores and tucked-away bays until it feels like it's just us on this lonely, mysterious planet.

"You hungry?" he asks.

"Always." I force a smile, but my stomach is a giant knot.

"Take the wheel?" He stands, and I go over and take the wheel, glancing at him. He avoids eye contact before moving to the back of the boat. It hurts, his distance, but I'm not sure what to do about it. So I turn my focus to the lake. Choppy waves grow bigger and meaner. The wind howls and threatens. I love storms, but I'm not thrilled at the idea of being smack in the middle of one on Lake Champlain. Maybe we *should* turn back.

I glance over my shoulder to suggest this, but I can't get the words out. I don't want this to end. He pulls a cooler out from beneath a seat. As he unzips it, he looks lost in thought, troubled, his expression grave and serious.

"Here," he says, tossing me a Mountain Dew. One hand on the wheel, I reach out to catch it, but the can slips from my fingers, clamoring onto the floor.

"Sorry," I stammer.

"No big deal," he says, picking up the can.

"What about the noise?" I ask. "We'll scare Champ away."

He stands next to me as I steer the boat, but he looks out at the water. I wish he'd look at me. "Oh. Champ. Right," he says, like he's completely forgotten about the mission.

He scratches his chin and bounces a little, like he's gathering courage before a big fight. He wants to say something. I wish he would say it. Unless he wants to have some kind of Our-Friendship-Is-Ruined-Forever Talk. Then he can keep quiet because that would devastate me.

He cuts the engine, and I move back to my seat. He sits in the driver's seat, but he's turned a little to face me. For a few minutes, we just glide and sip our drinks. I'm not sure how much longer I can stand the silence, but I'm afraid words will take us back home. And I don't want to go home.

After I finish my Mountain Dew—in record time—Micah reveals a container of whoopie pies. He grins as he hands me one. "Not the healthiest meal," he says with a nervous laugh.

I take a huge bite. Sweet. Lovely. Heaven. "Where'd you get these?" I ask, my mouth full.

"Brian."

I pick a hair from my black jacket. "You asked Brian for these?"

He shrugs. "They're *that* good."

I laugh. So true. After I inhale a second pie, Micah wipes a crumb from the corner of his mouth and says, "So..."

"So..." I mimic. The sky is almost completely black now. He flips on the pale boat lights, which dance across the water.

"Do you think he's listening to us?" Micah asks, his voice soft, like he's telling a secret. "Champ, I mean."

I hesitate for a moment. I feel safer, calmer, in the dim light. "I like to think he listens."

He stares down at the cartoon drawing on his shoes. The drawing we created together. "What do you think he'd say about us?"

I freeze, a half-eaten whoopie pie in my right hand. Is he really asking what *I* think about us?

"Us?" I gulp.

"You. Me." He looks up. Shadows play across his lovely face. I almost gasp. This is it. The time hidden feelings bubble to the surface. I'm terrified of saying the wrong thing. I like that it's just me and him out here, two old friends on the verge of discovery.

He fidgets with his snow cap. "Do you think Champ exists? Or do you think we imagined the whole thing?"

Okay. Maybe he's not asking about us. Maybe I'm reading too much into this.

"It's the not knowing that kills me," I say with a shrug.

"I know he exists." Micah moves to sit beside me. His knee touches my knee. His eyes light up. I drop the half-eaten whoopie pie. A second rumble of thunder sounds, louder this time.

Okay. Maybe he *is* talking about us. *Kiss me again.*

He meets my gaze. "Toni. I—"

BOOM! A gigantic roar of thunder interrupts, followed by cold fat drops of rain. The boat rocks. He tears his stare from mine and sighs, wiping water from his stubble.

"Wait. What were you going to say?" I shout over the wind. A little thunderstorm shouldn't stop him from saying that he loves me. If that is, indeed, what he was going to say.

"Damn it!" He yells. He hurries back to the wheel. I'm crushed. Stupid thunder. The wind sends the rain in sideways, straight into my face. I hunch over, shivering.

Micah squints and turns the boat back toward the dock. Another blast of thunder sounds. I stand and move in next to him, aching to be near him.

"What are you doing?" he shouts over the wind. "Sit down!"

"I want to know what you were going to say!" I shout back.

"What are you talking about?" Drops of rain stick to his thick eyelashes.

"You wanted to say something before the rain!" I sound desperate, but it's too early to give up now.

"Just sit, please?" he begs. Water stings my eyes. As the boat rocks, I hang on to the back of his seat for balance, but I can't pry myself away from him. Not when we're so close to discovering something.

BOOM! Another roll of thunder. The sky lights up with a slit of lightning.

"Okay, Toni. This isn't funny," Micah says. "Sit before you fall overboard."

"Not until you say what you were going to say." My teeth are chattering and my fingertips are numb from the cold. When the boat rocks again, I stumble. Micah grabs my arm, keeping me upright.

"I love you, okay?" he shouts. "Now will you sit down?"

I stare at him. His expression is a blur through the rain, but I'm flooded with relief. I'm not alone in this thing. Or is he just saying that to shut me up? He isn't trying to kiss me right now. He glares.

BOOM! Another roll of thunder. Slowly, I take a seat, soaked, freezing, rewinding the words Micah Garry said to me in my head. His warm, lovely words. Words I never thought I'd hear from him. My best friend. The boy who's always been there.

It's an odd feeling. Entirely new. And I'm not quite sure how to process the mix of happiness and confusion and newness running wild through my heart. I tremble. I feel like I need to examine his words, to hold them up to a bright light to see where they might lead. Does this mean we're together? Is this our beginning? Or is this our bittersweet ending before we start our separate lives?

We're at the dock.

Micah cuts the engine and goes to tie up the boat. He looks over his shoulder at me and asks, "A little help?"

I'm still frozen in place. I swallow the lump in my throat and nod. *Get it together, Toni.* I'd love to kiss the rain from his lips. I'd love to bury my face in his chest and begin the next stage of our relationship. Right this second. The best stage. Instead, I tie the back end of the boat to the dock while he secures the front end. His movements are harsh, jagged, like he's mad. Why is he mad?

I hop onto the dock and crouch down to secure the rope, but I keep looking up at him. His end of the boat is tied so he grabs the cooler, mumbling something underneath his breath, and climbs onto the dock. I try to will him to look my way, but he won't. Panic hits me. Everything's different now. What if it's ruined?

Absently, I tie the rope but my head spins. This wasn't how I pictured this going. Loch and I should be kissing. Shouldn't we? Proclamations of love have been made.

A gust of wind knocks me off-balance. I fall forward, headed straight for the water. I scream until he wraps his arms around my waist and pulls me back, into him. "You're okay," he whispers in my ear. "I got you."

He keeps his hands on my hips as I stand and turn around. I press my hands to his chest. The rain falls hard and fast. Another boom of thunder. Not nearly as loud as my heart right now.

"You're always doing that," I say.

"Doing what?" He brushes a wet strand of hair from my cheek.

I look up at him. "Catching me."

He clears his throat and looks away. "Did you hear what I said on the boat?"

I smile. "That you loved me?"

"You did hear." He sighs and frowns. My gut jerks as he lowers his hands from my hips and scratches his stubble. He steps away.

"Did you not want me to hear?" I ask, heart pounding. Oh my God. He regrets saying it. This has all been a huge mistake. A lump lodges in my throat, but I try to pretend that I'm not on the verge of tears.

"Let's pretend it didn't happen," he says with a wave of a hand. Like he can magically erase everything with a flick of his wrist. "It was dumb. I don't know what I was thinking."

It's like I've been kicked in the stomach. Hard. Breathless, I look down at the names carved in the wooden dock for I don't know how long.

Micah touches my shoulder. "We should get back, Toni. We're soaked. And it doesn't look like it's gonna clear up anytime soon." He tries to lead me forward, but I jerk away from his grasp.

"Did you even mean it?"

He rubs the back of his neck. "Of course I meant it!"

"Why take it back then?" I scoff. "Why pretend it didn't happen?"

His voice lowers. "You didn't say anything back."

I blink water from my eyes. "I didn't?"

Micah shakes his head. I process this bit of information. I'm a total idiot. Hadn't I responded to his intimate confession?

A loud splash startles us. I spin around to face the lake. Through the thick rain, there appears to be a black mass cutting through the water. There's definitely *something* out there. Something alive. Something legendary.

"Micah! Look!" I point at the thing moving through the violent waves. It's huge, elegant, breathing. A long tail rises above the choppy waters and splashes down.

I look over my shoulder, gripped with fear and excitement. He must be filming this, but he's just looking at me, not at the water, his expression full of longing.

"I'm going to say it one more time." He takes a deep breath. "If you don't feel the same way, that's something I will have to live with. I love you, Toni. I'm sorry if that screws everything up but—"

"I love you too," I blurt out. His mouth hangs open. I've stunned the poor guy. "Sorry," I continue, facing him again. "I just wanted to say it before I forgot to say it. I've said it so many times in my head that I guess I thought you knew. I love you. I love you, Micah."

When he takes my hands, his skin is cold, rough, the hands of an explorer. He touches my neck. My ear. My cheek. The space between us shrinks until I have to crane my neck up to look into his eyes, but I don't mind. Don't mind at all.

"This is like one of Ollie's romantic movies." Micah grins. "Here we are. Professing our love in the rain."

I laugh. "Don't worry. Our love story has a monster in it. Look at the water."

He looks out at the water, squinting, searching. "I don't see anything."

"Don't worry." I whisper in his ear. "He's been there all along. Like you said."

He pulls me closer. I step into this moment, and his lips find mine again. We're tangled with each other. This kiss is different from the others. This one is no longer an experiment but a certainty. I forget about the past. I forget about the future. I forget about the monster in the lake.

Here we are. We're the legend.

acknowledgments

. . . .

My deep gratitude and appreciation goes to my editor, Danielle Ellison, for loving Toni as much I did. Your phone call was a dream come true. Thank you to my other editors Lauren Meinhardt and Traci Inzitari for both discovering the manuscript. I've had such a blast working with all three of you.

Thank you to the entire team at Spencer Hill Contemporary and Spencer Hill Press.

Thank you to Patrice Caldwell, publicist extraordinaire.

Thank you to Rebecca Mancini for finding Toni a home overseas.

Thank you to Jenny Zemanek for designing a great cover. It's better than I could've imagined.

Thank you to the online writing community, including Evil Editor and the WriteOnCon team, without which this book may have never been discovered. Thanks goes out to my fellow Fearless Fifteeners for support throughout this whirlwind journey.

Thank you to my in-laws, Kevin and Kathy Aldin. Kathy, thank you for happily babysitting while I rushed off to finish edits before deadline.

A special thanks to my parents, Dan and Kathy Taylor, for nurturing my love of reading. Your support this year as I navigated the terrain of new motherhood and new authorhood at the same time means the world to me. Thank you. Thank you. Thank you.

Thank you, above all, to my husband Chris for taking such good care of me. Without you, this book would be unfinished.

At last, I thank my darling daughter, Charlotte. Due to your impending arrival, I found the courage to resurrect this story and submit it for publication. You are my heart.

about the author

· · · · · · · · · · · · · · · · ·

Lisa Aldin graduated from Purdue University with a B.A. in English Literature. She now lives in Indianapolis, Indiana, with her husband and daughter. *One of the Guys* is her debut novel.